Laurie Gilmore writes small-town romance. Her Dream Harbor series is filled with quirky townsfolk, cozy settings, and swoon-worthy romance. She loves finding books with the perfect balance of sweetness and spice and strives for that in her own writing. If you ever wished you lived in Stars Hollow (or that Luke and Lorelai would just get together already!) then her books are definitely for you.

instagram.com/lauriegilmore_author

Also by Laurie Gilmore

The Pumpkin Spice Café

The Christmas Tree Farm

The Strawberry Patch Pancake House

THE CINNAMON BUN BOOK STORE

Dream Harbor Series

Book 2

LAURIE GILMORE

One More Chapter
a division of HarperCollins*Publishers*
1 London Bridge Street
London SE1 9GF
www.harpercollins.co.uk
HarperCollins*Publishers*
Macken House, 39/40 Mayor Street Upper,
Dublin 1, D01 C9W8, Ireland
This paperback edition 2024
24 25 26 27 28 LBC 18 17 16 15 14
First published in ebook by HarperCollins*Publishers* 2024

A catalogue record of this book
is available from the British Library

ISBN: 978-0-00-864158-0

This novel is entirely a work of fiction.
The names, characters and incidents portrayed in it are the work of the author's imagination. Any resemblance to actual persons, living or dead, events or localities is entirely coincidental.

Printed and bound in the United States

This one's for the readers. Thanks for returning to Dream Harbor with me.

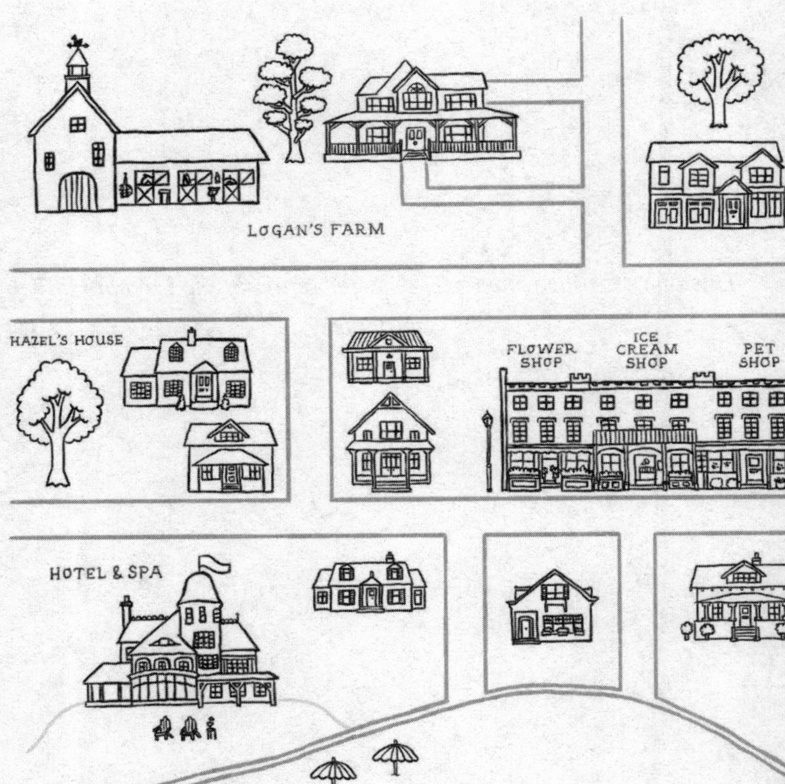

DREAM HARBOR

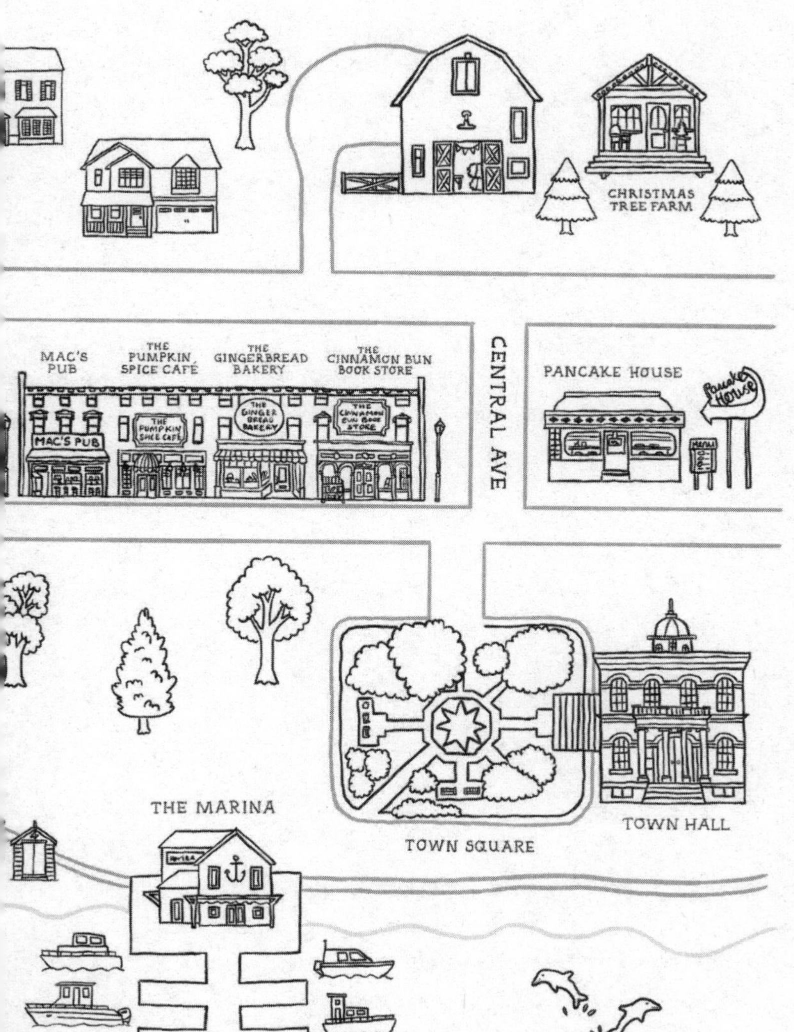
CHRISTMAS TREE FARM
MAC'S PUB
THE PUMPKIN SPICE CAFÉ
THE GINGERBREAD BAKERY
THE CINNAMON BUN BOOK STORE
CENTRAL AVE
PANCAKE HOUSE
THE MARINA
TOWN SQUARE
TOWN HALL
NOAH'S BOAT

Playlist

'tis the damn season - Taylor Swift
Scarlett - Holly Humberstone
October Passed Me By - girl in red
Scott Street - Phoebe Bridgers
Meet Me In The Woods - Lord Huron
gold rush - Taylor Swift
Little Freak - Harry Styles
I Know it won't work - Gracie Abrams
Bookstore Girl - Charlie Burg
Bags - Clairo
Cinnamon Girl - Lana Del Rey
End of Beginning - Djo
Nonsense - Sabrina Carpenter
Homesick - Noah Kahan, Sam Fender
Heaven - Niall Horan
Fade Into You - Mazzy Star
all my ghosts - Lizzy McAlpine
Too Sweet - Hozier
All My Love - Noah Kahan
Belong Together - Mark Ambor
Radio - Lana Del Rey
There She Goes - The La's
invisible string - Taylor Swift

Chapter One

Hazel Kelly loved a good story. She just didn't have any of her own, which became abundantly clear as she stood behind the counter at The Cinnamon Bun Bookstore, in the exact same spot she'd been for the last fifteen years.

Well, not perpetually. She did get to go home at the end of each day and all that, but still, the feeling was the same. Fifteen years in the same place.

Hazel sighed as she rearranged the piles of free bookmarks in front of her. It was a slow day, bright and sunny, the type of day people wanted to be running around outside, not browsing the shelves of a bookstore. Not that Hazel understood that line of reasoning. She *always* wanted to be browsing the shelves of a bookstore.

It wasn't that she didn't love it here behind the same counter she'd stood at for her first shift at the end of her sophomore year of high school, it was just that nothing else in her life had changed either. Same job. Same town. Same friends. In fact, the only thing that had changed, besides a slight twinge in her back when she woke up each morning, was the name of the bookstore, which her boss changed every other year or so.

Hazel was literally surrounded by amazing stories, books filled with love and adventure and *life*, but Hazel herself was stuck.

'And in two months, I'll be thirty,' she muttered to no one in particular since the shop was empty.

Thirty loomed in the distance, glaring at her menacingly. The date, September 28, was imprinted in her mind. For some people, Hazel assumed, thirty meant an end to the wild and storied days of their twenties. A time to settle down, to get serious, to be an adult.

Hazel had a different problem with thirty.

She'd forgotten to have wild and storied days. Her twenties had been ... calm? Responsible? Boring. Hazel had essentially been in her thirties since she was fifteen. Or more like her seventies if you asked Annie, without whom Hazel probably wouldn't have picked her head up out of a book at all.

And it had never bothered Hazel before. She liked her bookstore. She liked cups of chamomile tea and rainy days and the Sunday morning crossword puzzle. She liked her quiet life. Except now, all of a sudden, with thirty sticking its proverbial tongue out at her, Hazel suddenly wondered if she'd missed out on something. Maybe she'd forgotten to try some things. Maybe, shockingly, there was more life outside of her books that she should have experienced by now.

The sun mocked her through the large front windows. She'd just put up a display of 'Beach Reads' for August, but Hazel couldn't remember the last time she'd taken a book to the beach. She had a tendency to burn if she was in the sun for more than ten minutes at a time, which was perhaps indicative of her current problem and maybe a vitamin D deficiency that she should probably look into.

Hazel needed an adventure.

And soon.

Or at the very least a good story to tell the next time she was at Mac's pub listening to Annie's latest theories about him and how he was out to get her. Or Jeanie and Logan's plans to update the farmhouse whenever she finally decided to move in. Just once, Hazel would like to shock her friends, and shock herself. Just once, Hazel would like to do something very un-Hazel-like.

But not right now. Because right now Hazel's gaze snagged on a crooked book in the Romance section and the Hazel thing to do was to straighten it. And frankly, that was her job. She wandered over to the shelf, glancing out the door on her way just in case anyone was walking by and might stop in, but the streets were empty. It was a perfect late summer afternoon and it seemed the whole of Dream Harbor was at the beach or out hiking a trail or relaxing by a pool, trying to soak the warmth in before the weather turned.

Even Annie had declared the day too beautiful to be

inside and had closed up The Sugar Plum Bakery early to set off with some of her sisters to traipse around a vineyard. Hazel sighed. She was sure she'd hear all about it tomorrow while she had nothing to contribute to the conversation except the exciting tale of this crooked book.

She shook her head. She needed to snap out of this funk. And what better way to do that than tidying? The Romance section had grown exponentially over the past few years thanks to the lobbying of the Dream Harbor Book Club and their love of the genre. Hazel blushed just looking at some of the covers, but if it was good for business then she was on board.

The crooked book was not only crooked but also shelved in the wrong place so she pulled it out, avoided eye contact with the half-naked man on the front cover, and was about to reshelve it when she noticed one of the pages was dog-eared.

'What's this?' she muttered. Did people have no respect? They hadn't even bought the book yet but they marked the page? She nearly added, 'What is the world coming to?' but she tried to catch her old lady tendencies as much as possible these days so she only thought it.

She flipped open to the marked page and found a highlighted sentence. A highlighted sentence in one of her books! How totally unacceptable! Unbelievable! Someone just waltzed in here and defaced one of her books and hadn't even bothered to buy it!

Hazel would have kept raging internally for the rest of

the day if the highlighted line itself hadn't caught her attention.

It wasn't particularly good. Not pithy or profound. But it was like the book, or whoever had highlighted it, was speaking directly to Hazel.

'Come with me, lass, if you want an adventure.'

She nearly dropped the book.

She glanced around the store and half expected someone to be watching her and laughing. Surely this was a joke of some kind. But who would have left it? And who could have known what she'd been thinking about all day?

The store was still empty. Of course it was. This was some kind of weird coincidence.

Hazel looked back to the shelf. No other books were out of order. Just this one. The one she still held gripped tight in her hand. There was a pirate on the cover, his shirt torn open from the apparently very strong sea wind that was also blowing his hair back. *Love Captive* was scrawled across the top.

She had the strange and sudden urge to curl up somewhere and read the book cover to cover, but she was at work, and this book felt dangerous. Like something she certainly didn't want to read in the middle of her workplace.

It was just that it really seemed like this man, this theoretical, fictional man could in fact take her on an adventure.

She flipped back to the highlighted line, reading it as if she could solve the mystery of who'd highlighted it and left it crooked on her shelf just by looking at it. She was so caught up in her thoughts, she didn't hear the door to the shop open.

She didn't hear anything until a low voice rumbled right next to her ear. 'Whatcha reading?'

Hazel tossed the book across the room. It landed with a thud in the reading nook by the window. She spun to find Noah Barnett grinning at her.

Noah, owner / operator of Dream Harbor's one and only fishing-tour company. Noah who had showed up in town a few years ago, quickly became friends with Logan, and now hovered around the periphery of Hazel's life like a sexy satellite. She shook her head. Just because every woman and at least half the men in town found Noah attractive did not mean she would fall for his charms.

'That good, huh?' he said with a lazy smile.

Ugh, he was charming. Charming enough, in fact, that his exploits with female tourists were practically legendary. So why he kept hanging around her bookstore was still a mystery to Hazel.

'You scared me.'

'Clearly.'

Her heart was racing, and only partially because she'd been caught reading smut during work hours. The other reason was because ... well, because Noah was smiling at her like that again.

She couldn't really figure it out. Noah was objectively very handsome, she could admit that. And, objectively, very much not her type. She also knew for a fact that she was not his type, mainly because she actually lived in Dream Harbor, so she found it curious that he was always smiling at her like he knew something she didn't.

Annie said he had the hots for her, but Hazel knew that was absurd. No one, not even her handful of ex-boyfriends, had had the hots for her. Hazel was cute. She could admit that. Cute in like a koala-napping-in-a-tree kinda way. Not cute in a I-want-to-get-in-her-pants kinda way. And that was fine. She'd made her peace with it.

But Noah was still staring at her like *that*.

She turned and went to pick up the book, keeping the cover carefully hidden against her chest. 'Did you need something?' she asked, ignoring the way Noah was now casually leaning against the counter watching her walk toward him.

'Uh ... maybe?'

'Maybe?'

'Yeah, I just...' His gaze flicked from her face to the shelves behind her and back again. This was a typical Noah visit. He came in every other week for a book but never seemed to know what he was looking for.

Annie said it was evidence of his having the hots for her, but Hazel still wasn't convinced. Annie said he would need to pull his pants down in the middle of the store for her to be convinced, but Hazel very much hoped that wouldn't happen.

'I just need something new to read.' He crossed his arms over his chest, his forearms flexing as he did so. Warmer weather had brought less clothing with it and now all of

Noah's tattoos were on display. Hazel's cheeks flushed at the sight of the half-naked mermaid wound around his left bicep.

This was a man with stories. So many that he'd imprinted them on his body.

Hazel cleared her throat. 'Did you enjoy the last book I gave you? *A Curse of Blood and Wolves*.'

Noah nodded, his auburn hair glinting in the late afternoon light. 'Yeah, loved it.'

'Great. We just got book two in the other day. Let me grab it.'

She'd meant to go by herself but Noah followed her down the fantasy aisle, bringing with him his heady scent of sunshine and salt. Hazel had never noticed a man's scent before. Annie would take this as evidence that Hazel had the hots for Noah.

Which would be ... silly? Futile? Adventurous.

'Here it is.'

Noah was too close when she turned around and she nearly smacked into his broad chest.

'Oops.'

'Sorry!'

Both books fell to the ground and Hazel scrambled to pick them up, but Noah was faster and he already had his hands on the half-naked pirate before she could snatch it back.

'*Love Captive*?' he asked with a cocked eyebrow.

They were both squatting in the aisle now, too close for

Hazel to avoid his eye. 'It's not mine. I mean I wasn't reading it. I was just reshelving it.'

Noah's smile grew. 'It sounds good.' He flipped to the dog-eared page. 'I thought you weren't reading it?'

'I ... uh ... well...'

His gaze landed on the highlighted line. 'Come with me, lass, if you want an adventure.'

Oh, no, that line read in Noah's deep voice was doing things to her ... hot things. What was going on today?! Hazel shook her head.

'I was just reshelving it,' she repeated as she snatched it back and stood before Noah could read any more and make everything worse.

'But someone marked it up,' he said, standing and dwarfing her in the process. Why did he have to be so big and smell so good? He was confusing her and she didn't like it.

'I know.'

'So someone just marked it up and then put it back on the shelf?'

'Yes.'

'Weird.'

'I know, and they didn't even put it back in the right spot.' She shuffled past him, avoiding contact with his large, good-smelling body and made her way back to the relative safety of the front of the store.

Noah followed. 'Almost like they wanted you to find it.'

Hazel stopped and spun to face him. They nearly

crashed again, but Noah skidded to a stop, too. 'Why would you say that?'

He shrugged. 'Don't know. Just seems like a clue or something.'

'A clue?' Hazel narrowed her eyes. 'Noah, are you screwing with me?'

'Screwing with you?' He looked genuinely confused but Hazel wasn't buying it.

'Did you mess up my books as some kind of joke? You'll have to pay for this if you did.' She waved the book in front of him as his brows lifted higher on his head.

'Of course I didn't. I wouldn't ... mess with you. And I certainly wouldn't mess with your books.' He made a little 'x' over his chest. 'Cross my heart. Fisherman's honor.'

It was Hazel's turn to raise an eyebrow. 'Fisherman's honor? I don't think that's a thing.'

'Well it is now.'

'Hmm.'

'I still think it might be a clue, though.'

'Why would someone leave me a clue?'

He shrugged again but excitement lit up the light brown of his eyes. 'For an adventure, I guess.'

An adventure.

Noah grinned and Hazel's heart picked up speed and the book in her hands called to her and maybe it was a clue.

At the very least maybe it would make a good story.

Chapter Two

Noah had the hots for Hazel Kelly. It surprised him almost as much as it seemed to surprise her, but he did. She wasn't like any of the other women he'd been with. Take today, for example. With her loose button-down shirt tucked into her high waisted pants, a string of delicate gold chains around her neck, and a pair of cute little flat shoes on her feet, she looked ... well, she looked way too good for him. She looked smart and sophisticated. And don't even get him started on that cloud of soft curls around her face, or the adorable way she pushed her glasses up her nose, like she was doing now as she stared at him like he was some kind of alien species.

He had it bad.

Like *real* bad.

Which hadn't happened to him, well, ever. Noah liked women. A lot. And at least so far in his life, he'd been pretty good at attracting them. But he'd never felt like this before.

Which was unfortunate because he was fairly certain Hazel didn't feel the same.

She usually looked at him like she was right now. Like she couldn't quite figure him out. At least that feeling was mutual. He didn't know how much more obvious he could be. He was in here every other week doing his best to charm and flirt his way into her good graces but it didn't seem to be working.

Although, he had read more books in the past few months than in his entire life, so that was a bonus.

He should probably just be honest and ask her out or something. It had worked for Logan, eventually anyway, and now he had Jeanie and they were sickeningly happy together and all that.

But they were different. Hazel was different. And Noah was completely out of his element.

'An adventure?' she asked, startling him out of his swirling thoughts about her cuteness and his ineptitude.

'Yeah. I don't know. Maybe someone is leaving you clues, like a scavenger hunt or something.'

'Hmm.' Hazel frowned, a little crease forming between her brows. 'Seems unlikely.'

'Maybe. But unlikely things happen all the time.'

Like you agreeing to go on a date with me sometime...

He almost said it, almost asked her but then she was moving briskly back behind the counter and ringing up his new book.

'Is this all?'

'Uh ... yep. That's all.'

'Twenty-one ninety-five, please.'

That definitely wasn't all but Noah handed over his card. There was no way this smart, adorable woman would want to date him. There was a reason Noah went for girls that were only here for the summer, tourists and one-night stands. Noah was good for fun, for a fling. Not for serious girls like Hazel Kelly.

She handed him his book and his fingers brushed against hers. She held his gaze for a breath and in that moment Noah could almost believe that she felt it too, the spark. But then she looked away and was saying goodbye and his feet were moving him toward the door.

Girls like Hazel Kelly were not for him. He was at least smart enough to know that.

He stepped out of the bookstore and into the heat of the day. It was the first sunny day after a wet July and the town had swung directly back into summer mode. Summer was short in New England. If you didn't dive right in, you'd miss it entirely. Even though it was August, Main Street was still decked out from its Fourth of July celebration, with red-white-and-blue banners and flags on most stores. Summer had always been Noah's favorite season. Summer meant the beach and endless ice cream and no school. Freedom. He'd never been good at school. Too much sitting. He'd never been good at sitting. Or staying in one place for too long. After he left home, he hadn't stayed anywhere for more than a month or two, picking up and leaving once he got bored. But something about Dream Harbor, had him sticking around. At least for the moment.

Noah considered stopping into The Pumpkin Spice Café for an iced tea but he was exhausted and just wanted to get home and take a nap. His first tour of the day had him up at 4am and he'd spent the morning teaching a group of dude-bros from the city how to fish. Unfortunately, the bulk of Noah's business came from guys who knew nothing about the water or boats or fish and it was his job to take them out and make them feel like they did.

In reality, Noah did most of the work, made sure fish were caught, cleaned, and packaged up to take home, while the guys got drunk in the sun. But it paid the bills and he got to be out on the water so it wasn't a bad deal.

And it was better than taking over his family's seafood empire up on the North Shore. His sisters were better at running it anyway – he hadn't needed to stick around to know that would be true, even if he did still feel guilty for leaving. But that was less about the business and more about the people. He knew that too, he just didn't feel like dealing with it yet.

Noah wasn't cut out for running a business. Not one that big anyway. His parents had taken their small fishing business and over the years turned it into a multi-million-dollar company that supplied seafood to hundreds of restaurants across the country. After his parents retired, his older sisters took over as CEO and CFO. And Noah ran away.

He wiped the sweat from his brow as he walked, the familiar mix of guilt and shame rolling through him. There were only so many times someone could disappoint their family before it was time to cut and run, and he'd hit his quota pretty early in life.

Besides, his little fishing tours he could handle. He could schedule them and run them all on his own. And that meant there was no one to let down when the whole enterprise inevitably went under. Much simpler that way.

He made his way through town, thinking about how he should probably call his sisters and about Hazel and about how many tours he had scheduled for the rest of the week, letting his mind bounce from topic to topic as he walked, slowly letting go of the memories of his past mistakes.

By the time the house was visible, his thoughts had circled back around to Hazel and that book she had been reading and if she liked guys with boats. Because he happened to be a guy with a boat. Maybe he should ask her out after all.

Noah started his climb down the rocky shoreline. There used to be a path here from the road to the beach but it had eroded away over the years, so now to get down to the sand you had to climb over some large boulders and chunks of concrete. But Noah didn't mind. The public beach a few miles down the road had much better access and would be packed on a day like this, but here, it was quiet.

He toed off his shoes when he made it to the sand and dug his feet in, immediately feeling calmer.

When he had landed in Dream Harbor a few years ago, Noah had lived on his boat for a while until he'd found a row of old fishermen shacks on a forgotten stretch of beach, sure that if someone fixed them up, they'd do great as short-term rental properties. He'd started doing just that to one of them, as a little side project, about a year ago, half expecting someone to show up and tell him he couldn't. But so far no one ever had.

So now he secretly camped out here sometimes. He still stayed in the apartment above Mac's bar most of the time, and as far as the nosy townsfolk knew that apartment was his home. Someday he'd get around to telling Mayor Kelly about his ideas and see about buying these old shacks. Maybe.

Maybe it was a stupid idea. He'd had no shortage of those in his life.

Or maybe he'd get arrested for squatting. He wasn't really sure. But for now, he liked it here. He opened the door to the little house and stepped into the cool interior. The sea breeze that came in through the front windows kept the house comfortable even on hot days like today. They'd need better insulation if anyone wanted to stay through the winter but Noah had already patched up the roof and laid new flooring. Luckily, he'd followed his grandfather around a lot as a kid and asked endless questions. All his grandpa's tricks and tips had finally come in handy.

The whole house was maybe 400 square feet if he was being generous, but it fit a kitchenette, a queen-size bed – and a bathroom with plumbing that was older than him and questionable, at best.

Noah tossed his new book on the bed and pulled a cold beer out of the cooler he kept in the kitchenette. Electricity was the other thing, besides the plumbing, that he hadn't been able to fix on his own, so he was still roughing it, but it was so peaceful here he didn't mind. The sound of crashing waves filled the house and Noah knew he'd be asleep before he even cracked open his book.

He stretched out on the mattress he'd been using as a bed and took a sip of his drink, letting his thoughts wander back to Hazel. What would she think about this house and his ideas? Would she think he was ridiculous? He didn't have time to wonder about it for long before he drifted off to sleep and dreamt about capturing a certain bookseller and whisking her away on his boat.

Chapter Three

Another book was crooked. And backwards. And Hazel was refusing to look at it. She didn't care. It was just a poorly shelved book that some customer had haphazardly put back on the shelf. It happened all the time.

Alex would handle it later when they came in for their shift. Hazel had more important things to do, like work on next month's book order and schedule September's author events. She was the operations manager after all. She could leave the book straightening to Alex or Lyndsay or the new hire who came in on Sundays or literally anyone else but her.

Damn it. She was looking at it again.

It had been two days since the last crooked book incident and Hazel had officially decided it was a weird occurrence that definitely wasn't about her and definitely wasn't going to happen again. And now look. Another one.

Someone was messing with her.

An image of Noah's excited face when he'd thought maybe it was a clue flashed in her mind. She'd shut that down quickly. Too quickly. His handsome face had fallen in disappointment when she'd dismissed the idea.

She'd felt bad about it, but clues, really? That was absurd. And just because she'd gotten in her own head about her stuck-ness and then Noah had flittered in with all his confusing handsome-ness, did not mean there were suddenly secret messages in her books. Because that would be crazy.

Hazel tapped her fingers on the counter. Another slow day. Did people not read in the summer? She straightened the already straight bookmarks and sipped her tea.

Damn it.

Hazel marched over to the Romance section to fix the book and possibly give it a piece of her mind because she was that kind of crazy lady today. She pulled it out and found a corner turned down, just like in the other book. She couldn't just put it back on the shelf if it was highlighted, too. She couldn't sell a defaced book.

She had to check.

The blueberries popped tart and bright in her mouth. They tasted like summer and new beginnings.

Hazel was instantly transported back to picking blueberries as a kid, the sweet burst of fruit on her tongue, scanning the bushes for the ripe ones, and the ice cream her dad would buy her on the way home. She closed her eyes and leaned against the shelf. When was the last time she'd gone blueberry picking?

'Napping on the job?'

Hazel's eyes snapped open at the sound of Annie's teasing voice. She had to stop getting caught doing weird things in the Romance section. She shoved the offending book back on the shelf and turned to greet her friends.

'No, of course not.'

'We brought you lunch,' Annie said, dropping into her favorite comfy chair by the window.

'And an iced tea.' Jeanie held out the drink and Hazel took it, happy for the distraction.

'Thanks.'

'Everything all right?' Annie asked. Her blonde ponytail slipped over her shoulder as she tipped her head, studying Hazel. They'd been friends since Hazel's family moved here in the ninth grade and Annie knew her a little too well.

'Yep. Fine.' Hazel grabbed the other half of Annie's sandwich and sat across from her. She slipped her feet out of her shoes and tucked them underneath her. Normally she would have insisted they eat in the backroom but the store was empty enough that it didn't seem to matter.

'You sure? You look kinda strange.'

'*You* look kinda strange.'

Annie stuck her tongue out and Jeanie giggled.

'The heat always makes her grumpy,' Annie whispered to Jeanie, like Hazel couldn't hear her.

'It doesn't make me grumpy. It's just not my favorite.'

'Hazel hates sunshine. She's like a vampire.'

'I am not! I just prefer to be inside. I'm an inside cat.'

Jeanie laughed again, her gaze flicking between the two

old friends. 'Well, since you're an inside cat, you may not want to come, but I convinced Logan we should have a bonfire tonight.'

'A bonfire?'

'Or like a regular campfire. I don't know. But there will be s'mores!'

'And drinks?' Annie asked.

'And drinks.'

'Great, I'm in. And you, little inside cat? Can you manage the outdoors for a few hours to have fun with your friends?' Annie was just teasing but her words hit a little too close to home. Hazel's friends thought she couldn't even tolerate a campfire?

She scowled. 'Of course I can.'

'Perfect!' Jeanie clapped her hands in excitement and Hazel realized what she'd just signed on for. Bugs and smoke and dirt. And quite possibly Noah, considering he was Logan's friend. Her stomach did a concerning swoop at the thought of the fisherman.

Damn it.

It was too late to back out. Jeanie was already packing up the rest of her sandwich and hustling out the door. 'I gotta go. I left Crystal alone with the lunch rush, but I'll see you guys later. Around eight!'

Hazel gave her a weak wave before meeting Annie's eye again. Her best friend raised a blonde brow. 'You sure you're okay?'

Hazel sighed. She wasn't okay. She was having some kind of mid-life crisis. Or quarter life crisis? Was that a thing? Either way, she was considering going on a scavenger hunt, inspired by some town book-defacer, just to have something to show for herself by her thirtieth birthday. None of that really seemed okay, but she didn't feel like sharing it all with Annie just yet.

'Yep. I'm good. Just a little worried about the lack of customers.'

Annie glanced around the empty store. 'I wouldn't worry too much, Haze. Everyone is just a little stir crazy after that long, wet July. They'll be back.'

Hazel nodded. 'Yeah, you're right.'

Annie smiled and passed her a fresh baked cookie. A peace offering.

They ate the rest of their meal in companionable silence but Hazel's attention kept slipping back to the crooked book and the blueberries and the rest of the summer stretching out, hazy and hot and wide open in front of her.

Hazel had already been bitten by no fewer than fifteen bugs and no matter where she sat around the fire the smoke seemed to blow in her face. She held a lukewarm beer in one hand and a s'more with a burnt marshmallow in the other hand. She was pretending to have a good time.

She wasn't having a good time.

And Noah had just strolled in all sun kissed and freckled and her stomach was doing that swooping thing again.

'Hey, everyone.' He held up a hand in greeting and everyone called their hellos.

Hazel was flanked on either side by Annie and book-club Jacob, who were sitting in camp chairs while she got stuck with an old kitchen chair she was pretty sure might give out at any moment. George from the bakery was also here, standing with his beer while toasting a marshmallow. Isabel, Jeanie's other book-club friend, had wandered away from the group to call home and make sure the kids had fallen asleep without her. Everyone seemed happy and relaxed. No one else seemed to be getting eaten alive.

Logan was tending the fire with more concentration and strategy than Hazel felt should be needed to tend a fire, but even he seemed pleased with how the evening was going. Annie was right. Summer made Hazel grumpy.

'Hey, Noah!' Jeanie greeted him with a hug before he grabbed a beer from the cooler and joined the rest of the group. 'So happy you could make it.'

'Uh, yeah, of course. I'd do pretty much anything for a s'more.'

Hazel thought she was sufficiently hidden in the shadows but somehow Noah's gaze found hers and his mouth tipped into that confusing smile. She looked away and focused on her s'more which she had to admit was pretty good despite the charred flavor. When she glanced up again, Noah was watching her lick marshmallow goo from her fingers.

'Hey, Noah, I've been meaning to ask you something.' Annie's voice tore his attention from Hazel's fingers, thank

God, because Hazel was about to turn as gooey as the marshmallow she was licking off of them.

'Oh?' He lifted an eyebrow and smirked in that way he did when he was amused. Hazel paid attention to her sticky fingers and not his face.

'How come you never smell?'

A laugh burst from Jacob's mouth. 'What the hell kind of question is that, Annie?'

'He's on a stinky fishing boat all day and I've never once smelled fish on him!'

'So are you accusing him of lying about what he does all day?' Jacob asked, taking a sip of his beer.

Annie shrugged. 'I don't know, it's kind of suspicious.'

Noah laughed. 'I find showers work pretty well.'

Annie narrowed her eyes, studying him. 'You must have some really strong soap.'

'I scrub really hard.' He winked at her and Annie laughed.

Everyone was laughing now, actually. Except for Hazel, who was using all her mental energy to not picture a soapy, naked Noah scrubbing himself in the shower.

'What did I miss?' Isabel asked, re-entering the ring of firelight.

'Just discussing Noah's showering habits.' Annie gestured to Noah with her beer and he held out his arms as though to let Isabel admire his cleanliness.

She didn't seem impressed, which was strange because Hazel could swear the heat of the fire increased when Noah's biceps flexed against the sleeves of his T-shirt.

'Wow, my first night out away from the kids in months and we have to talk about Noah showering?'

'I also vote for a change of topic,' Logan muttered, standing from his crouch near the fire. Jeanie planted a kiss on his cheek.

'How about our August book choice?' Jacob chimed in and Logan groaned.

'We're going to go from discussing Noah in the shower to smutty books?'

Jeanie giggled. 'Yep.'

'We need something summery. Ooo, maybe pirates!' Isabel's eyes lit up with her idea.

'Hazel was reading an interesting pirate book the other day.' Noah met Hazel's gaze with a playful grin.

'I wasn't reading it. I was reshelving it.'

He shrugged. 'It looked good.'

'What was it?' Jacob leaned forward, all interested now in this smutty pirate book and Noah was still looking at her and another mosquito landed on her thigh. What fresh hell was this?

'*Kidnapped Lover*... Or no, that wasn't it ... Trapped? Caught? *Bound up by the Pirate*?'

Oh. My. God. If Noah uttered another word about this book or being tied up by pirates, she was going to skewer him with this marshmallow stick.

'It was *Love Captive,*' she ground out, happy for the semi-darkness to hide her heated cheeks.

'That sounds perfect!' Jeanie clapped her hands.

'I bet pirates smelled pretty bad.'

Jacob reached over Hazel to smack Annie on the arm. 'Don't ruin sexy pirates for me!'

Noah was still looking at her while the rest of the group descended into chatter about the cleanliness of pirates. He was looking at her like he knew that she had taken that book home and read it cover to cover and that the pirate she was picturing looked nothing like the one on the cover...

'I need to g—' Hazel stood too fast and her chair tipped over. 'Uh ... to the bathroom.' *You did not need to announce that to everyone!*

'Just be careful making your way back to the house. It's getting dark and the Bobs got out again,' Jeanie said with an apologetic smile.

'Okay, yep. No problem.' Hazel scurried away from the ring of light around the fire and the laughter of her friends. The sun had dipped low enough in the sky that long shadows concealed the dips and pits of the field. *Great, I'm either going to break an ankle or get attacked by goats.*

She knew her way from the back field to Logan's grandparents' house well enough to do it in the dark; she'd been coming here for years. But in her current state she wouldn't be surprised if she ended up in a ditch. Or worse, pecked to death by Logan's precious flock of chickens.

Hazel shuddered and hurried to the house. She didn't even have to go, but she did need to get away from good-smelling fishermen and bloodthirsty bugs, so this seemed as good a plan as any.

She let herself in the house and found Nana and

Grandpa Henry dozing in front of the TV in the living room. They startled awake when she walked in.

'Hazel Kelly is that you?'

'It's me, Nana. How are you?'

'Oh good, good. There's leftovers in the crockpot if you're hungry.'

'No one wants that, dear.' Henry patted her leg lovingly and Estelle shot him a glare. Hazel smiled. It was like coming home with Logan in high school all over again. They'd adopted each other as siblings a long time ago since neither of them had any.

'I'm full of s'mores actually. Just came in to use the bathroom.'

'Okay, dear. You let me know if you need anything.'

Hazel nodded and made her way down the hall to the little bathroom off the kitchen. It still had the same faded wallpaper, the same blue-tiled floor. She looked in the mirror and found the same reflection she'd seen in high school.

Well, maybe a little different. A little older.

But she felt the same.

Same old Hazel.

Could you have memories of things you hadn't done? Standing in Logan's bathroom, Hazel couldn't help but remember everything she didn't do. Like the fact that she never skipped a single day of school because she'd been too worried she'd miss something important. Or the fact that she'd only ever gotten tipsy in high school once and it was here at the farmhouse and then she'd felt so guilty she'd confessed to Nana.

She lived at home during college, too. Hadn't gone out to clubs, hadn't ever had a one-night stand, hadn't been arrested.

Okay, so maybe it was good she'd never been arrested, but the point was she had never been reckless, not even a little bit.

Hazel liked herself in general. She liked her life. But she still couldn't help feeling like something was missing. That all those holes in her memories were turning into something like regrets. Regrets she didn't want to bring with her into her thirties.

She thought about Noah's smiles and those crooked books and blueberry picking. Maybe she didn't have to be stuck. Maybe for the next two months she could be ... fun. She could have fun, right? That's what summer was for, wasn't it?

The floorboards creaked under her feet as she went through the kitchen, grabbing the wine on the table that Jeanie had forgotten to bring out.

Fun. Adventure. A teensy bit of recklessness...

She could do it.

She would start tonight.

She went out the side door, the one that led to Grandpa Henry's private garden, and found an unexpected surprise. *Blueberry bushes*! Blueberry bushes she had totally forgotten existed on Logan's farm. She stood there on the edge of the garden, darkness creeping in around the edges of the sky, and felt every bit her age. She wasn't in high school anymore, or college. She couldn't go back and change the past and she didn't want to, not really. But in the months leading up to her birthday, she wanted to step outside herself. To let go. To be young and fun and twenty-something before it was too late.

And maybe she'd inhaled too much woodsmoke but the fact that she'd ended up right where the crooked books had pointed her just felt like too much of a sign to ignore. The books were the key to her adventure. It was time she started paying attention.

Chapter Four

Noah found Hazel a little bit drunk in the small garden. The air smelled like dirt and woodsmoke. It was full dark now and Hazel was sitting at the edge of the garden holding a half empty bottle of wine.

'Hey, we got worried about you. Thought you might have been eaten by goats.'

Hazel gazed up at him. 'It was in the book.'

Maybe she was more drunk than he thought. 'What was in the book? You sure you're okay? Want me to get Annie?'

Hazel wrinkled her nose and tugged him down next to her. 'There was another book.' She was looking at him like he should know what she was talking about but he definitely didn't and frankly all he could think about right now was how close she was and how sweet she smelled and that she was wearing shorts which he'd never seen her do and the beautiful, soft skin on her legs, and...

'Another clue!' she said, dropping her voice like it was a

secret. He wanted to have secrets with Hazel Kelly. 'I found another book with another clue.'

'Oh! Right. The book clues.'

'Yeah.' She nodded her head and her curls bounced around her shoulders. 'And it was about eating blueberries and look!' She flipped up the leaves of a nearby plant and exposed the fresh fruit underneath. 'Blueberries.' Her tone was hushed, like these berries held some kind of answers for her.

'That's ... cool.' That was an inadequate response but Hazel nodded again and plucked one of the berries.

'They're really good, too.' She brought the fruit to her lips and popped it in her mouth and Noah's world ground to a halt. The only thing that existed in that moment was Hazel's mouth and her little sigh of happiness and the fireflies lighting up around her head.

Her eyes closed as she ate the berries and Noah just stared. Anyone that didn't realize that Hazel was hot as hell had their head up their ass.

'You want one?' she asked, her eyes fluttering open again. She picked a few more berries and placed them reverently in his palm.

'Thanks.' The word came out strangled and Noah cleared his throat.

'Here.' Hazel passed him the wine and he took a long swallow before eating the berries. The combination was tart and sweet and summery.

Hazel smiled at him. His head spun.

'I think I need your help.'

Anything. 'Okay.'

She pushed her glasses up her nose. 'I need help with my summer... I mean... I need help having fun.'

'You need help having fun?'

'An adventure.' She waved her hand around, gesturing to ... everything? 'I want to follow the clues, assuming there will be more, and I want to just ... I don't know... I want to be reckless. I've spent my whole life being safe and now I want ... adventure, excitement. I want a good story to tell over drinks.'

'And you want me to help you?'

Hazel shrugged, looking away from him now. 'It seems like you'd be good at it. At fun, summer adventuring. That's what you do, right?'

'Are you ... hiring me?'

'No!' Hazel's eyes went wide. 'No, that's not what I meant. Sorry, I'm messing this up. I just thought you seemed excited about the clues and you're just more ... I don't know ... interesting than anyone else I know ... and I thought you might want to help me. Sorry I shouldn't have said anything.'

'Hazel.'

'Yeah?'

'Of course I'll help you.' Did a part of him wish this help had something to do with anything other than reckless fun? Sure. But Noah recognized his strengths.

'You will?'

'Yeah, I'd love to help with your book clues.'

Her eyes lit up. He'd made Hazel Kelly happy.

He didn't get to savor that thought because her mouth crashed into his before he could register what was happening and oh God, she tasted like berries and wine. A soft groan left his mouth before he could stop it and Hazel leaned deeper into him. Her hands had come to rest on his chest and she twisted her fingers in his shirt, pulling him closer.

And Noah wanted to kiss her. He wanted to do so many things to Hazel Kelly and his mind was filling with all of them and she was sighing against his lips, but Hazel was drunk. And even though she'd just asked him to help her be reckless, he was pretty sure this wasn't what she meant.

And Noah had no intention of being something Hazel regretted.

'Haze,' he whispered. The name felt newly intimate on his tongue. He'd never called her that before, but he'd wanted to.

She yanked back, her eyes huge behind her glasses. 'Oh God, oh my God. I'm sorry. I'm so sorry. I don't know what is going on with me.' She tried to stand but her shoes were hanging off her feet and she couldn't seem to get them back in.

'Hey.' He grabbed her hand, keeping her next to him. 'We'll just blame it on the blueberries.'

Hazel softened and her mouth tipped into a smile. 'They are really strong blueberries.'

A surprised laugh burst from Noah. 'Yeah, they are.'

'I shouldn't have done that.' Her chin was resting on her pulled-up knees now and she directed her words to her bare toes, her shoes forgotten. 'That's not what I meant about needing your help.'

'You don't need to apologize.'

'I do!' Her expression was earnest when she turned to him. 'That isn't what I was asking for and I don't want you to think I was trying to ... I don't know ... take advantage of you.'

Noah would have laughed if she didn't look so sincere and worried. 'Haze, if you weren't kinda drunk I woulda kept on kissing you.'

Somehow her eyes widened even further. 'Really?'

'Yeah.'

'Oh. I didn't ... I mean you're ... you.'

'Right.'

'And I'm...'

'Hot.'

Hazel's laugh burst through the quiet around them. 'And I'm not your type.'

'Hot is definitely my type.'

She just shook her head, like she couldn't possibly believe he was serious. And now he had a new mission. To convince Hazel Kelly she was hot as hell and that he wanted her.

'So you'll do the clues with me?'

'Of course. Who do you think is leaving them?'

She shrugged. 'Maybe the book club? Although I don't know why they would, but they're always up to something. Plus, all the books have been in the romance section, and that's their usual haunt so ... I don't even really know if the clues are meant for me but I just feel like ... I don't know ... like maybe they'll help.'

Noah still didn't really know what she meant but he nodded like he did and pulled his knees up to his chest. He rested his forearms across them and looked out over the plants. Besides the blueberry bushes there were strawberry plants too, but the fruit had already been picked earlier in the summer. This must be where Henry's famous strawberry jam came from. For a minute, Noah worried the old man might come out and yell at them. Something about sitting outside in the dark with a cute girl and a possibly stolen bottle of wine made him feel sixteen again.

'I'm about to turn thirty.' Hazel's voice was quiet in the darkness, nearly drowned out by the chorus of crickets chirping around them. 'Well, in two months I am.'

'I'll be sure to get you a gift.'

She huffed a little laugh before going on. 'I feel like I forgot to do my twenties. Like I didn't fully live them, or something. I feel ... stuck.'

'And the clues are going to unstick you?'

Hazel's breathy laugh sent a little thrill down Noah's spine.

'It sounds stupid.'

'Not stupid.'

'I just want to have a fun summer. What's left of it anyway.'

'Well, you hired the right guy.'

'I'm not paying you.'

Noah laughed. 'Good. That would make me feel dirty.'

Hazel smacked his arm, tipping into him slightly before righting herself. 'Wait, how old are you?' she asked, like this was suddenly very important. He liked tipsy Hazel. She was more honest. And looked at him less like she didn't understand what planet he was from and more like she wanted to kiss him again.

He liked that a lot.

'Twenty-five.'

She groaned, covering her face with her hands. 'Noooo...'

'No?'

'No, you cannot be twenty-five! God, now I'm a lecherous old lady!'

'If lecherous means you want to get in my pants, I'm totally fine with it.'

Another playful smack, another delicious Hazel giggle.

'And almost thirty is not old.'

'It's a lot older than twenty-five. And if you ask most of my friends they'd tell you I act more like I'm seventy.'

'Your friends? Logan talks to animals, Jeanie can't decide if she lives here or in her own apartment, and Annie is engaged in a one-sided feud with the owner of the only good bar in town. These friends should not be telling you how to behave, Haze.'

She was laughing again, doubling over with giggles now, her hair falling into her face. 'What I want to know,' she said, between gasping breaths, 'is do the animals talk back?'

Noah took another swig of wine. 'Oh God, I hope not.'

'I love them, though,' she said, her giggles petering out.

'Of course you do. I just meant, don't let them dictate how you think about yourself.'

'Very wise for someone so young.'

Noah huffed and nearly protested but Hazel was leaning into him now, the side of her body pressed against the side of his and he couldn't form sentences or complete thoughts so he just took another sip of wine and then passed her the bottle.

She took a sip too and sighed. Her head was nearly on his shoulder, her soft curls brushing against his chin.

'What's this one from?' Her finger traced lightly over the tattoo of a scorpion on the inside of his forearm. Noah shivered.

'Senior year of high school. Thought it would look cool and impress a girl.'

'Did it?' The question was soft and sleepy. Her finger was still tracing his arm and Noah had to force his brain to think.

'Look cool? Not really. Impress the girl? Yes.'

Hazel's small puff of laughter skated over his arm. 'I bet you always impress the girl.'

Noah cleared his throat. 'Some of them.'

'Where do you get these? I've always wondered.' Her fingers ran over the colorful braided bracelets he wore on his wrist. Friendship bracelets, the kind girls make at summer camp.

'My nieces make them for me and send them in the mail.'

'And you wear them.'

'They require photographic evidence of me wearing them at all times.'

Another quiet laugh. 'You're a good uncle.'

He would have shrugged but he didn't want to do anything to dislodge Hazel's head from where it was now resting on his shoulder. He was actually a pretty crappy uncle, avoiding going home as much as possible, but he didn't want to tell Hazel that, either. He wanted her to think he was a good uncle. And wise beyond his years. And really anything other than just a reckless, fun time.

But if reckless fun was what she needed, then that was what he'd give her. Anything to spend more time with her.

'There you two are! We thought you left.' Annie's voice cut through the silence and sent Hazel careening away from him. She would have tipped over if he hadn't caught her elbow and held her upright.

'Or got murdered,' Jeanie added, following behind her with a flashlight.

'No one is going to get murdered here.' Logan pulled up the rear, a small black cat snuggled in his arms. Where the hell had that thing come from? It was like the man attracted strays.

'It's just so dark out here. We'd never see it coming.' Jeanie shone the light across the strawberry patch, lighting up the incriminating scene of Hazel and the wine and Noah beside her. Jeanie's eyebrows rose.

'Whatcha guys doing?'

'Eating berries,' Hazel said, shielding her eyes from the light.

'You and Noah were just sitting here in the dark, eating berries?' Annie said 'eating berries' like it was the most absurd thing she could imagine.

'Yep. That's what we were doing.' Noah stood and held a hand out to Hazel, who took it and let herself be hauled up. She brushed the dirt off her butt and faced her friends.

'Sorry I drank all your wine.' She handed Logan the empty bottle on her way past, weaving dangerously in the dark.

'I'll drive her home.' Noah followed her toward the driveway, ignoring the surprised and curious faces of their friends.

'To her home! Not yours!' Annie called after him and he waved her off. He stopped that kiss in the field, didn't he? He would never take advantage of Hazel, or any other woman for that matter, but he was more than excited to start their adventure together.

By the end, she'd be kissing him with no wine required.

Chapter Five

Hazel was hungover. But it was Thursday and she had a standing breakfast date with her dad on Thursdays, so here they were in their usual booth at the diner on the corner of Main and Central, the one with the best pancakes and mediocre coffee. She'd stop at the Pumpkin Spice Café on her way to work for something actually drinkable.

The diner was filled with the usual weekday crowd, which consisted mostly of very loud seniors. Hazel's head pounded every time Amir Sharma raised his voice to argue with Rico Stephens about their ongoing football pool, and the crowd of retirees in the back corner was getting rowdier by the second.

'You look terrible, Hazelnut.'

'Thanks, Dad. That's sweet of you to say.'

Her dad took a sip of his coffee. 'You know I value honesty.'

'I'm hungover.'

'On a Thursday?' The mayor looked truly scandalized. So maybe, 'act like a teenager' mission accomplished?

'Yep. Logan and Jeanie had people over for a bonfire last night.'

'And things got rowdy?'

Hazel snorted into her orange juice. Things hadn't gotten rowdy, she'd just lost her mind, got drunk in a berry patch, and assaulted a fisherman. She wasn't entirely sure this was the kick off to the last months of her twenties that she wanted, but it sure was reckless.

'You could say that.'

'I hope you didn't drive home in that condition.'

Hazel refused to think about the drive home, or Noah's forearms flexing as he turned the wheel, or the way he walked her to the door and helped her inside. She was not thinking about the kiss he left on her cheek or the way he said, 'Goodnight Haze.' Her nickname whispered in his deep voice sending chills through her body. Nope. Nope she wasn't.

'Of course I didn't drive home like that.'

'Just making sure.'

'I'm twenty-nine, Dad.'

'And yet somehow, still my baby.'

Her father was ridiculous and also adorable so she let it slide. Today he was wearing a tie covered in rubber duckies, a sky-blue button down, and his signature glasses that kept slipping down his nose. It was hard to stay irritated at him.

'How's Frank?'

'He's good, sends you a kiss.' Frank was her dad's husband and the whole reason they moved to Dream Harbor in the first place. He was another father to Hazel, but she'd probably always call him Frank.

'And Mom?'

'Mom's good, starting to gear up for the school year.' Hazel's mother made the move with them to Dream Harbor and lived upstairs in the two-family house they all shared. Some people seemed to find it odd, but Hazel never did. Her parents had never been together in that way. Just two friends who decided to make a baby together and it had worked out just fine for everyone.

Hazel had no siblings unless you counted her mother's two French bulldogs, Diego and Frida, which her mother definitely did. She taught art at the middle school and was known for the often scandalous, always nude, sculptures she made in her spare time.

'Middle-schoolers are rough. I don't know how she does it.'

'Your mother loves a challenge.'

'Hmm. I guess so.' Hazel smiled at the new waitress as she set a heaping plate of pancakes in front of her. 'Thank you.'

'Mayor Kelly.' Her father stuck out his hand as soon as the woman's hands were empty. 'I don't believe we've met.' He smiled his biggest smile and Hazel bit down on her lip at how delightfully nerdy her father was.

The woman smiled back and took his hand. 'Maribel. Nice to meet you.'

'Are you new to town?'

'Yes. We moved in a few weeks ago.'

'And how are you finding things so far?'

'Very well, thanks.'

Hazel tuned out her father's welcome speech as she dug into her breakfast. She already knew the ins and outs of Dream Harbor plenty well by now. But Maribel seemed pleased with the chat as she moved on to take Dot and Norman's order, who were snuggled up together in the next booth over.

'You know you can't know every single person in this town, right?'

Her dad smiled indulgently, cutting into his omelet. 'I can try.'

'Dad, do you ever feel ... I don't know ... stuck?'

He paused with a forkful of omelet halfway to his mouth. He lowered his fork. 'Sure. Sometimes everyone feels that way, I think. Why? Is everything alright?'

Hazel waved his concern away with a hand. 'It's nothing serious. Just been feeling, I don't know ... restless.'

Her father smiled, resuming his eating. 'Sounds like you just need a fun summer,' he said between bites.

A fun summer.

I woulda kept kissing you.

Noah's words echoed through her brain like they had been all night. She felt the heat rush to her face. She loved her dad, but she certainly wasn't going to discuss *that* type of fun summer with him.

'Yeah, you're probably right.'

'Of course I'm right. I'm your dad.'

Hazel smirked, shoveling in the last of her pancakes. 'Right. Okay, well I gotta get to work.' She slid out of the booth and planted a kiss on her father's cheek. 'Love you.'

'Love you.' Her father waved goodbye as she left and by the time she was outside he'd already joined his deputy mayor, Mindy, and her best friend, Tammy, at the next table over. Hazel smiled at them through the window. Her father never tired of talking to people.

It was a warm morning, but not hot yet, and Hazel let herself appreciate the early sun on her face. The walk to the bookstore was short, and even with a stop at the café for her new favorite apple cider iced tea, Hazel was early. The store wasn't supposed to open for another half hour which made it all the more surprising to find a certain fisherman propped against her emerald green door.

'Noah.'

A slow grin crossed his face and Hazel clutched her iced tea tighter. Protection against that smile.

'Hey,' he said, all low and deep, the sound vibrating through her in that way that made her lose all coherent thought.

'What are you doing here?'

'I just wanted to make sure you were okay.'

'Of course I'm okay.' She sounded grumpier than she meant to, but she was not prepared to face Noah yet, certainly not after last night. She was hoping to avoid him for at least a week or two. Or possibly forever.

'Well, last night you seemed...'

'I'm fine. I just need to get to work.' She gestured toward the door where he was still leaning and blocking her escape.

'Right, sorry, I just thought...'

He shuffled out of the way and Hazel unlocked the door, but she couldn't very well slam it in his face, so she had no choice but to let him follow her in.

'Was this place always called The Cinnamon Bun Bookstore?' he asked, following along behind her.

'Nope.'

'Why'd you change it?'

'The owner likes to keep things fresh.'

'So ... are there cinnamon buns?' he asked, hope clear in his voice.

Hazel bit down on a smile. 'Every Sunday morning.' It was Hazel's favorite thing about the rebranding; the smell of cinnamon and sugar every Sunday made working on the weekends a pleasure.

'How did I not know this?'

Hazel shrugged. 'It's kinda new.'

'Anyway, I just wanted to make sure you were all right,' he tried again and Hazel turned to face him. The morning sun highlighted gold streaks in his copper hair. He had a sunburn across his nose and cheeks but somehow he looked healthy and sexy instead of like a giant crustacean as she usually did. He had an uncharacteristically worried crease between his brows.

She sighed. He looked genuinely concerned about her. 'I'm fine. Really.'

His gaze raked over her like he was assessing for

damage, like somehow after he left her house last night, she'd managed to fall down a well or something. Her first big reckless night and Hazel had set off alarm bells in two of the men in her life. And she hadn't even left the garden. A clear sign that she had been living far too safely for the past twenty-nine years.

Noah met her gaze and nodded, apparently believing that she was fine. 'Great.' His expression turned from worried to mischievous. 'So, when do we start the clues?'

Heat crept up her cheeks at the memory of all the things she said last night, the things she asked for and confessed. That insane kiss. She hadn't been that drunk, just loose enough to be honest. To do the things she'd really wanted to do.

'You don't have to do that. It was a crazy idea.'

His smile slipped. 'Oh.'

I woulda kept kissing you.

What was she doing? This man, this very sexy man, was offering to spend the rest of the summer with her and she was just, what? Not going to do it? Wasn't this exactly what she'd wanted? A chance to spend the last days of her twenties having reckless adventures?

And looking at Noah right now, sun-kissed and windswept, his brown eyes watching her, this idea felt *very* reckless. Spending time with Noah could backfire in any number of ways ranging from her going overboard off his boat to developing actual feelings for this man who had no real ties to this town and could up and leave at any time.

But Hazel was officially throwing caution, sense and

practicality out the window. For the next two months. This morning, completely sober and in the bright light of day, Hazel was making a decision. She was going to do this for herself. She was going to take Noah up on his offer. And whatever else this summer handed to her.

'However, there aren't any new clues yet.' She pointed to the neatly organized shelves behind him. His face lit up again. She was quickly learning that Noah's emotions were never far from the surface of his handsome face and maybe all that staring at her and smiling that he did was ... him *actually* having the hots for her?

She was getting ahead of herself. Noah offered to help her have a fun summer not be her summer fling. Right? Right. That would be weird. You don't just ask someone to have *that* kind of fun summer with you.

Damn it. She was probably blushing up to her ears right now.

'But you'll let me know when there is?'

'Uh, yeah. I mean if there are any more. Who knows.'

'Well, if there isn't then we'll just have to make our own fun.' His smile grew and thankfully Hazel's iced tea was in a metal travel mug or she would have crushed the cup by now. 'I've got a tour this afternoon but text me if you find anything.' He tossed the words over his shoulder like it was all very casual. Like Hazel didn't feel as though she just made some kind of nefarious deal with a very handsome pirate.

She was being crazy.

Noah was a friend. They were just two friends who

decided to follow the clues left in her bookstore. Nope that still sounded crazy.

'Okay, sure.' She raised a hand in goodbye as Noah left. She watched him walk past the front windows and then disappear down the street. He was far too good-looking for this to end well, but it was too late now. She'd recruited the sexy, town fisherman to help her have an adventurous end of summer/end of her twenties and she was suddenly feeling as though she was in way over her head.

Hazel sighed and went to hang her bag up in the back office before it was time to open. She didn't really think of it as her office since it was where everyone kept their coats and bags and contained the sofa where staff usually ate their lunches. But the desk was hers.

And it was the perfect spot to rest her head and think about what she'd just agreed to.

Chapter Six

It was nearly a week before Hazel found the next clue. Enough time to almost forget about them, to realize the whole thing had been a silly misunderstanding. Enough time to decide spending the next few months with Noah was actually a terrible idea.

Even though she still kinda wanted to.

But the real reason she didn't tell Noah about the clue was because it was actually pretty mundane. A clue she could follow completely on her own. One she was planning to do anyway, really. So she didn't need a guide or an adventurous companion at all.

That was why she was at the grocery store buying ingredients for milkshakes by herself. And also why she was hiding in the frozen-food aisle because she'd just seen Noah walk in and now she was trying to calculate if she could check out before he spotted her. Which was crazy. He didn't need to know she'd found another marked book today, this one with a line about drinking vanilla shakes like the person leaving the clues wanted to make sure she enjoyed all her favorite tastes of summer before it was over. He didn't need to know she had broken her promise.

She could just be at the grocery store. Like a normal person. Which she just happened to be.

Right. No problem. She grabbed a carton of vanilla ice cream and put it in her basket next to the milk and the sprinkles she'd chosen to add to the top. And she was ready to confidently walk to the register when a voice behind her stopped her in her tracks.

'Hazel Kelly.' A low, deep rumble that did things to her that she'd rather not explore in the frozen food section. Or maybe ever.

She turned to find Noah leaning against the freezers with a mischievous grin on his face.

'Fancy meeting you here,' he said, prowling closer.

Hazel clutched her basket to her body. 'Just getting some groceries.'

Noah peered into her basket. 'Ice cream and sprinkles, yum.'

'And milk.' Hazel pointed out like it mattered that she was also buying milk, like that absolved her of her lies.

'Making milkshakes?' he asked, still smiling as though he knew her secret.

'I had a craving, and my favorite shake place closed last year so I thought I would make one instead.' She was rambling. This was ridiculous. Noah had no right to make her so flustered all the time. He was just a regular human

man. And Hazel refused to think about the fact that this was the second time he'd shown up at the scene of one of her clues. It was the grocery store. Plenty of people were here.

It wasn't weird that she'd just run into Andy in the produce department and Joe in the baking aisle, also looking for sprinkles. It was a small town. That was to be expected. This was all to be expected, including the handsome man staring at her like he wanted to eat her and wash it down with a milkshake.

Hazel swallowed hard.

'So...' She shifted the basket to her other arm.

'So, enjoy your shake, Haze.' He was about to walk away and she couldn't let him because he was here. *Again.* And she didn't want to drink her shake alone anyway. And she did promise...

'It was a clue!' she blurted out and Noah's eyebrows rose. 'I didn't tell you. I found another book clue and it was about milkshakes but that seemed boring so I didn't tell you.'

Noah's smile grew. 'A clue?'

Hazel sighed. 'Vanilla milkshakes are objectively better. Colder and Sweeter. Evie smiled around her straw and took another sip.' Hazel quoted from memory the clue she'd found this morning, looking somewhere over Noah's shoulder instead of at his face while she said it.

'Perfect!' he said like she'd nailed her line for the school play.

'Perfect?'

'Yeah, I couldn't agree more. Vanilla shakes are the best.'

'True.'

'And we're both here now ... so...'

Hazel couldn't help her smile at Noah's hopeful tone. 'Do you want to have a milkshake with me?' she asked.

'There is literally nothing else I'd rather do.' He held her gaze and Hazel believed him. She couldn't think of a single thing she'd rather do either, as it turned out.

'Sorry I broke my promise.'

'I forgive you.' He linked his arm with hers and escorted her down the frozen-food aisle. 'But for future reference, Haze, milkshakes are never boring.'

Hazel laughed, relief and warmth and excitement flowing through her.

Okay, universe, or whoever you are, I'm officially done fighting this thing. Lead the way.

'Your blender or mine?' Noah asked as they walked out into the warm air of the evening.

Hazel didn't feel prepared to let Noah into her space yet. That felt like a step too far. 'Yours,' she said, letting Noah put the shopping bags in the trunk of her car.

'Perfect. Meet you there.'

It wasn't until she was driving away that she realized Noah hadn't bought whatever it was he'd come to the grocery store for in the first place.

Maybe she flustered him, too?

Noah probably should have mentioned that he didn't actually own a blender, but Hazel had a tendency to scramble his thoughts.

But it was working out okay.

It was a slow night at Mac's and the pub owner/landlord didn't seem to mind them coming down to the bar and borrowing his. Or at least he hadn't kicked them out. Yet.

'Are you sure we're allowed to be back here?' Hazel whispered, crowding closer to him in the cramped kitchen.

'Of course. As Mac's favorite employee...'

Danny snorted loud enough to be heard over the dishwasher.

Noah cleared his throat. 'One of Mac's favorite employees.'

Hazel laughed.

'There are certain perks,' Noah went on, grabbing the blender from the top metal shelf. Mac only busted this thing out on frozen margarita nights. Noah set it down on the counter as Hazel pulled the ice cream and milk from her bag.

'Oh, really?'

'Sure. I pop down here for late night snacks all the time.'

Hazel laughed again, her gaze drifting over his shoulder. 'Is that so? And Mac doesn't mind?'

'What Mac doesn't know can't hurt him,' he said with a wink.

'You know we have security cameras, right?' Mac's voice scared Noah enough that he clapped a hand over his chest.

'Jesus! Why are you so quiet?'

'You couldn't hear me over your bizarre bragging.' Mac quirked a dark, unamused eyebrow. 'Hey, Hazel.'

Hazel was doubled over in giggles and Noah would let Mac make fun of him all day just to keep listening to that sound.

'Hey, Mac,' she said, gasping a little for breath.

'You're cleaning this up.' Mac gestured to the mess they were already making. 'And put some damn clothes on if you're going to sneak down here in the middle of the night. I'm tired of seeing your skinny ass on video.'

Hazel laughed so hard she snorted, making her laugh even harder.

Noah grinned. 'It's not that skinny. Muscular is how I would describe it.'

Hazel wiped her eyes with the back of her hand. 'Muscular?' she squeaked, the giggles still fizzing out of her.

'Yeah, right,' Mac muttered, making his way to the back office.

'Is he angry?' Hazel asked, finally getting her laughter under control.

Noah waved the other man off. 'You know Mac.'

Hazel nodded. Of course she knew Mac. She'd known him most of her life, like everyone else in this odd little town, and for a minute Noah was almost jealous. Jealous of all the people who'd had so many more years with Hazel than he had.

He shook his head. She was here now, smiling at him, her eyes still full of laughter.

'Ready?' he asked, reaching for the ice cream.

'Very.'

They filled the blender with ice cream and just enough milk to make the shakes drinkable and then poured the concoction into tall beer glasses, the only things they could find that made sense for a shake.

Hazel shook sprinkles on top of each one with a flourish. 'There. That makes them special.'

Noah resisted the urge to tell her they were special because she was here and she was special. He'd already cornered her in the grocery store after he'd vowed to himself to let her come to him next. That was enough overdoing it for one day.

Instead he sipped his shake, barely able to get it through the straw. It was thick and cold and sweet.

'So good,' Hazel moaned and Noah forcibly shoved his thoughts away from where they wanted to go, which was hearing Hazel moaning those words about something very different. Something involving him between her thighs.

'Thanks,' she said.

Noah blinked. 'Uh ... for what?'

'The shake. It came out a lot better than mine usually do.'

'Must be the fancy blender.'

Hazel smiled, the straw between her teeth. 'Must be.'

'Or that we make a good team.'

She tipped her head, studying him. Deciding something. Something about him. And the moment felt monumentally important. Even though it shouldn't. Even though they were just drinking milkshakes in the kitchen at Mac's with Danny washing dishes a few feet away. Nothing about this moment was important.

And yet...

'Yeah, I guess we do.'

He couldn't help but feel like he'd passed the test.

Chapter Seven

'Alex?'

'Yeah?' Hazel's best employee looked up from where they were picking crayons up off the carpet. Alex had purple hair, an amazing read-aloud voice, and an encyclopedic knowledge of Dream Harbor history. They were beloved by the youngest and oldest customers alike.

'Did you happen to see anyone messing around by these shelves during story time?'

Alex came to stand next to where Hazel was staring at the Romance section. 'Did I see any preschoolers messing up the romance books? Uh, no.'

Hazel huffed. 'What about their grown-ups?'

'A few people bought some books while they were here. I don't really remember if they were romance or not. Want me to check?' Alex pointed to the computer, but Hazel waved them off.

'No, no it's fine.' She'd already grabbed the upside

down, dog-eared book off the shelf before Alex could ask questions, but she was still curious if Alex had seen anything ... suspicious. She couldn't very well say that without explaining the whole thing which she was not at all prepared to do.

Preschool story hour tended to be crowded and today was no different. Hazel booked a different local author every month to share their latest book and read an old favorite. Annie's bakery sent over treats and the parents and kids loved it. Hazel did, too. But she'd been so busy, she had completely forgotten about the clues until the last tiny customers filed out and she'd spotted an upside-down book.

Her mind raced over who had been here today. Isabel and her kids, George had come by with his little nephew, Annie of course to drop off the cookies, Tammy with her granddaughter, and that was just the beginning. It had been a zoo. There was no way Hazel could narrow down the suspects.

She wasn't sure it really mattered, but she wanted to know who was leaving these messages. And even if she had her own reasons for following them, she still wanted to know why they were doing it. Was it all a big joke?

She didn't like to think she was the butt of a joke.

Alex had gone back to their clean-up efforts, scraping stepped-on crayons from the carpet, so Hazel ducked behind the counter and peeked inside the book.

The descent of the Ferris wheel made her stomach swoop with nerves.

Hazel hated Ferris wheels. Or heights in general.

But that obstacle would have to wait.

There were crayons to scrape and surfaces to disinfect. Preschoolers were savages.

Noah was just getting off his boat when a text pinged on his phone. It was a picture of a page in a book. A page with a single highlighted line.

He grinned.

A ferris wheel, huh?

He leaned against a post on the dock, waiting for her response. It didn't take long for another text to appear.

I hate heights.

Sounds like this mystery person wants you to face your fears

That's crap

He laughed out loud, startling a nearby seagull.

I thought you wanted a reckless summer?

Reckless like fun, not like terrifying

Sometimes the two go together

All she sent after that was a grumpy-face emoji so Noah continued his trek back to his car parked in the marina parking lot. It was a small marina; the harbor Dream Harbor was named after wasn't much more than an inlet with a rocky coast. Besides Noah's boat, there were a handful of other fishing boats and a few pleasure boats docked alongside.

Dream Harbor wasn't a big tourist destination, at least not compared to other towns up and down the coast. Other than the old inn up on the hill and the new, swanky spa and resort they'd put in a few years ago, there weren't many places for people to stay, but still the population grew every summer with guests looking for a relaxing vacation. Noah was convinced his little beach-cottage idea would draw people to town looking for a quiet seaside getaway without the jam-packed beaches and overcrowded restaurants in other destinations. And due to the fact that there were only a handful of houses, even a steady turnover of guests wouldn't actually add to the town's population much at all. He hoped this would alleviate some of the townsfolk's concerns.

It was a good idea. He knew it was, even when he didn't really believe it. He just had to wrap his mind around how to sell it to the town council. They were incredibly protective of the town's ascetics. According to Logan, it had taken years and many heated arguments and multiple Mayor Kelly dreams to convince the good people of Dream Harbor that putting in one spa would not in fact destroy the entire town.

And if it wasn't for the inn, Noah wouldn't have a business at all. Can't take out-of-towners on fishing tours if they have no place to stay afterwards. But Noah grew up in a tourist town. He understood why Dream Harbor didn't want to turn itself over completely to impermanent residents.

He was sure there was a way to balance the two, though. Someday he'd get around to presenting his idea. Maybe.

Noah climbed into his car, leaving the windows down. Despite what Annie said, he did in fact smell pretty fishy when he got off the boat and he was looking forward to a shower. He shot Hazel one more text before pulling out.

Sounds like we're heading to the carnival this weekend.

Her response was immediate and he couldn't help his smile.

I'll go to the carnival but no ferris wheel

We'll see . . .

NO FERRIS WHEEL

He laughed and tossed his phone aside. He didn't care if they went on every ride or did nothing but stand around. He had a date with Hazel Kelly. And all he'd needed to get it was for some cryptic messages to appear in the pages of a book. Not his usual style, but he'd take it.

By the time he was out of the shower and sprawled on his bed, he had three more messages from Hazel.

I think we should meet at the carnival.

Around 8.

And maybe don't mention this whole clue thing to anyone.

He frowned.

Why?

I don't know, I still feel kinda ridiculous about it. Also we need to figure out some suspects.

Suspects?

Yeah, like who is leaving them and why.

He rolled over onto his back, a smile on his face. He liked talking to Hazel. He liked that he got to.

I didn't realize there would be a mystery-solving component to this arrangement.

Don't call it an arrangement. That sounds weird.

Okay. What should I call it? Hazel and Noah's Summer of Fun!

No.

HANSOF for short

Definitely not.

HANSOF!!

Summer is nearly over anyway

Yeah but 'Hazel and Noah's two months before her thirtieth birthday of fun' just doesn't have the same ring to it.

Dear Lord, what have I gotten myself into?

The best summer you've ever had.

He was making big promises here, but he had to. Go big or go home, right? And if this was his one shot with Hazel he sure as hell was going to take it. Whatever the bizarre circumstances that got them here.

Oh yeah?

Guaranteed.

Wow.

I'm very good at fun, Hazel.

He thought of Hazel's wine-flavored lips. She was very good at fun too, whether she knew it or not.

I believe it.

Noah had never attended the Dream Harbor PTA presents A Midsummer Night's Carnival before. It hadn't felt like the sort of thing a single man should attend by himself. He imagined it would be filled mostly with small children, dragging their parents along to play a few games and stay up past their bedtimes, and not much else. A small, school-run affair for kids to celebrate their freedom before school started up again. Not something anyone else attended.

He was very wrong.

Like most things in Dream Harbor, the town locals had turned out in force. Add to that the influx of tourists for the event and the carnival was packed. The town green was filled with rides. Teacups, spinning swings, and a small roller coaster had sprung up overnight. The giant lit-up Ferris wheel loomed over it all. Main street was closed to traffic and filled with game booths. Giant stuffed animals hung from wooden booths, attracting large crowds of kids and adults trying their hand at winning one. Lining the park were food trucks from every nationality and culture Noah could think of, filling the air with scents of fried dough to jerk chicken to gyros. His mouth was watering by the time he stepped up to the ticket booth.

'Hey, Noah.' Isabel smiled at him as he approached, still a bit shell-shocked by the whole thing.

'This is amazing.'

Isabel laughed. 'Yeah, the PTA goes hard for this one, but it funds most of the kids' activities for the next school year so it's worth it.'

'It's really impressive.'

Andy sat next to her, doling out tickets to a pack of middle-schoolers hopped up on cotton candy. Noah could feel the energy vibrating off them. Andy shook his head as they ran away.

'Hey, Noah.'

Noah smiled. 'I'll take whatever forty bucks will get me.'

Isabel took the cash and Andy handed him a string of the ubiquitous red tickets.

'Thanks for your support!' Isabel said before turning to her daughter, Jane, who had come running up to show her the stuffed dog she'd won.

'And it only took twenty-five tries,' her father, Marc, said with a laugh.

Isabel rolled her eyes. 'At least the money goes back to the school.'

'Cool dog,' Noah said, turning his attention to Jane. 'Maybe I'll win one, too.'

Jane looked up at him with pity. 'It's a pretty hard game. You might not win anything.'

Noah nodded, biting down on a smile. 'Okay, thanks. I'll try my best.'

'That's all you can do. Try your best.' The little girl's face was solemn as she delivered the advice before running off in the direction of the rides.

Marc shook his head. 'Much better at giving advice than taking it. Kid would not budge from that booth until she won.'

Noah laughed, clapping Marc on the shoulder. 'Good luck, man.'

'I'm going to need it.' He planted a kiss on Isabel's cheek before running off to follow his daughter.

'Have fun!' she told Noah with a wink, her gaze flitting to where Hazel was waiting for him. He didn't have time to wonder how much the Dream Harbor Book Club knew about Hazel's clues before his brain stuttered at the sight of her.

Activity and noise and lights and bodies swirled around her, but Noah only saw her. It was as though everything else was blurred but Hazel was crystal clear.

She was standing next to the cotton-candy stand, where her dad, the mayor, was cranking out big tufts of fluffy sugar. She was wearing shorts again, which Noah found wildly distracting. Her thighs felt like a personal attack. He dragged his attention back to her face. She was smiling. At him.

If there wasn't a growing line of people behind him and

Isabel staring at him like she knew exactly what was going on in his head, he might have stayed frozen there forever. But he had to move or risk causing a riot at the Midsummer Carnival ticket booth.

Hazel raised a hand in greeting as he approached. 'Hey.'

'Hi.' Very smooth opening line. He was good with women, wasn't he?

'You know my dad.'

'Noah, how are you? How's business?' Mayor Kelly smiled as he handed a stick of cotton candy to a small child. The spun sugar was larger than the kid's head.

'Business is good.'

'Wonderful, wonderful.' The man kept spinning the paper sticks through the candy as he spoke. 'I've been meaning to talk to you...'

'They're not here to talk business, hun.'

'Right, right. Sorry.'

'Do you know Frank?' Hazel asked, her hand on the other man's arm. 'This is my other dad.'

Frank gave Noah a shy smile. 'Nice to meet you.'

'Nice to meet you, too.' Noah would have reached out to shake the man's hand but Mayor Kelly was already putting a giant blue cotton-candy stick in his fist.

'Have fun you two!' Did the mayor just wink at him, too?

'Come on.' Hazel tugged him by the hand away from the stand before he could think too hard about that. 'You don't have to eat that,' she said when they were out of earshot from her dad's booth.

'Why wouldn't I eat it?'

Hazel wrinkled her nose. 'Because it's disgusting.'

'Disgusting?! What?'

A small laugh escaped her. 'It's just sugar-flavored air.'

'And why wouldn't I want sugary air? In fact, I wish all the air was sugar flavored. That would be amazing.'

'And sticky.'

He shrugged. 'I guess.' He dropped Hazel's hand to pick off some sugary fluff. It melted as soon as it hit his tongue, sending sweetness through his veins. He licked the stickiness off his fingers and he could have sworn Hazel watched him do it before tearing her gaze away.

'So what do you want to do first?'

'Well...' Noah let his gaze wander suggestively toward the Ferris wheel.

'Nope. Not ready yet.'

'Okay, no problem.' He looked around. 'How about we play some games?'

Hazel nodded. 'I can do games.'

'Great.' He pulled off some more cotton candy but before he could put it in his mouth, Hazel grabbed his forearm and rerouted the candy into her mouth instead. Her lips ghosted over his fingers and he nearly dropped the whole damn thing.

She gave a little sigh. 'Might not be as bad as I remembered.' She walked off ahead of him and he was forced to follow or risk getting lost in the crowd.

Who was this Hazel Kelly and what was he going to do with her?

He ignored the list of ideas that immediately popped into his head, starting with feeding her more cotton candy and ending with her very naked in his bed. This was a family event. Those thoughts needed to be tamped down along with the other ones about Hazel's ample thighs, her bare shoulders and all that skin he'd never paid attention to before that he now couldn't seem to stop staring at.

She glanced over her shoulder to make sure he was still behind her and a mischievous smile played around her lips.

If she kept looking at him like that he could no longer be held responsible for where his thoughts wandered off to. This Hazel Kelly was trouble.

And Noah liked trouble.

Chapter Eight

Hazel usually avoided the carnival like the plague and so she hadn't been here in years. Probably since she was in high school. In fact, she was pretty sure the reason she broke out into a cold sweat every time she looked at the Ferris wheel was because she once got stuck at the top with Annie for nearly an hour in a lightning storm and she was convinced she was going to die unkissed.

Annie had offered to do the job but it just didn't seem the same as kissing Heath Ryan, who she had a horrible, unrequited crush on at the time. So she politely declined even as the two girls huddled together, shrieking at every rumble of distant thunder.

By the time the fire department arrived, she and Annie were both soaked and terrified. And she hadn't been back to the carnival or on a Ferris wheel ever again. But that traumatic moment wasn't actually why she avoided the carnival.

She just didn't think she liked it.

Too hot.

Too crowded.

Too noisy, and chaotic, and buggy, and...

She couldn't really remember her other reasons because Noah had stepped up to the ring toss and flashed her a cocky grin like he had big plans to win her a stuffed animal. And since Hazel was a fully mature, grown woman she was not at all excited about that prospect.

She was holding his cotton candy and shoved another piece into her mouth. Sugar moved fast through her bloodstream, which was obviously why her stomach was doing weird things as she watched Noah toss three yellow rings one at a time toward the wood pegs. He missed every time.

He handed the teenager working the booth more tickets. 'That was just a warm-up.'

'Hmm. Yes, important to warm up.'

Noah grinned at her and then turned his focus back on the pegs. He missed again. Three times in a row. He groaned.

'Jane did warn me this was a tough game.'

Hazel laughed.

'She said try to do my best.'

'Good life advice.'

'Smart kindergartener.' He winked at her and then tossed another ring. It spun around the peg and then clattered to the ground. Noah hung his head. 'Damn.'

'Come on, champ. Maybe you'll have better luck at the next one.' Hazel put a hand on his arm to guide him away from the game and found her fingers lingering there on the muscles of his bicep. His arm was so ... solid.

He let himself be led and caught Hazel's hand in his before she could pull it back. His hand was solid too, big and strong and probably capable of doing so many more interesting things than ring toss.

She cleared her throat. 'You know if we hold hands the whole town will have us married off by Monday.'

His laugh was low and just for her when he leaned down to whisper in her ear. 'Fine by me.'

She peered up at him, a frown on her face as they meandered through the crowd. 'Oh, please.'

'Oh, please, what?'

Hazel let out a little disbelieving huff. 'Everyone knows you don't date women for longer than a summer. Two months max. At that rate, you'd be dumping me on my birthday.'

His copper brows rose. 'Oh, really? This is common knowledge?'

'Yep. You like tourists, temporary guests, out-of-towners. There was even a rumor that you spent a very interesting weekend with an entire bachelorette party.' Her cheeks burned at the thought. Why had she brought any of this up? Well, it was one thing to engage in this ... flirtation for the duration of their summer of fun, but to pretend it was anything more would just be ridiculous.

Not that she thought Noah actually wanted to marry her by Monday, but the town would talk. They would make assumptions. And she wanted Noah to be clear on what was going on here.

She'd like to be clear on what was going on here.

She expected him to grin and make some kind of joke about the bachelorette party but he'd gone quiet instead.

'Sorry, I didn't mean to insult you. I only ... I just ... people will talk. And I know we're just doing this as friends. A friendly summer of fun...' Hazel trailed off when Noah's gaze met hers and the look in his eye said he wanted to be something other than friends. Her breath stuttered. Oh, damn.

'No, no. You're right. I don't do long-term relationships.'

'Right.'

'And it wasn't the *entire* bachelorette party.'

'Oh.'

'But there's a first time for everything.' He winked at her, the smile back on his face as he pulled her through the crowd. A first time for everything? Wait ... for the entire bachelorette party or the long-term relationship thing?

She was about to ask more questions she shouldn't, but he was already at the next game booth, handing tickets to the perky high-school attendant and assuring Hazel that squirting targets with a water gun was more his game. And it didn't matter anyway because she hadn't intended on anything serious happening between her and Noah this summer. In fact, serious was the opposite of what she intended.

A buzzer sounded and the players, seated on small stools, started shooting their targets. The more you hit it, the faster your little racehorse ran. Noah was competing against two eight-year-olds and the mailman, Mr. Prescott.

Lights flashed and tinny music blared from the speakers. Noah was all focus, though. Hazel couldn't help but smile as he crouched over the fake gun, a furrow of concentration in his brow. And she also couldn't help the cheer that escaped her when he won.

'For you.' He proudly presented her with a giant penguin. It was easily three feet tall and stuffed with material she could only assume was carcinogenic. The entire thing felt highly flammable and utterly toxic but she held it to her chest like a kid on Christmas.

'I love him.'

Noah laughed, his eyes crinkling in the corners. 'Just imagine what the rumor mill will crank out now.'

'Noah and Hazel elope in Antarctica. Bring home new pet.'

'Hazel gives birth to three-foot-tall tuxedoed baby.'

Giggles fizzed from her as they walked away from the booth, penguin tucked beneath her arm. The cotton candy was long gone.

She grinned up at him. Maybe she liked the carnival after all.

'Noah's much more handsome brother comes to town and sweeps Hazel off her feet.'

He feigned offense at that one. 'Hey. More handsome? Now that just hurts, Haze.'

'Do you even have a brother?'

'Nope. Two sisters. Both older than me. Both smarter and more responsible.'

'But definitely not handsomer.'

He laughed again, taking her free hand in his. She let him. Let the Dream Harbor rumor mill say what it would. She wasn't afraid of them.

'Definitely not. But don't tell them I said so.'

'Never.' They'd wandered toward the food trucks. 'Should we get something to eat? Like some real food?'

'Sure.'

After much deliberation they settled on chicken gyros and an absurdly large fresh squeezed lemonade to share. They sat at a sticky picnic table across from each other while small children ran screeching by. The night was hot and humid and Hazel's thighs stuck to the metal bench, but somehow she didn't seem to mind as much as she usually did.

'I'd like to meet them,' she said.

'Meet who? The bachelorette party I allegedly debauched? Lovely girls.'

She smacked his arm. 'No! Your sisters.'

'Really?'

'Yeah, of course.'

'Why?'

She shrugged. 'I don't know. You're kind of a mystery around here.'

'A mystery? I like that.' He waggled his eyebrows, taking another bite of his gyro.

'I'm serious. You just kinda showed up here one day and I feel like I don't know much about you.'

'Believe it or not, Haze, there are a lot of towns out there that people come and go from without anyone noticing.'

'Well, that's sad.'

He shrugged but was no longer meeting her eye. His playfulness was gone. Hazel had managed to suck the fun out of the freaking carnival.

'I'm sure plenty of people noticed when you moved here.'

'Oh, they definitely noticed when I bailed on the family business.'

'Oh.'

'I'm not so much a mystery as a screw-up. Sorry to disappoint.'

'You don't disappoint me at all.'

He met her gaze again, a look of quiet surprise on his face. He quickly covered it up with a charming grin. 'I think we need to get back on track.'

'We do?'

'Yep. I promised you a fun night. HANSOF, remember? We can't be sitting around talking about my family drama on a HANSOF night.'

'Sounds like a German cousin or something.'

Noah laughed, the playfulness back in his eyes.

'And HANSOF says no more family talk. It's time for the Ferris wheel.'

Hazel hugged her penguin tighter. 'I think I've had plenty of fun for one night. I should probably get to bed.'

'Haze, it's nine o'clock.'

'I'm tired.'

'Haze, nine o'clock is an old-lady bedtime.'

'I'm an old lady.'

'No, you are young and vibrant and fun. And sexy.' Another wink. How did he make winking not creepy?

'Sexy?'

'Terribly.'

She rolled her eyes, but heat had crept into her cheeks anyway. Noah, debaucher of entire bachelorette parties, thought she was sexy. It made her head spin.

'Okay, fine. We can do the Ferris wheel, but if I vomit on you, that's your fault.'

'Understood.' He held out a hand and helped her up from her sticky bench. 'Kinda wishing we did the rides before eating, though.'

She laughed. 'No turning back now.'

He held her gaze another second, something heavier there now, before pulling her toward the rides. *No turning back now.*

The Ferris wheel couldn't do anything to her stomach that Noah's stare wasn't already doing.

'Just squeeze my hand ... oww ... a little less squeezing.'

'Sorry.' Hazel eased her grip but did not open her eyes. She was crammed into a Ferris wheel seat with Noah and her penguin, slowly rising up over the carnival, but she wasn't thinking about that. Or about the fact that this Ferris wheel had literally been assembled that morning, and by whom?! And what if they'd missed a screw or something? She wasn't thinking about any of that.

She was focused instead on Noah's fingers wrapped around hers, and his warm body against her side, and his deep voice in her ear. And frankly, all of that was making her dizzy in an entirely different way.

'You should really open your eyes. It's beautiful up here.'

'Why are we stopping?' Hazel's heart lurched as the wheel stopped.

'They're letting more people on.'

'I hate that.'

'That other people get to ride, too?'

She had to open her eyes to smack his shoulder and found him grinning at her. 'No. I got stuck at the top once.'

'For how long?'

'Like an hour. But it was storming.'

'Shit, Hazel. You didn't tell me you had like actual trauma around the thing.' He loosened his fingers from hers and wrapped his arm around her instead. She didn't hate it.

'I'm fine. I think.' She peered over the front of the carriage and found the carnival lit up below her. Music and laughter drifted on the evening breeze, muting the frenetic energy of the fair and giving an ephemeral quality to the night. Beyond the carnival, the twinkling lights of Dream Harbor made the town feel both cozy and distant, like another world she had the opportunity to see just for a moment. She could even spot the marina from here and the lights on the docks. The beauty was nearly enough to make her forget to be afraid.

'Any urge to puke?'

'Uh ... no. Not at the moment.' The wheel started turning and they continued their descent. Hazel's stomach dipped and she squeezed her eyes shut again, burrowing her face into Noah's shoulder.

Salt air and sunshine and soap. She breathed deep. Noah's arm stayed firm around her shoulders as they reached the ground and swooped back up for another rotation. Hazel looked this time.

'This might be fun.'

'You sound surprised.'

'I am.'

He laughed, the feel of it ghosting over her cheeks. Their heads were close together, the seat was small and the penguin was big. They didn't have much choice.

'You know what might be even more fun?' he asked.

'What?'

'If we made out up here.'

His smile said he was teasing but his eyes said he was dead serious. He was closer now, his nose brushing against her cheek, his forehead leaning against hers. And everything about this felt reckless.

Hazel leaned in.

Her lips brushed against his. Noah made a sound somewhere between a groan and a sigh so Hazel deepened the kiss, her tongue swept into his mouth and he was cotton candy and lemonade and summer and Hazel *liked* it.

She pulled away as the wheel turned to bring them back down and caught Noah's dazed expression in the multi-colored lights of the rides.

'Damn, Hazel Kelly,' he whispered.

And she smiled.

Chapter Nine

Noah had still not recovered physically or mentally from kissing Hazel the night before, and he needed an iced coffee before his first tour of the day.

The cool air of The Pumpkin Spice Café hit him as he walked in. The place was bustling as usual, with the morning rush getting their caffeine fix for the day.

He got in line, stooping to give Casper a scratch between his ears when the little ghost cat came over to greet him. The cat purred happily before sauntering off to curl up on the lap of a college student sitting in a cozy chair by the window.

'Noah!' Kaori appeared behind him in line, her briefcase slung over one shoulder. 'What did you get up to last night?' she asked, all smiles. But Noah had lived here long enough not to be fooled. Kaori was fishing.

'Oh, you know, the usual. Visited a few of the local

sorority houses, made some new friends. How about you? Read anything good lately?'

Kaori's smile grew shark-like. Suddenly, Noah felt bad for everyone she'd cross-examined as a trial lawyer. She must be terrifying to face in court. And she wasn't fooled by Noah's lies, but he wasn't scared of the book club.

'Oh, plenty of good reads. Just finished one about a reformed rake.'

'Well, everyone loves a reformed rake.' He winked and turned toward the counter with Kaori cackling behind him.

'Hey, Noah.' Jeanie was at the register this morning and she was also smiling at him like she knew things, or thought she knew things.

'Hey, Jeanie.'

'How was your night?'

Before or after Hazel kissed him and rearranged his brain chemistry?

'Fine, thanks.'

She was still staring at him, her dark brows lifted like she was waiting for him to go on.

'Uh, I'll have an iced coffee with milk.'

'Okay, sure.' She called his order to Joe who was making the drinks this morning while Jeanie manned the register.

'Has Hazel been in yet?'

Jeanie's smile grew. 'No, not yet.'

'Then I'll get an apple-cider iced tea, too.'

'You know her drink order.'

He was sure Kaori had just sighed dreamily behind him but he refused to turn around.

'Stop looking at me like that, Jeanie.'

'Like what?'

Noah narrowed his eyes. 'Like that. Hazel is a friend.'

'Uh-huh. Right. A friend. Got it.' She handed him his drinks, a look on her face like she didn't believe a word he said which was fair because he didn't either, but he wasn't about to discuss what he and Hazel were to each other with half of Dream Harbor, the nosy book-club president included, waiting in line behind him.

'See you later.'

'Bye, Noah.'

'Bye, Noah!' Kaori chirped, stepping up to the counter. Noah did not want to know what she and Jeanie were immediately giggling about.

He was nearly free of Jeanie's insinuating looks and Kaori's probing questions when Logan walked in. He really needed to find a different coffee shop.

'Noah.'

'Hey, man. I was just on my way out—'

'What happened last night?'

Good lord, this town.

'I had a lovely time at the carnival. Where were you by the way? Didn't feel like supporting the school?'

Red was creeping up Logan's neck and into his cheeks. 'Jeanie put on a sundress.'

'Excuse me?'

'We didn't make it out of the house, okay?' Logan ground out the words like they were choking him and Noah burst out laughing.

'Damn. Must have been one hell of a dress.'

'It was. But that's beside the point.'

'And what is the point exactly?'

'We heard you were there with Hazel. Like a date.'

'You really shouldn't believe everything you hear in this town, man. You of all people should know that.' He flashed Logan a grin before scooting around him and out the door. Hazel was not kidding about the town talking about their little outing. But let them think what they wanted.

He'd had an amazing time.

The best time.

Such a good time, in fact, that he hadn't been able to sleep last night. Instead, he'd tossed and turned and thought about how sweet Hazel tasted and how soft her hair was as it brushed against the arm he had around her shoulders.

And most of all, he thought about the satisfied smile on her face when she'd pulled away. He wanted to see more of that.

He walked next door, drinks in hand, suddenly finding it necessary that he see a certain bookseller before he started his day.

'Hazel, you're here!'

Hazel looked up from her laptop at the sound of Annie's voice. She'd let herself in the backdoor of the shop like she always did when they were closed.

'Of course, I'm here. And shouldn't you be at your own place of business?'

Annie waved away her concern. 'I heard Noah carried you out of the carnival over his shoulder last night after winning like ten stuffed animals.'

Hazel blinked. 'Uh, no. That's not what happened.'

Annie dropped onto the couch. 'Then what happened?'

She still didn't feel like explaining the whole book-clues summer-of-fun, hots for Noah situation so she went with the simplest lie. 'Noah asked me to go with him, so I did.'

Annie's eyes widened. 'And...'

'And that's it. It was fun.'

'Fun?'

'Yes, fun. I am in fact capable of having fun.'

Annie's brow creased. 'Of course you are, Haze. But you hate the carnival. Especially ever since the Ferris wheel debacle of junior year.'

Hazel shrugged. 'Turns out Ferris wheels are kinda fun.'

Annie studied her, the crease in her forehead deepening. 'You sure you're okay?'

'Yep.'

'And this thing with Noah is...'

'Casual.'

'Casual?'

'Yep. Fun and casual.'

Annie snorted.

'What?'

'Haze, we've known each other for a long time, right? And you've never done casual in your life.'

Hazel opened her mouth to speak but then shut it again. Annie wasn't wrong. Hazel was a serial monogamist. She'd had exactly three boyfriends in her life, each one lasting a year or two and then petering out somewhat unspectacularly. Her break-ups weren't even dramatic or interesting. Each time, they'd parted amicably and agreed to be friends. In fact, she still wrote semi-regular emails to her college boyfriend who'd moved back to Japan. It was all very ... boring.

'Well, now I am doing casual.'

Annie considered her, tipping her head to the side as though she was looking at Hazel from a different angle.

'I support this.'

'So happy to get your okay on the matter,' Hazel said dryly.

Annie smirked. 'I think this could be good for you. I mean, Noah clearly wants to get in your pants.'

'Don't get carried away. All we did was kiss.'

'You kissed!' Annie nearly shot up off the couch. 'Way to bury the lead, Haze.'

She shook her head at her friend. 'It's not that big of a deal.'

'It definitely is.' Annie leaned forward. 'How was it?'

Hazel's cheeks heated. 'It was...' *The best kiss ever.* 'It was really nice.'

Annie frowned. 'Nice? Hazel, this man is known for his sexual prowess. You need to get more than nice.'

'God, Annie. Don't talk about him like that.'

Annie lifted an eyebrow. 'Wait a minute. You can't get

feelings for him. I mean, Noah is fun to hang out with, but he doesn't have serious relationships. Like, at all. You know he only sleeps with tourists.'

'I'm aware. And I don't want serious this time. I'm tired of serious.'

Annie was still looking at her skeptically, but she nodded. 'Okay. As long as you're going into this with your eyes open.'

Hazel widened her eyes behind her glasses. 'They are wide. Very wide. I know what I'm doing.'

'All right, babe. I believe you. I gotta get back. I left George up to his elbows in cookie dough and we open in like half an hour. Love you.'

'Love you, too. Lunch?'

'Definitely.' Annie nearly collided with Noah on her way out of the office. 'Oh hello, Noah. And how are you today?' Her voice was loud and strange and Noah glanced over her shoulder at Hazel with a look on his face that clearly said *what is with her today?*

Hazel shrugged and couldn't help the small smile that tugged at the corner of her lips. She hadn't expected to see Noah today, but now that he was here her stomach started its usual flipping and dipping.

'I'm good. How about you?' he said, answering Annie's high-pitched question.

'Good. Very good. Gotta run!'

He shook his head as Annie scampered out of the office.

'How'd you get in?' Hazel asked.

'Back door. Sorry, was I not supposed to?'

'Well, you brought me a drink, so I'll allow it.'

The smile that lit up his face took her breath away. He put the iced tea on her desk and sat across from her, swirling the ice cubes in his drink. He was watching her in that way he did, with dark eyes and a playful smirk.

Even in this dim back office, he was bright. His copper hair and tangle of tattoos, the sunburn that had turned slowly to tan, the colorful braids on his wrist. It was like he'd brought the sea air directly into her office.

She breathed it in before she spoke. 'So ... what are you doing here?' she asked, thankful when her words broke his stare.

'Just bringing you a drink. And I wanted to see you.'

'You wanted to see me?'

'Of course.'

'Right.' She swirled her drink too, and took a long sip, avoiding his eye. She'd kissed him last night. On purpose, fully sober, but now she didn't know what to do about that. Or about any of this. Annie's warnings echoed in her head.

'Look, Noah. About last night...'

'I had fun. Did you?'

'I did, but...'

'No buts.'

'What?'

'You recruited me to help with your summer, right?'

'Yes, but...'

He shook his head. 'No buts. We had fun. Mission accomplished.'

'But the kiss...'

'Was fun.'

'Very. I just don't want things to get weird between us or I don't know ... confusing.'

He leaned forward, forearms on his knees. Hazel counted five stars and two large dahlias on his right arm. Her gaze flicked back to his and worry had crept into his playful stare.

'I don't want to do anything you don't want to do, Hazel. But if you're having a good time then let's just see what happens. Okay?'

Hazel swallowed her protests. This was what she wanted. This was why she'd asked Noah to help her. She wanted to see where the summer took her. She wanted more kisses. It didn't have to be confusing. It could be painfully simple.

'Okay.'

His grin grew. 'Okay, great. Any more clues?'

'I doubt it, but I haven't checked yet.'

'What are you waiting for?' He was already up and out the office door before she could respond. He was in front of the romance shelves when she caught up to him.

'Look! A crooked one.'

'Hmm.' Hazel pulled it from the shelf and found the dog-eared page.

Noah's little intake of breath caught her attention. She raised a brow in question.

'This is exciting.'

She laughed and ran her finger down the page.

'She dug her toes into the cool sand and dipped her

head back, letting the warm sun caress her face.' Noah read the highlighted line out loud in that low rumble of a voice and Hazel repressed a shiver.

'Looks like we're going to the beach,' he said, still close enough that his breath stirred the curls around her face.

Hazel sighed.

'Please don't tell me you don't like the beach.' A pained expression crossed his face as if Hazel had personally insulted his mother.

'I just always get sunburned, and sand gets everywhere, and last time a seagull pooped on my sandwich.'

Noah was fighting a laugh. She could tell. 'I promise no wildlife will poop on your lunch this time.'

'I just don't think those are promises you can make.'

'Fisherman's honor.'

She tried to frown, she tried to be grumpy about sand and errant bird poop and the inevitable sunburn, but it was impossible. Not with Noah nearly glowing with excitement.

'Okay, fine.'

'HANSOF!' He took the book from her hands. *Seduction Cove* was scrawled across the cover. 'Also I'm taking this one.'

Hazel scoffed. 'No, you're not.'

'I'll pay for it.'

'You don't want to read that.'

'Of course I do.' He flashed her a smile as he wandered toward the register. 'Looks educational.'

Hazel bit down on her laugh. 'You're ridiculous.'

'It's what you hired me for, isn't it?'

His smile was still firmly in place but a shadow of doubt had crossed his features.

'That's not why at all. And I didn't hire you.'

'Right. Just kidding.'

Hazel came around to the other side of the counter and took the book from his hands. 'I want to do this with you because I like you.'

'Oh.'

'And you're good at it.'

A new mix of emotions flitted across his face but Hazel couldn't catch them before he was smiling again.

She wanted to say more. That he was a breath of fresh air in her musty life, that he was slowly reminding her how to let go, that he was waking her up like the sun after a long winter. But none of that seemed casual.

And this thing between them was very casual.

A few months of excitement and flirting and nothing more.

Regardless of how he looked at her.

Chapter Ten

Noah had insisted she leave all their beach-trip planning to him. So she found herself wandering down to the shore with a straw bag tucked under her arm and no real concept of what the day would hold. The weather had turned again and despite the bright August sun, the day was cool and breezy. Hazel wore her favorite hoodie over her tank top and had opted for hot tea in her mug over iced tea.

It was a Tuesday morning, her day off, and Noah was free too, so they'd agreed to follow the book clue today. He'd told her to meet him at the end of one of Dream Harbor's many little side streets that ended up at the water's edge. But this wasn't the public beach with its sandy shoreline and snack stand. Hazel was standing next to the rocky edge before the sidewalk turned into coarse sand.

She hadn't ever been to this part of the shoreline,

although she knew plenty of kids in high school who had partied here on the weekends. Not surprisingly, she'd never joined them. But she could see why this was the big meet-up spot; once you got over the large rocks, the beach was mostly obscured from the street. It was quiet and secluded. On a Tuesday morning there were no partying teenagers in sight.

'Hey, there you are.' Noah's head popped up over the rocks, the usual smile on his face.

'Hi.'

'Come this way, there's more of a path.' He led her to where there may have once been a path but was now more like crumbled concrete. She took his hand as he led her over the rough terrain.

'You thought this was the spot to convince me to like the beach?'

He grinned at her. 'Yep.' He hadn't let go of her hand and she liked the feeling of her fingers intertwined with his, so she didn't pull it away. 'It's like our own private beach down here.'

Hazel frowned, glancing down the narrow strip of sand. About a hundred yards down a mother was building a sandcastle with her toddler. Every time she tipped the bucket over and dumped out a castle, the boy stomped it and giggled manically.

'Well, mostly private.' He led her to where he'd spread out a blanket. A cooler sat next to it and the flip flops he'd already discarded. 'This is for you.' He grabbed the large straw hat that sat on the blanket and placed it on her head with a flourish.

It was huge and flopped over one eye. 'Why would I wear this?'

Noah peered under the brim. 'To protect you from sunburn.'

She wanted to protest. The hat was big and ugly but ... it was casting a nice wide shadow around her. There was no way the sun was getting through this thing. And then there was the way Noah was looking at her, waiting for her approval.

'Do you like it?'

'I like the shade it provides.'

'Great!' His smile grew as he tapped the hat further down on her head, adjusting the strap beneath her chin. 'My grandfather always used to say, there's no such thing as bad weather, just bad equipment.'

Hazel huffed a small laugh. Only for her was a sunny day 'bad weather' but this big, dumb hat, did seem to be working.

'Okay, next thing.' He clapped his hands and started rummaging through a backpack he'd placed next to the cooler. He pulled out a spray can and shook it.

'What's that?'

'Bug spray.'

'You brought bug spray?'

'Yep, close your mouth.' She held her breath as he sprayed the bug repellent over her legs and arms. 'I noticed you had a lot of bug bites.'

'Uh, yeah...'

Pink had washed over Noah's cheeks as he said it. He'd noticed her *legs*. He'd noticed an awful lot about her and he'd brought all these things to make her beach trip comfortable. A new sensation settled in Hazel's stomach. It was warm and happy.

'Thanks.'

'Sure.' He shrugged, tossing the canister back in the bag. 'Okay, now for the fun part.'

Hazel raised an eyebrow although she was sure he couldn't see it from under the brim of her hat. 'The fun part?'

'Well, there's multiple fun parts, so I'll let you pick what you want to do first.'

'Okay.' A smile was working its way across her face, the one she couldn't seem to tamp down whenever Noah was around.

'We can build a sandcastle.'

Hazel glanced down the beach at where the toddler was now crying because the waves had knocked his creation down. 'Um, what else you got?'

'We could play frisbee.'

She scoffed. 'Do I look like a frisbee on the beach kinda girl?'

Noah laughed. 'Okay, how about a treasure-hunting walk?'

'Treasure hunting?'

'Yep.' He winked. 'Come on.' He twined his fingers with hers again and tugged her along the sand.

'So what kind of treasure are we looking for exactly?' she asked as they strolled. The waves washed over her feet, the shock of the cold water leaving her toes numb. But in a way that she didn't seem to mind.

Small rocks that lined the shore rolled in and out with the surf creating a soft shushing sound and even the squawking of sea birds in the distance was peaceful. Now that she was here it seemed rather insane that she didn't come more often. How lucky that something so beautiful existed mere blocks from her house.

Her hand was still in Noah's and he swung their arms gently as they walked. 'We won't know it's treasure until we see it.'

'Hmm.' Hazel tugged him to a stop. 'How about this?' She squatted to pick up her find. A tiny, pure white shell that she placed in the palm of her hand.

'A bay scallop. One of my favorites.'

'So ... treasure?'

'Definitely.' He grinned and she tucked the shell into the pocket of her sweatshirt.

They kept walking with Noah stopping every few feet to pick up a 'perfectly round rock' or any pebble that looked like a jelly bean or the white shells with purple inside. She added it all to her pouch until it was sandy and damp and sagging. The shells and rocks clicked against each other as they walked.

'I kinda thought the treasure was going to be like the experience of being here or something metaphorical like that.'

Noah glanced at her, a smirk teasing around his mouth. 'I'm not that deep, Haze. And I like treasure.'

Hazel huffed a laugh and Noah's smile grew. The day was slowly warming up but that wasn't what had Hazel's cheeks heating. It was him. It was that smile directed right at her. She dipped her head so the brim of her enormous hat blocked Noah from her view.

'Look!' The tiniest crab she'd ever seen had emerged from the wet sand and was scuttling past her feet. As soon as her shadow passed over it, it froze.

'He thinks you're going to eat him.'

Hazel scrunched up her nose. 'You're safe little guy.' She moved to the side and once he was back in the sunlight the little crab skittered off between the rocks.

'And too tiny for lunch, anyway,' Noah said and Hazel could imagine him talking to his tour customers that way, too. *Too small, guys. Throw it back.*

'Speaking of lunch...'

'You hungry?'

'Well, I am curious what you packed in that cooler but I'm still not trusting of these seagulls.' She glanced up to find several of the large birds circling overhead. Good thing her little crab friend had found shelter among the rocks.

Noah slung an arm over her shoulder as they turned back to the blanket. 'Trust me. I promised you no harm would come to your lunch, remember?'

'I remember. But they look ready to attack.'

Noah laughed. 'I'm a man of my word, you'll get to eat your lunch.'

Hazel let herself relax into his side on the way back to the blanket. He was warm and solid and her body seemed to melt against him regardless of how her brain felt about the situation. Her brain had no place here. Not during her fun, reckless adventures with Noah.

The water had begun its trek back to low tide and even more rocks and shells were exposed. Water ran in rivulets through the sand and out to the ocean. Hazel's toes were used to the chill of the water now and she didn't mind stepping in the little streams. She spotted more crabs but they didn't stop to chat. All this salt air had made her hungry.

The cooler was waiting for them right where they'd left it and Hazel plopped down next to it on the blanket. She tossed her giant hat to the side.

'Woah, playing a little fast and loose with the sun protection, Haze.'

She stuck out her tongue and Noah laughed. 'I have sunscreen on. And I'm being a little reckless, remember?'

'Oh, I remember.' He said it like he remembered just how reckless that Ferris wheel kiss was and like he wanted to do it again. He held her gaze and for a second Hazel thought he might close the distance between them, but instead he turned and started rummaging through the cooler. 'Turkey BLT or ham and cheese?'

She might have been disappointed that he didn't initiate a repeat of their kiss if her stomach wasn't grumbling. 'BLT.'

'Good call.' He tossed her the sandwich, a very risky move on his part, but miraculously she caught it.

'Did you make these?'

'Nope. Got them from the deli next to Mac's.'

'Yum.' Hazel loved that deli, especially the pasta fagioli soup in the winter time. She unwrapped her sandwich and they ate in peace for a while, forgetting about the imminent threat of sea-bird excrement.

Or at least Hazel had put it completely out of her mind until Noah leapt up and darted away from the blanket.

'Noah, what—'

He was gone before she could finish her sentence, running down the beach, sending a group of seagulls squawking angrily into the air. Hazel clapped a hand over her mouth. He was chasing birds for her. He ran, kicking up sand and waving his arms until the birds were a satisfactory distance from their spot. She held in the unhinged giggles that threatened to spill out.

Noah returned out of breath and with a triumphant gleam in his eye. 'Got 'em.' He sat down again, sprawling out with his sandwich on his lap. 'They won't be bothering you anytime soon.'

Hazel couldn't bring herself to tell him that the birds had already begun inching closer again. She was too busy grinning like an idiot, as though Noah had slayed dragons for her instead of chasing away some pesky birds.

It was the thought that counted, right?

'Thanks. I feel much better.'

He squinted up at her, using a hand to block the sun. 'Do you like the beach yet?'

With you, I do. 'I'm warming up to it.' She plopped the giant hat on his head. 'I think it's your turn for the hat.'

'Thanks,' he said, taking another big bite of sandwich. 'So, I've been thinking about the clues.'

'Oh?'

'About suspects.'

'Really? Who do you think's doing it?' Hazel had forgotten that she even cared who was doing it, but it was cute that Noah had been thinking about it.

Noah stretched his legs out in front of him. 'What about Annie?'

'Annie? No, I don't think so.'

'She's in the bookstore all the time. And she knows you the best. She would know what clues to leave.'

'Hm. Yeah, I guess so.' Would Annie leave her a scavenger hunt of clues? Maybe. But Annie was also terrible at keeping secrets. 'I just don't think she could pull it off without me knowing.'

'Okay, what about your dads?'

Hazel paused, considering that idea, too. 'Neither of them have been in the shop in a while.'

'So who do you think is doing it, then?' Noah asked, folding up his empty sandwich wrapper and tucking it back in the cooler.

'I don't know. I thought maybe it could be Alex. They have the access but not the motive.'

Noah laughed. 'The motive, huh? This is getting serious.'

Hazel threw her balled-up sandwich wrapper at his

head, but he caught it before it hit him. 'Of course it's serious.'

'Right, very serious,' he said with a teasing smile. He pulled out a bag of chips and Hazel was really starting to like this whole beach picnic situation.

'Well, whoever it is, this clue wasn't the worst idea.'

Noah's shoulder bumped lightly against hers. 'Phew. I'd hate for your beach day to be the worst.'

She let herself lean into his body. Definitely not the worst. When she did figure out who left the clues, she'd have to remember to thank them.

They finished eating with no further attack from the local shorebirds. Hazel dug her toes into the sand beyond the blanket and let the sun warm her face. A cool breeze came in off the water and made the day comfortable instead of hot and Hazel could almost feel fall heading her way.

Change was coming soon.

Hazel breathed in the briny air and felt just the tiniest bit unstuck. Here she was, on the beach in the middle of a Tuesday with a pocket full of treasure. Not a bad HANSOF day.

'Hey, did you read that book? The one with the beach clue?' she asked.

Noah grinned up at her from where he was now laid out on the blanket. The giant hat was covering his eyes and he didn't bother to move it so Hazel was free to watch his mouth as he spoke. It was a good mouth. Soft and sweet. Quick to smile. Hazel had become quite fond of it. In a casual way of course.

'I sure did.'

'And?'

'And it was a good one.' His smile grew. 'Very educational, just as I thought it would be.'

It was good the top half of his face was still covered so he couldn't see Hazel's face turn pink, as she was sure it was. She shouldn't have brought up the book but before she could admonish herself for that, Noah tugged her down beside him.

'Now we nap,' he murmured, his deep voice doing things to her that were not at all sleep-inducing. 'Beach naps are the best naps.'

It was impossible to argue with that, so Hazel closed her eyes and let Noah's breathing and the sound of the waves lull her to sleep.

Chapter Eleven

Hazel was stretched out on the blanket beside him, her head resting on her crossed arms. She had her hood up and she looked like a little sea creature peeking out of its shell. Noah was on his side facing her and he found himself cataloging all the delicate features of her face. She'd taken her glasses off and he could see that the warm brown of her eyes contained a silver ring around the pupil. He didn't know of any other time he'd noticed a woman's eyes, beyond light or dark, interested or not.

Her curls spilled from her hood and framed her round face. Her mouth ... well, he couldn't look at her mouth for too long without wanting to cover it with his, but it was soft and relaxed at the moment, a small tip up at the corners. She looked happy, peaceful.

'Tell me something no one else knows,' she said now, the late afternoon sun slanting across her face. They'd dozed for a little while and waking up next to a drowsy and warm Hazel was something Noah liked a little too much.

'I hate pickles.'

Hazel scrunched up her nose, not satisfied with his answer. 'No, something real. A secret.'

A secret? *I like you way more than I should, Hazel Kelly.* How was that for a secret?

'Only if I get one of your secrets in return.'

'I don't have any.'

'Everyone has secrets.'

She paused, her wide eyes studying him. 'Okay, deal.'

He could have made something up, told her any number of stories from his life that no one around here knew, but he found himself wanting to tell her a real secret. He didn't know if it was the grogginess from their nap or the soft lines of Hazel's face but he wanted to know what she would think of him if he told her something true.

'I never graduated high school.' The beach was quiet. The mother and her little boy had gone home, the seagulls were asleep, their heads tucked against their white bodies. Even the tide had gone out far enough that the waves were a faint whisper.

Noah's words fell quietly between them.

Hazel blinked. Once, twice. 'Well that makes sense.'

What? That certainly wasn't the response he was expecting. Maybe a 'why not?' or the always dreaded 'you could go back and finish.' But not a very matter of fact 'that makes sense'.

'It does? Wow, I didn't think my inability to use the

quadratic equation was showing.' He sounded snarkier than he meant to, old wounds opening up and threatening to ruin their afternoon.

She shook her head a little, pressing her cheek into her arms. 'No, that's not what I meant. It makes sense now why you're always disparaging your own intelligence.'

He wanted to laugh that comment off, but did he do that?

'I do?'

'Yep. You make little comments about how not smart you are. Just today you told me you're not 'that deep'. Remember?'

Huh. Was he making this thing he'd always kept as his shameful little secret obvious with his own words?

'I guess I didn't realize.'

'So, it bothers you? That you didn't finish?'

Did it bother him? He'd never been good at school. He hated sitting inside all day. It made him itchy and prickly. He was happiest out on the water, so at the start of senior year he'd decided to stick with what he did best. It had made sense to him at the time even when his parents lost their minds about it. His father had told him in no uncertain terms that he'd ruined his life. Only when he promised to start working full time for the seafood business did his dad calm down. And then Noah had screwed that up, too. But instead of confessing any of that, he said, 'Not really.'

She raised a disbelieving eyebrow.

Noah sighed. 'It's just not something I like to broadcast.'

'And it's why you left your sisters to run the family business. Because you don't think you're smart enough?'

'Damn Haze, this line of questioning isn't exactly fun beach talk.' Of course he didn't think he was smart enough. What the hell did he know about running a multi-million dollar company? He couldn't even pass pre-calc. And he'd tried. He really had. He'd gone to work with his father every day for a year after he quit school. He'd sat in that office and tried to understand the inventory spreadsheets and the delivery schedules and the restaurant contracts. And he'd never been more miserable in his life.

So, one day he just took off. Took one of his family's old boats, scribbled his dad a check to pay for it, and left. It was a shitty way to leave but he couldn't face his father's disappointment again. It was why he rarely went home, rarely talked to the old man, rarely saw his beautiful little nieces.

But Noah had no intention of talking about his family today. One open wound was enough.

She winced. 'Sorry. I have a bad habit of doing that.'

'Doing what?'

'Spoiling the fun.'

He inched a little closer and ran a finger down the bridge of her nose to un-crinkle it. 'You don't spoil the fun.'

'Well, I turned this little secret-telling game into a terrible therapy session, so...'

'Tell me your secret, then, and I'll psychoanalyze you. It'll be fun.' He flashed her a grin and she let out a quiet laugh.

'I mean, I already told you my whole afraid to turn thirty thing...'

'There must be something else. Some deep dark secret ... something not even Annie knows.'

Her eyes widened at that. She clearly told her best friend everything, but Noah wanted a little piece of Hazel Kelly that no one else had. A little treasure he could put in his pocket at the end of this day and keep with him when she decided she didn't require his services anymore.

Hazel blew out a long sigh like she was strengthening her resolve. 'Okay, there is something I've never told anyone else.'

Noah rose up on his elbow, his curiosity piqued even as Hazel stayed in the protection of her hood.

'I don't ... I don't actually believe my dad is clairvoyant.'

'What?'

'I know a lot of people in town think his dreams are real or have real meaning or whatever and my dad does too, but I just can't ... I don't know ... I can't truly believe that his dreams are anything more than random and the decisions he makes based on those dreams are just good decisions for the town.'

Hazel looked truly stricken like she had confessed to the worst possible thing. Noah stared at her for a second before he rolled onto his back, laughter bubbling out of him.

'Haze,' he gasped between laughs. 'Are you kidding?' Noah had been to enough town meetings to know Mayor Kelly loved to talk about his dreams, but he honestly thought everyone was humoring him. Did the town *really* think he had premonitions? This place just got weirder and weirder. He loved it.

She was up on her elbow now, looking down at him with a crease between her brows.

'Of course I'm serious.'

He wheezed, the laughter making his stomach hurt. 'From the way you were acting, I thought you were going to tell me you killed a man or you liked some kinky sex thing.'

'The town is very serious about those dreams!'

Tears had started to fall from the corners of his eyes and he wiped them with the back of his hand. 'I thought everyone was just playing along!'

Hazel shook her head. 'Nope. It's all very real to them.'

His laughter petered out as he looked at her serious face. He tucked an errant curl behind her ear, letting the back of his hand brush against her cheek.

'So what do you believe in?'

'What do you mean?'

'Well, you don't believe your father receives messages from the universe in his dreams, but what do you believe in? What makes the world make sense to you?'

She stared past him down the beach, the crease between her brows deepening and he could tell she was really considering it before she answered. He liked that about her. Hazel didn't say things unless she meant them. It made everything she said that much more important.

'Good books,' she said after a minute, her gaze returning to his. 'Good friends. Good food.'

He smiled up at her. 'What more do you need?'

'Exactly.' She smiled back. 'What about you?'

'Hmm.' He twisted his mouth to the side as he thought, loving the way Hazel tracked the movement with her gaze. 'The love of a good woman.'

A laugh burst from Hazel's mouth. She shoved his shoulder playfully and he caught her wrist and tugged until she landed on top of him. Her face was a breath away from his.

'I was serious,' he said with a teasing grin.

'I bet.' She hadn't moved, hadn't pulled away and instead had left the weight of her body on his. He could feel every line of her, every dip and valley she'd been hiding under her bulky sweatshirt all day.

'What more is there to believe in than love?' He was still teasing, still trying his best to charm her, but he wanted to know more about her. Hazel Kelly was the only thing he'd felt like learning about in years.

'Have you ever been in love?' she asked, resting her hands on his chest and placing her chin on top of them.

'Nope. Unless you count *Ginger*.'

'Ginger?'

'My boat.'

She giggled and he could feel the vibration through his chest.

'I don't count that.'

'Okay, then no. How about you?'

'Not really.'

'Not really?'

'I mean, I don't think so...'

'Haze...'

'Yeah?'

'I'm pretty sure you would know. I mean, I think it should be obvious.'

She scrunched her nose again. 'I guess you're right. It just feels like maybe I should have been. I had a few long relationships and I was ... comfortable, I guess. For a while anyway. And then it was always like I outgrew them or we outgrew each other.'

'Hmm, yeah I get that.'

'You do?'

'Not really. Just trying to be nice.'

Hazel laughed.

'Hey, Haze?'

'Yeah?'

'Are you sure you don't have any strange sex kinks you want to confess? I'm very open.' He waggled his eyebrows and her laugh fizzed through him again.

She was grinning up at him, her body still pressed against his and he thought maybe his weird sex kink was Hazel. Just ... all of her. But not in his usual way. Not like when he spotted a woman at the bar and knew they'd have fun together for a weekend or two, when he didn't want to know much more than her name and what would make her come.

Hazel was different. He wanted Hazel in bed and out of it. He wanted to lie here and talk to her all day and then bring her home and do everything but talk. He wanted to know what she loved and also what she tasted like.

But none of that was what *she* wanted.

She wanted him for a good time. An adventure. A diversion. She might live here in Dream Harbor but he needed to remember to think of her like every other tourist. Hazel Kelly was passing through his life and he needed to shake off all these crazy feelings he was having. He needed to stop noticing her eye color.

'I'm sure you are very open but I have nothing like that to confess.'

'We could remedy that, if you really wanted to kick this summer of recklessness into high gear.' He'd let this conversation get too deep. It was time to steer things back toward what he did best. Flirting. Charming. Entertaining.

It was what Hazel had signed on for. Not some sad dude pining after her.

She laughed again, but had somehow inched forward so her breath teased across his lips. 'How about we just start with making out on the beach?' That mischievous glint was back in her eyes, the one he selfishly hoped only he got to see. Even though he shouldn't. Even though this thing was temporary. He'd take this image of Hazel above him, looking wind-blown and sun-kissed, with him. Another little Hazel treasure.

'Hell, yeah.' He cupped her face with his hands and brought her mouth down to his. Her soft sigh ricocheted through his body. Hazel Kelly was going to be the death of him. He rolled her onto her back, suddenly needing to take control of the situation. She'd blindsided him with too many kisses, left him dizzy and reeling. He was taking the lead this time.

Or he thought he was, anyway. With Hazel's arms wrapped around his neck and her breathy little sounds against his mouth, Noah had lost all sense of reason once again. He kissed down her neck and Hazel arched into him and he suddenly hated the damn sweatshirt she was wearing. He sucked on a particularly sensitive spot on her neck and she groaned.

Oh, God, he wanted more of that.

He let a hand wander to Hazel's hip, letting his fingers slide along the skin above her waistband. Soft and warm. He traced further, over the soft curve of her stomach, the dip of her waist. His mouth was on hers again, the kiss deeper, more urgent. And the way Hazel had started squirming against him meant she felt it too, just as desperate. Just as—

'Wait.' The word combined with her hand clamped around his wrist, stopped him in his tracks. They were both breathing heavily and Hazel looked up at him with dark eyes. 'Can anyone see us?'

Noah blinked. Right. They were outside on the damn beach and he was feeling her up. Or was about to, anyway. He looked up, glancing down the beach in either direction. Empty. He turned his grin back to Hazel.

'Not a soul around.' He dipped his head and kissed her again. Softly, repeatedly. Little kisses along her lips and jaw, to the place behind her ear where she smelled like coconut sunscreen. 'But we can stop if you want to. Exhibitionism wasn't part of the clue.'

She squirmed a little as he continued his way down her neck, her hands roving over his back now, the gentle scrap of her nails through his shirt doing more for him than they probably should.

'I mean ... our clothes are still on ... so I don't think we're breaking any laws.' Her words were interspersed with sighs and Noah couldn't help but smile against her skin.

'Very good point. HANSOF is a law-abiding endeavor.'

She started to laugh, but his hand had resumed activities under her shirt and her laugh dissolved into a soft groan. Her skin was warm and a little sticky from the sea air and Noah knew if he ran his tongue down her body she'd taste like salt. He wished he could see more of her, but he had to settle for the feel of her beneath his fingers.

He pushed up beneath her tank top and found the edge of her bra. It was soft cotton, with no padding to block the peak of her nipple. Hazel gasped when his thumb traced over the top of it. He grinned against her lips.

'I'm starting to like the beach even more,' she sighed as he cupped her breast, his thumb running back and forth over her nipple.

He huffed a laugh. 'Yeah, you're really getting the hang of it.' He pushed up her bra and somehow having Hazel's naked breast in his hand, even under the bulk of her sweatshirt was the most erotic moment of his life.

He groaned, pressing his forehead against her shoulder.

'You okay?' she asked, her voice breathy and tight.

'Fine. Just trying not to come in my shorts.'

Her surprised laugh made him smile even though it was true. He was harder than hell and they both still had all their clothes on. He rolled her nipple between his fingers and she gasped, her body bowing toward his.

'Noah,' she groaned and he nearly lost it right then and there. How would he ever live his life normally after hearing Hazel Kelly groan his name? He really didn't know, but he didn't have time to think about that right now.

'What do you want?' he asked, brushing his lips against hers. He'd do anything. Strip down right here and take her on this beach blanket, despite his concerns about sand in unfortunate places and public indecency charges.

'I want...' She groaned a little in frustration, her hips moving on their own accord, rolling against his. She sighed. 'We can't.'

He looked down at her, her cheeks pink from desire. 'Well ... we could...' He took his hand from her breast and let it slide back down her stomach, pausing at the waistband of her shorts. 'Let me make you come.'

Her eyes got impossibly wider. 'Here? On the beach?' She looked truly scandalized, but also like ... like she wanted to. And whether this was all part of her 'live the last months of her twenties like a reckless teenager' or not, Noah was here for it.

'Yeah, here on the beach.' He tore his gaze from Hazel's to check up and down the beach again and saw no one. 'Do you want to come, Hazel?'

Desire flared in her eyes, the flush on her cheeks deepening. She hesitated. 'Okay.'

'Okay? I'm going to need more enthusiastic consent than that,' he said with a teasing grin, his fingers still running along the edge of her shorts.

She huffed. 'Yes. Please. A big enthusiastic yes.'

He kissed the word from her lips and flicked open the button of her shorts with one hand. The zipper came down just as easily. He dipped his hand in, under her panties, not wasting any time. He was dying to know what color they were, but he could tell they were simple and cotton, no lace or frills and somehow this thrilled him even more. This wasn't a hook-up. She wasn't some girl he met at the bar.

His fingers brushed against her soft curls, dipping lower into the wet heat of her.

She bucked beneath him, her groan vibrating against his lips. 'Holy crap, Noah.'

He stroked her, learning what she liked, letting her sighs and whimpers guide him. He kissed her, letting his tongue match the rhythm of his hand. He forced himself to stay in the moment, to not dwell on everything else he wanted to do to her, everywhere else he wanted to touch and taste.

Because right now, he had Hazel in his arms, whimpering his name as he circled his fingers faster, backing off and picking up again, until she was breathless.

'Noah, please.'

He wanted to make it last longer, didn't want the moment to end, but they were outside, in public. The beach was empty for now but people could show up at any time.

The last thing he wanted to do was embarrass her or cause a town scandal. Showing up at the carnival together was one thing, public sex was another.

He worked his fingers faster until Hazel gasped, her nails digging into his shoulders. She squeezed her eyes shut, a shudder running through her whole body.

'That's it ... Noah ... that's it.' Her voice broke as the orgasm crashed over her, Noah could feel it pulsing beneath his fingers. He slowed his movements, letting his hand linger in that private place against her for a moment longer before pulling it out.

Hazel stared up at him with a dazed expression. 'That was...'

'Good? I hope.' He propped himself up on one elbow to look down at her.

'Good is an inadequate word for what that was. That was incendiary ... transcendent...'

Noah laughed. 'I've never heard anyone call an orgasm transcendent before.'

Hazel grinned. 'Well, they should. That was amazing.' She was buttoning her shorts and her gaze snagged on the raging erection still pushing against the front of Noah's pants.

'Uh ... I don't think there's a way to reciprocate that's as discreet,' she said.

'No need. I'm fine.'

She frowned. 'Are you sure?'

'I'll take care of it later.'

This seemed to catch her attention. A new flush worked its way up her cheeks. 'You will?'

Noah gave her a slow smile. He liked this Hazel, this daring, sexy Hazel. 'Does that turn you on, Haze? To think of me touching myself later?'

Her eyes widened like she was shocked at his words, but her tongue darted out and traced her bottom lip.

'Maybe...'

'Maybe?' He raised an eyebrow. 'What if I told you, I'll be thinking about you when I do.'

She swallowed hard. 'You will?'

Noah's smile grew. 'I'll be thinking about how sexy you sound when you come and how your body felt in my hands.'

Her breath had gone shallow again, her gaze dark. God, what was he doing besides torturing them both? But he couldn't stop. Not with Hazel looking at him like that.

'I'll be thinking about all the things I want to do to you next time.'

'Like what,' she breathed.

He brushed the hair from her face and her eyes fluttered closed. 'Next time, I want to lick between your thighs and see how you taste.'

Hazel trembled against him.

'I want you completely naked so I can see how beautiful you are. I want to suck on your sweet little nipples. I want to make you come again and again until you beg me to stop.'

'Shit, Noah.' She breathed out a long sigh and opened her eyes again.

'Yeah.' He cleared his throat, pressing a hand against his aching erection. This was a bad idea.

'That was hot.' She smiled up at him.

'You are a little bit kinky, after all, Hazel Kelly,' he said with a wink, needing to steer them back to safer ground before he really did come in his pants in the middle of the beach.

She sat up with a laugh and he sat, too. The sun had dipped lower in the sky, painting the water gold. It had gotten chillier, but their recent activities had kept him warm. Now, with no blood left anywhere else in his body, he was feeling the cool air.

Hazel nudged him with her shoulder. 'This was a really fun day.'

He peered at her from the corner of his eye. The sea breeze swept through her curls, tossing them around her shoulders. Goosebumps ran up and down her legs.

'It was very fun.' He picked up the back half of the blanket and flipped it up and over their shoulders. Hazel leaned into his side and he put an arm around her so they were snuggled beneath it as they gazed out at the water.

'I mean, even before that last part.'

'So do I. I think you're better at having fun than you think you are.'

He could feel her shrug against him. 'Maybe. I think you bring it out in me.'

'Happy to help.' He turned and pressed a kiss to the top

of her head and it was that touch, that kiss, that settled into him even more than anything else they'd just done. This moment right here, him and Hazel tucked together under his old beach blanket, this was the one that would haunt him.

Noah could do casual sexual encounters. He did them all the time. But this was different. Hazel was different.

'I really appreciate you helping me with my little quarter-life crisis. You help me get out of my head. I don't take everything as seriously when you're around. It's nice.'

She put her head on his shoulder and he knew she meant the words as a compliment. She was having a good time. She was doing things she didn't usually do. He was happy to help with that, he really was.

But he was doing things he didn't usually do, either.

He was falling hard for Hazel Kelly.

And it wasn't exactly what she said, but her words twisted in his mind, turning over until he was convinced she wouldn't take him seriously, either. She didn't see him that way. She *couldn't*. Noah was her adventure guide until she turned thirty.

And then what?

What more could Noah offer other than orgasms on the beach? Certainly not as much as a girl like Hazel deserved. She was smart and sweet and deserved a guy with more than a battered boat and a half-baked idea to renovate some old fishing shacks. He'd be better off if he remembered that. This thing with Hazel was temporary.

He gave her a little squeeze. 'Happy to help.'

Chapter Twelve

'What do you think, Hazel?'

Jacob's question, shouted across the front half of the bookstore, snapped Hazel out of her daydream. She blinked. It was a wildly inappropriate daydream. Well, not so much a daydream as the vivid memory of Noah getting her off on the beach yesterday, playing over and over in her head.

'Uh ... what do I think about what?'

The members of the Dream Harbor Book Club grinned at her from their seats around the little coffee table Hazel had set up in the reading nook. They sat in various chairs they'd pulled from other corners of the shop for their weekly meeting. Their books and coffees were scattered across the table. They had been here for nearly an hour already dissecting their latest read. The one with the pirate.

The way their eyes were lit up, their cheeks pink with

delight, she knew whatever they were asking her was also wildly inappropriate for a Wednesday morning.

She came out from behind the counter and hurried over to where they were set up before Jacob had the chance to yell his question again.

'We were wondering,' he said, his mouth tipping into a nearly evil grin, 'What do you think about sex in a hammock? Personally, I think there wouldn't be enough resistance, you know ... for the thrusting.'

Hazel's cheeks went up in flames. The Hazel that existed on the beach, the one that kissed Noah, the one that let him debauch her on a public beach, was not here. That Hazel seemed to only come out when Noah was around.

'I think the rocking motion might be nice, though,' Linda weighed in, oblivious to Hazel's growing embarrassment. Linda smiled at her wife, Nancy, and Hazel was sure the two were silently sharing some kind of memory she didn't want to get into in the middle of her place of business.

'I told you before, you need to keep the conversations PG.' Hazel glanced over to where a mother was shopping with her toddler in the kids' section. She gave them a little wave and turned back to the giggling group in front of her.

'Sorry, Hazel,' Jeanie said, the pirate romance clutched to her chest. 'We'll tone it down.'

'We definitely won't,' Kaori said with a laugh. 'But we'll lower our voices.'

'Thank you,' Hazel said with a nod, intending to turn and go back to the safety behind the counter when she stopped herself. 'I'd been meaning to ask you all something, actually.'

'Was it about hammocks?' Jacob asked with a laugh.

'Definitely not.' Hazel cleared her throat, ready to get some answers about her little mystery. Her prime suspects for who was messing with the romance section were all sitting right in front of her. Despite the suspects Noah had suggested, Hazel still thought the book club was the likeliest culprit.

As much as Hazel had been having fun following her little clues, she was starting to wonder if it was all a joke. Or worse, some kind of Dream Harbor plot to help poor Hazel and her boring life. Hazel's face burned with a different type of embarrassment. The type that came from wondering what people thought of you and being sure it wasn't good.

Not that she thought her friends and neighbors didn't like her, but what if they saw her as pitifully as she saw herself? Or worse, what if they didn't think about her at all and these clues were meant for someone else and she'd just inserted herself into the story where she didn't belong. What if she was stealing someone else's adventure?

Horribly embarrassing.

'Have you noticed anything strange in the Romance section lately?'

Isabel tapped her chin with her pen. 'Stranger than moth men with vibrating tongues or giant blue aliens or minotaurs donating their—'

Hazel held up a hand to stop her. What did these people

read? Although that vibrating tongue sounded interesting... No. She shook her head. Not the time for that.

'I mean, I've found some defaced books.'

Heads shot up at that, all eyes on her.

'Someone has been defacing romance novels?' Kaori asked like she was preparing for battle, like she would defend the romance section with her life. Hazel had to admire their dedication to the genre.

'No, no. Not like that. I just noticed a few books were ... marked up.'

'That's weird,' Jeanie said. 'Why would someone do that?'

'I don't know. But I didn't know if you guys were doing some kind of ... I don't know, a secret romance thing...'

'A secret romance thing?' Isabel asked, handing Mateo another crayon. The little boy sat at her feet scribbling on a coloring sheet. 'Not sure what that means, Hazel, but now I kinda want to do a secret romance thing!'

'Ooo we could do like a blind date with a book sort of thing!' Jacob piped in.

'Now, how would that work exactly?' Kaori asked, leaning forward, the book defacing crimes already forgotten.

'Yeah, would it be sort of like a Secret Santa where we gift each other a secret book?' Jeanie was all in, already writing notes in the notebook she'd brought along. And just like that the Dream Harbor Book Club was off and running on their next secret-romance book idea and Hazel had no more answers than she had this morning. Although, Nancy and Linda were suspiciously quiet when Hazel asked about the defaced books and even now the two women were studiously avoiding her eye.

Were the two oldest members of the book club messing with her books? Were they messing with *her*? Nancy looked up and flashed her a smile before jumping into the conversation.

Maybe she'd been imagining it.

Maybe that beach orgasm had scrambled her brain.

Maybe she should just be happy that the clues were taking her down some very enjoyable roads so far.

Jeanie grabbed her hand before she could walk away and tugged her down onto the arm of her chair. 'We'll let you know if we notice anything,' she whispered as the rest of the group continued their chatter. 'We can't have people ruining your books.'

Hazel smiled at her friend. 'Thanks, Jeanie.'

'Maybe it's a ghost,' she said with a smile.

Hazel laughed. 'I don't think Casper can hold a highlighter.'

Jeanie's response was cut off by her phone vibrating on the table. 'Sorry, sorry!' She reached for the phone but not before Jacob spotted who was calling.

'It's Bennett!' he said, clapping his hands. 'Answer it.'

Jeanie rolled her eyes but answered the call. Her brother's face filled the screen. He looked remarkably like Jeanie, same dark hair, same expressive eyebrows, but where Jeanie's eyes were a dark brown, Bennett's were light blue, almost gray, and a dark stubble covered his jawline. If Hazel wasn't in over her head with a certain ginger fisherman, she would probably find Jeanie's brother to be quite cute. But she had enough on her plate.

'Hey, Ben, I'm at book club.'

'Hi, Bennett!' Jacob called and Jeanie rolled her eyes with a laugh.

'Hey, book club.'

'Hi Bennett!' The other members echoed. Ben's smile grew.

'When are you coming for a visit?' Jacob continued, scooting closer to Jeanie so their faces shared the screen. Hazel had to laugh at the bemused expression on Bennett's face. Apparently, Jeanie's brother had become an honorary, long-distance member of the book club, although Hazel had no idea if he read the books.

'Actually,' Jeanie cut in before her brother could answer. 'I've been trying to convince Bennett to come stay for the holidays.'

Jacob's eyes lit up. 'You definitely should! It's so beautiful here in December and then you can meet my new boyfriend.'

'Boyfriend, huh? Hope this one treats you better.'

Jeanie waved a hand between them. 'You two can have your little guy-chat later. Have you considered my idea?'

'I've considered it.'

'And?'

'Jeanie, a month away is a long time.'

'But you can work remotely!'

'I have the dogs...'

'Bring them!'

A dog barked somewhere on Bennett's end as though agreeing with her and Jeanie grinned. 'See. They want a vacation, too.'

Bennett rolled his eyes, but Hazel could see his resolve cracking.

'We can go get a tree and go ice-skating and do all the winter stuff you never get to do anymore!' Jeanie was on a roll now and she got up to finish the call away from the group.

'Tell him we will pick a sweet holiday read so we don't damage his delicate sensibilities!' Isabel called as Jeanie walked away.

Hazel hoped Ben would say yes. Jeanie missed him and she would love to meet her friend's brother. But thinking ahead to the holidays also left a panicked feeling in her stomach, a feeling of already missing something. Missing *someone*.

What would her and Noah be by the holidays? Friends? Back to acquaintances? How do you go back to casual conversations and friendly smiles with someone who previously put his hand down your pants?

This was why Hazel didn't do casual.

She didn't know how.

But Noah did. He'd teach her, right? He'd show her how to end this thing between them, just like he ended all his other summer flings. She'd chosen him for her summer of fun for a reason. She could learn to be reckless and he could get her out of his system – after their interlude on the beach, Hazel could no longer deny that Noah did in fact have the hots for her. But it wouldn't last. They didn't make sense together. Noah needed a girl who would go rock climbing with him or jet skiing or... or... other adventurous things like that. And he certainly wouldn't be content to spend the weekend in bed reading and working on the Sunday crossword puzzle. Right? Right. Keeping this thing short and sweet was a win win.

Somehow this line of reasoning was doing nothing to stop the dread in her gut. She didn't want to think about the holidays or what her life would look like then. Would she be exactly the same as she was now but with one less Noah in her life?

A depressing thought she quickly shook off.

This was her wild and crazy twenties condensed into two months. She refused to overthink it.

The book club meeting was slowly breaking up so she got up and wandered back to the front counter, straightening a pile of books on the New Releases table. The latest autumnal themed romance novels were selling fast and she'd have to order more soon. It turned out the book club wasn't wrong about what people liked to read. At least her boss would be happy.

Melinda Church was the current owner of The Cinnamon Bun Bookstore but she only made an appearance here once every quarter or so. Her rich father had swept into town about ten years ago and bought it for her when she was only eighteen. The entire town had gone into a panic that he would change everything about their quaint bookstore, or worse, tear it down completely. But the store was a gift and he let his daughter do what she wanted with it.

As it turned out, after the first couple of years when she went wild with bizarre decorating choices (one whole wall was still covered in chalkboard paint, though Hazel had moved the children's section over there and let the toddlers take out their artistic inclinations in a sanctioned area) and questionable book orders (for a few months they had nothing but self-help books and psychological thrillers doing nothing good for the mental health of the town), she tired of the whole enterprise. She gave Hazel a promotion and a raise and left her in charge of the store. She came in from the city four times a year to make sure the place was still standing and to occasionally change the name of the shop when she felt bored.

Hazel didn't mind. The situation worked well for her.

She finished her straightening and went back behind the counter as the book club trickled out. It was a good job, running the bookstore. She loved it, but she couldn't help but wonder what she might have done instead if she hadn't been made manager so early on. Had she intended to work here forever?

She honestly couldn't remember.

Jeanie wandered back into the shop, saying goodbye to her fellow book clubbers as they made their way out the door. She came over to the counter.

'So did you convince him?' Hazel asked, gesturing toward the phone.

Jeanie shrugged. 'Maybe. He's still not sure, but I think it would be good for him.'

'And good for you.'

Her friend smiled. 'And me. I miss him. And he could stay in my apartment above the shop and I could stay at Logan's.'

Hazel lifted her eyebrows. 'So ... you're moving in with Logan?'

Jeanie's cheeks colored. 'It could be a good test run.'

'Yeah, and you're there all the time anyway.'

Jeanie's dark brows knitted together. 'True ... but officially moving in feels like a bigger deal.'

Hazel shrugged. 'He adores you.'

Jeanie's smile bloomed at Hazel's reminder. 'I know.'

'And he doesn't care that you leave your dirty socks around the house.'

'Hey! He told you that?'

Hazel laughed. 'He said it like it was cute!'

Jeanie made a face and went to grab her notebook and romance novel from the reading nook. 'I have to get back to the café and then I have to tell Logan to stop literally airing our dirty laundry.'

'Your secret is safe with me.' Hazel assured her with a smile.

Jeanie pretended to scowl at her but the woman was too cheerful to pull it off. 'Oh, so what about the defaced books? Are they just scribbled in or what?'

'Oh ... uh...' Hazel pushed her glasses up her nose. A need to protect her clues flared up inside her. It didn't make sense but she wasn't ready to share them, to share this whole bizarre summer. She wasn't ready for everyone to think she was so pathetic that she had latched on to some randomly highlighted lines and based the last two months of her twenties on them. 'Yeah, just seems to be some random marks. Probably a kid or something.'

'Hmm. Strange.'

'I'll keep a better eye on things. I'm sure it won't happen again.' Even as she said it she hoped her words wouldn't come true. If the clues stopped, what excuse would she have to keep hanging out with Noah?

His face above her as she came apart yesterday, the blue sky, bright behind his copper hair, flashed through her mind. Right. That might be a good enough reason. For the next few weeks anyway.

'Okay, let me know if you need anything!'

'Thanks, Jeanie.'

'See you later!'

Hazel watched Jeanie walk past the large front windows of the shop before turning back to her work. She had orders to put in for next month and all the chatter about Bennett coming for Christmas reminded her she needed to get the holiday books in ASAP. It might still feel like summer outside but cozy season was rapidly approaching.

She had been very cozy yesterday, huddled under Noah's blanket into the late afternoon. She'd returned home a little sunburned, very wind-blown, and more than a little bit ... happy.

For better or worse, Noah and the clues were making her happy.

And as a birthday gift to herself she refused to think about all the ways it could go horribly wrong.

Chapter Thirteen

Noah glanced at his phone for the twelfth time in the last half hour. Nothing. No word from Hazel, at all. He grimaced and dropped the phone back in his pocket.

Mac was watching him when he looked up. 'Waiting for a call?' he asked, a dark eyebrow raised.

'Uh ... no ... not really.' Noah went back to wiping down the bar for something to do with his hands that didn't involve reaching for his phone again. He'd come in for a shift at the bar since he didn't have a tour today, but the bar was disappointingly empty. Which made sense for a Wednesday evening, but Noah had really been hoping for a distraction.

Mac didn't push further but Noah could feel the man's eyes on him before he went back into the kitchen. His head cook had come down with flu and Mac was on the grill tonight. The man owned the bar but also seemed to do most of the jobs within it as well. Noah never saw him not working.

Amber came up to the bar with her tray and an order for a round of beers for the rowdy table in the corner.

'That's your tour for tomorrow,' she said, laying her tray down and pushing the honey-colored curls from her shoulder.

Noah grimaced. 'They look like fun.'

'Oh, definitely. Should get a lot of good fishing done.'

Noah glanced over at the table where the guys were loudly arguing over the difference between a first mate and a skipper.

Amber laughed, her green eyes dancing. She was dressed in her usual waitressing uniform of a tight tank top and shorts and Noah couldn't help but appreciate the long swaths of skin exposed to him. He happened to know she was just as gorgeous naked, but he hadn't hooked up with Amber since last summer, and had no intention to now, despite the knowing smile she was giving him.

'Still not dating locals?' she asked, leaning on the bar as he poured the drinks.

He shrugged, trying to play it cool even as all his thoughts turned toward Hazel. 'Rules are rules.'

Amber laughed. 'Let me know when you feel like breaking them again.' She winked at him before walking away and he'd be lying if he said he wasn't tempted. Not because Amber was sexy, which was objectively true, but because things with Amber were simple. Sex and nothing else. They'd made it clear from day one. And when things between them petered off no one was hurt.

And now here he was checking for messages from Hazel every two minutes like a teenager. His feelings were already hurt. Why hadn't she texted? Was he supposed to text? He didn't want to come on too strong. Maybe he was supposed to wait until the next clue? He didn't know the rules to this game anymore.

But all he could think about was Hazel. The taste of her and her little sighs and moans and the way she'd held onto him when she came and the feel of her head resting on his shoulder . . .

He wanted more of that, of her.

He tried to lose himself in the repetitive tasks of the night and luckily as the evening wore on more folks came in for dinner, giving him more to do, more to think about that wasn't a certain bookseller.

Cliff and Marty sidled up to the bar. The two old fishermen had bailed him out of a crisis or two since he'd moved here, like the time he had a full bachelor party on board and an empty gas tank. Not a great way to start a new business. But they had happily filled him up and laughed their asses off about how stupid he was. It was a ... layered relationship.

'What can I get you gentlemen?' Noah asked.

'A beer for me,' Cliff said, and Noah didn't have to ask which one. Cliff would only say 'the usual' anyway.

'Coke, please.' Marty hadn't had a drink in nearly a decade but he came to the bar every Wednesday with his friend to get out of his wife's hair, as he said, and to make fun of Noah.

Noah poured the drinks and served them under the watchful eye of the older men.

'How's business?' Marty asked.

'Not bad. Been a pretty good summer despite all the rain.'

Cliff harrumphed at the mention of rain as though it didn't rain back in his day or they didn't let it stop them anyway.

'And how are the girls?' Marty asked with a wink.

'I wouldn't know.'

Both men burst out laughing and Noah just chuckled along with them. There was no way he was about to divulge his currently way-too-desperate feelings for Hazel to these two. Not if he didn't want to get laughed out of town anyway.

He'd almost managed to stop thinking about her for more than five minutes when the door opened and the air in the room shifted.

Just like that, she was here, and Noah would swear the room slowed down, blurred, frozen in place. Everything but her. She caught his eye and gave him a little wave before making her way to the bar.

'Hey,' she said.

'Hey.' He tried for cool but knew it didn't land. His smile was too big, his 'hey' was far too enthusiastic. But Hazel's smile grew so maybe it was okay.

'Oh, now I see,' said Cliff from down the bar.

'I did always like a girl with glasses. I like 'em smart,' Marty added.

Hazel glanced at the men with a confused smile but Noah waved them away, hoping they would kindly shut up.

'I just came in for some dinner.'

Noah blinked. 'Yeah, sure, of course. Do you need a menu?'

'No, I'll just get the fish tacos.'

Mac had added to the tacos last summer when Noah offered to supply him with whatever whitefish he managed to catch in his spare time. Tonight they were made with deep-fried cod and Noah felt an absurd flair of pride that Hazel had ordered them. Like he had personally invented fish tacos.

'Sure. I'll get that right in for you.'

'Thanks.' She settled in on the bar stool and Noah rushed off to put her order in with Mac. And then the fates conspired against him. A bachelorette party arrived for night one of their five planned days of events. A group showed up for a twenty-first birthday. And at least four families arrived with kids in tow for dinner. Suddenly, Noah was overwhelmed with orders, pouring drinks as fast as Amber could put the orders in. Mac was slammed in the kitchen with his two line cooks and poor Danny was drowning in dirty dishes.

It was two hours before Noah glanced down the bar and found Hazel still perched on her stool. She was curled over the bar top, her intense gaze focused on the book in front of her. Hazel had brought a book to the pub. Of course she had.

Noah couldn't help but smile as he headed toward her.

She glanced up just as he landed in front of her.

'You're still here.'

Her cheeks pinkened. 'I was just going to read one more chapter.' She shrugged, gesturing toward the book. 'Guess I read a bit more than that.'

'You brought a book.'

'Of course I did.'

His mouth tipped up in the corner, unable to resist the little smirk on her face. 'Of course you did.'

'I always bring a book, just in case.'

'Just in case of what?'

'Just in case the person I wanted to see gets very busy doing his job and I have to wait to talk to him.'

Noah leaned toward her, his elbows on the counter. *She wanted to see him*. 'Oh, really?'

'Yeah. Is that okay?' Her expression was suddenly worried behind her glasses and Noah wanted to kiss the frown from her lips but since they were in public and he still didn't understand the rules, he settled for running his finger down her nose and smoothing out the crinkles.

'Definitely okay.'

'Good.' Her smile grew again. 'The tacos were delicious by the way.'

'I'll let Mac know.'

'So,' she said, leaning in, her head tipped toward his. 'I questioned the book club today.'

'Oh, really. About what?'

'The clues!'

'Right. Of course. And...'

Hazel gave her head a slight shake, her curls sliding across her shoulders. He wanted to touch them but kept his hands planted on the bar instead.

'And,' she frowned, 'they didn't seem to know what I was talking about.'

'So they didn't do it?'

'I don't know. I guess not. But now I really can't imagine who would have. I guess you could be right about Annie, although I still don't think she's sneaky enough.'

'Does it matter who's doing it?'

Hazel shrugged, but her gaze slid from his. 'I would just feel kinda ... silly ... if they're not meant for me. Or if it's all some kind of . . . joke.'

'Haze.'

'Yeah?' She turned back to look at him and she was close enough that he could see the silver ring around her pupils.

'So what if it is a joke?' He kept his voice soft, not wanting to make it sound like her worries weren't valid but just wanting to understand why she was so concerned about the origin of the clues.

She shrugged again, the crease forming between her brows. 'It's just embarrassing if everyone gets it and you don't.'

'I feel like we're not talking about the clues anymore.' He straightened and wiped his hands on the towel he kept behind the bar. The dining room had emptied out now and other than a few stragglers it was just him and Hazel at the bar. Marty and Cliff were long gone, thank God. He didn't need them chiming in with ill-timed comments about him and Hazel.

He poured her a fresh glass of wine.

'Is this like a bartender thing where you're going to get me to spill all my issues to you?'

'Oh, come on,' he said with a teasing grin. 'I told you mine.'

Hazel huffed a quiet laugh.

'It's not some long-simmering trauma or anything, it's just we moved here at the start of high school and everyone had already known each other forever and I don't know ... I just felt left out or something. Or like I didn't really belong here.' She sighed. 'Sometimes I still just feel like ... I don't know. Like I'm missing something. Or I'm going to commit some kind of Dream Harbor faux pas. I nearly got run out of high school for not dressing up for school spirit week. Anything less than a face painted with the school colors was considered a crime against the town. If Annie hadn't adopted me, I probably wouldn't be the well-rounded woman you know today.' She gave him a self-deprecating smile.

'So, worst case scenario...' Noah leaned against the counter behind him, arms over his chest. 'We've inserted ourselves into someone else's prank and are now having the best summer ever. Even if the Dream Harborians—'

'Dreamers.'

'Right, Dreamers. Even if the Dreamers think you're

some kind of ... clue stealer ... that doesn't sound so bad to me.'

'That doesn't sound embarrassing to you?'

'Nope.'

'Do you ever worry about what other people think of you?'

'Pretty rarely.'

Hazel raised her eyebrows like she didn't believe him, but she lifted her glass and took a sip instead of calling him out on it. Maybe he did care about what *some* people thought of him, but certainly not the general opinion of the Dream Harbor residents.

'You didn't care that everyone saw us at the carnival together,' he pointed out, for reasons he couldn't fathom. Was he trying to make her doubt being seen with him? *Real smart move.*

'That wasn't embarrassing.'

Being 'not embarrassing' was something, anyway.

'But,' she went on, 'being the neighborhood crazy, book lady who thinks the books are talking to her so she plans the last two months of her twenties around them . . . is definitely embarrassing.'

'You gotta let that shit go, Haze.'

She narrowed her eyes at him but there was no heat behind it.

'There is no room for self-consciousness in HANSOF.'

Her lips tipped into a smile despite her efforts to tamp it down.

'We are having fun . . . remember?' he said with a wink

and watched in delight as a blush crept up Hazel's cheeks. She remembered. 'Speaking of which, did you find any more clues today?'

'No.' Hazel's voice was tight and she cleared it before going on. 'No clues today.' He felt the disappointment in her face reflected on his own. 'Maybe it's over?'

It couldn't be over.

He shook his head. 'Nah, not until your birthday.' He forced a smile on his face. 'I'm game to keep going, if you are. I'm sure we can find ways to be adventurous on our own...'

Hazel nodded, the smile blooming wider on her face. 'Yeah, I'm still in, too.' She glanced around the nearly empty room 'I should get going, though.'

'Hang on, let me just say goodnight to Mac and I'll walk you home.'

'Are you sure?'

'Yeah, definitely.' He had no set hours at Mac's and the other man was usually just grateful for the extra hand. Now that the dinner rush was over, Amber and Isaac, Mac's other regular server, could handle things fine on their own.

He said goodbye to Mac and settled his tips before meeting Hazel outside. She stood under the streetlight, the soft light gilding her curls. She was wearing her typical work outfit, tan chinos with a tucked-in button-down shirt. The shirt looked soft and loose and he had more than one perverse fantasy of slowly undoing each and every button...

'Ready?'

Noah cleared his throat. 'Uh ... yeah. Ready.' He

followed her down Main Street, past The Pumpkin Spice Café, the bookstore, and Annie's bakery, all closed for the night. They paused briefly in front of the pet shop so Hazel could peek inside at the kitten she wanted but couldn't have because of her allergies and continued on past the other various restaurants and shops on Main Street.

The town had replaced the modern fluorescent streetlights with ones that looked old-fashioned and filled the center island in the road with flowers. Noah couldn't identify most of them but he knew in daylight the street was full of late summer color.

A cluster of sunflowers rose particularly high, their giant heads looking almost eerie in the dark.

Hazel's hand brushed against his and he grabbed it, twining his fingers with hers. She leaned against him, her touch lighting up the side of his body with little pinpricks of starlight. Her soft sigh drifted across his skin.

'I think I like this time of year,' she said as they walked.

'You sound surprised.'

'I am.'

Noah laughed. The night was cool, the sound of crickets buzzing loudly as they moved toward the more residential side of town with manicured lawns and front gardens. He'd been to her house only once when he dropped her off after Logan's bonfire.

'I always liked summer.'

'Oh, yeah? Why?'

'No school,' he said with a laugh. 'I liked being outside. The winter involved a lot of my mom yelling at me to stop jumping on the furniture and my teachers yelling at me for not paying attention.'

'Hmm.'

He shrugged. 'I liked being out on my dad's boats. So ... summer was it for me.'

'It's growing on me, for sure. Even though I still strongly identify as a cozy-season girl.'

He gave her hand a squeeze and she glanced up at him with a quick smile. 'Sure, cardigans and knit socks and a lot of ... pumpkin-flavored things...' His voice trailed off and was buried by Hazel's laugh.

'Yep, you nailed it. Very cozy.'

'Hey, I like fall as much as the next guy. As long as no one is making me do homework, I'm all about it.'

Hazel nudged his shoulder. 'Do you read all those books you buy from me?'

'I *can* read, Haze.'

'I didn't mean it like that! It's just ... do you like them?'

'I do. I like them a lot. Much better than *The Scarlet Letter* and that one with the kids killing each other... What was that one?'

'*Lord of the Flies*.'

'Yeah, much better than that.'

'Agreed. I don't know why they still make kids read such horrible stuff when there is so much amazing YA literature out there.'

'Totally.' He wanted to listen to Hazel talk more about books because he loved it when she did that. Especially at random times like in the middle of trivia night at Mac's or when there was a long line at the Pumpkin Spice Café and she'd strike up a conversation with the person behind her. She never seemed self-conscious when she was extolling the virtues of her latest read with the inhabitants of Dream Harbor. Maybe he should remind her of that.

But right now they had stopped at her little bungalow on the end of a quiet street.

'This one's mine.'

'I remember.'

'Oh. Right.' They stood awkwardly out front at the end of the little path that led to her door. He should go. He should definitely walk away and go home and not linger here in front of Hazel's house like he wanted to kiss her goodnight, as though this was some kind of date, because it wasn't.

She looked up at him, the streetlight reflected in her glasses. 'Want to come in?'

Noah nearly groaned. Of course he wanted to come in. Did she know how much weight that innocent question held? Did she know that if he came in he would want to do so many other things, too? Did she want that?

'Sure.' His mouth answered before his brain could catch up and spit out an excuse. And maybe that was fine. Maybe he got two months with Hazel and he should take full advantage of that time right? Like, for whatever reason he'd developed some kind of sexy-librarian kink and he just needed to play it out. And then at the end of this they could go back to normal. *He* could go back to normal. So, yeah, he would come in and do whatever else Hazel wanted. And maybe he'd finally get Hazel Kelly out of his system.

He followed Hazel to her front door, thinking about how her lawn was a bit overgrown and wondering who mowed it for her, because he couldn't picture her doing it given her alleged aversion for the outdoors. His fingers tapped nervously against his thigh.

Wait, was he nervous?

The answer was a loud, resounding yes rattling through his brain.

He didn't know how to do this. He was adrift and suddenly, all he wanted to do was get back to his safe little island of casual sex with strangers.

Hazel turned to him and smiled in the mischievous way that told him she was about to blow him even further out to sea.

Chapter Fourteen

Noah was in her home.

She'd invited him in of course and now here he was. Standing in her entryway looking all large and sexy and she couldn't quite remember why she'd invited him in. He'd scrambled her brain again.

'I like your plants.'

Her what? Right. Her plants. 'Thanks.'

The front bay window was filled with plants, Hazel's babies. She couldn't have pets thanks to her allergies – although Casper never seemed to make her sneeze so maybe it was time to get that rechecked – but she could have as many plants as she wanted. And she did. They'd gotten a bit out of control at this point and Hazel could barely see out the window past the various hanging vines and potted trees.

'I thought you didn't like nature.'

She shook her head. 'No, I don't like bugs and heat and dirt.'

Noah gestured toward the potted plants. 'They have dirt.'

'Right, but I don't have to sit in it.'

Noah laughed, the sound low and rich in her small home.

'Uh ... So, can I get you a drink?'

'Sure. What do you have?'

What didn't she have? For as long as she could remember Hazel equated the number of available beverages with the coolness level of the house. If there was an entirely separate drink fridge in some basement or garage area, forget it, that house was by far the coolest. When she moved to Dream Harbor all her dads ever seemed to keep stocked was milk or OJ. These are not cool things to offer to your friends.

She rattled off the several types of beer she kept stocked for Logan, the wine she liked best, plus Annie's favorites, various teas, coffees, several flavors of White Claw and sparkling water. Noah stared at her like she'd grown an extra head.

'Are you opening your own bar, Haze?'

Her cheeks heated but something about the way Noah teased her never made embarrassment flair in her belly.

'I like people to have options.'

'I'll take one of those local beers Logan likes.'

Hazel nodded and popped down the few steps to her basement to grab the beer. When she came back up, Noah was in her kitchen admiring the shells she'd put on the little window sill above the sink.

'You kept the treasure,' he said, a secret smile playing around his lips.

'Was I supposed to bury it?'

Another laugh burst out of him and he turned to face her with sparkling eyes. 'Nah, that's when all the trouble starts.' He leaned against the counter, his arms crossed over his chest and Hazel's gaze flicked to the images inked into his skin.

'Why the mermaid?' she asked.

He flexed his arm and the woman seemed to undulate. 'Seemed right for a fisherman, I guess. Got it the same day I left home with *Ginger*.'

'So, do they all mean something to you?'

He shrugged. 'Some more than others. They're kinda like souvenirs, I guess. Memories from different times in my life.'

'You're only twenty-five.' Hazel winced at the thought, the reminder of just how ill-advised her attraction to him was. 'You're going to run out of room.'

'I've got a lot of body parts left.' He said with a wink, and heat rose to Hazel's cheeks. She really needed to spend more time outside. Maybe with a little tan on her skin she wouldn't go bright red at every other word Noah said.

But now all she could think about while crammed into her tiny kitchen with him were his *other* body parts. She should steer the conversation back to safer ground.

'Why do you always look at me like that?' she asked,

steering the ship right into the rocks of awkward conversation instead.

'Like what?' He grinned. 'Like I want to undo every one of the buttons on those shirts you love to wear?'

Hazel swallowed hard. 'That's what that look means?' Her voice came out embarrassingly squeaky.

He nodded.

'Oh.' More breathy sigh than actual word. Hazel thought she might expire on the spot when Noah's gaze flicked down to said buttons.

By the time his eyes met hers again, she had apparently lost her mind because the next words that came out of her mouth were not something she would have ever said had she still had her wits about her.

'Maybe we should have sex.'

Noah choked on his beer. 'What?'

'Oh, God, oh, no. Sorry. I just thought ... maybe I misread the situation ... but I thought maybe you might want to ... Shit. I ruined it.'

He pushed off the counter and stalked toward her. The kitchen was small. Really only big enough for one person to cook in at a time which was normally fine. But now, with Noah prowling toward her across the worn linoleum and her back suddenly against another set of cabinets, it was frighteningly small.

He took her chin between his fingers and tilted her face up to his. 'Stop saying that.'

'Saying what?'

'That you're ruining things. You don't ruin anything, Hazel.'

Her eyes widened at his words but she couldn't respond before his mouth curved into a wicked smile.

'And hell, yeah, I want to have sex with you.'

'You do?'

He sighed like she was frustrating him and then planted a kiss on her forehead before releasing her chin. 'I told you before. You. Are. Hot. Of course I want to have sex with you.'

'Oh. Okay. Great... I mean right ... so...'

'What's the matter? You sound like you're malfunctioning.'

'I think I am.' She shook her head, hardly believing the turn this night took. She just needed some dinner, she just wanted to see him. She just...

'Show me how you do it.'

Noah's eyes widened. 'Show you how to ... have sex?'

Oh, God she was screwing this up so many different ways she'd completely lost count. This was why she only had sex within the safe boundaries of a long-term relationship. There was nothing to explain when you wanted to have sex with your boyfriend. You simply both worked it into your schedules. Right? Right?! Oh God, what was wrong with her?

'No, no. Not how to have sex. I mean, I know how to do that.' Although now she was doubting literally every sexual encounter she'd ever had.

'I mean, I want to keep this casual.'

He looked like he might protest but Hazel plowed forward. She didn't want to make this weird for him. She didn't want him to think she was expecting anything to come of it. But if he wanted to undo her buttons and if she definitely wanted a repeat performance from yesterday then maybe she should go for it.

Casual sex with Noah was perfectly aligned with her goals for an adventure. And so...

'I know you don't date people long term and that's totally fine because obviously it would be weird for us to get together and it would never work out and...'

Noah was staring at her again. 'Wait, why would it be weird?'

'Oh. Uh. Well, I don't know. Too many overlapping friends and we have to see each other all the time in town and stuff and then when it doesn't work out it would be awkward.'

'And why wouldn't it work out?'

Hazel huffed and gestured between them. 'We don't make sense together.'

Noah blinked. 'Right.'

Wait, did she hurt his feelings? Shit. This was officially the world's worst seduction. 'I just meant, you don't do long-term and I'm not looking for that anyway and I just thought while we are having fun together anyway, we could add this ... component, but obviously I'm terrible at this so ... we can just forget it.'

'No way.' Noah's words were fast and sharp and Hazel's

head snapped up from where she'd been staring at her feet to avoid his gaze.

'No way?'

'No way we're forgetting it.' His mouth tipped into a slow smile and Hazel's breath caught. 'I can teach you.'

'Oh.' Heat crept up her neck but it wasn't just her face that was warm, it was all of her. Heat pooled in her belly and between her thighs. Just a look from Noah had her hotter than all her past relationships combined.

'When should we start?' he asked, taking another step toward her until she could feel the rise and fall of his chest against hers.

'Um ... as soon as possible, I would say. Unless...' The words stuck in her throat when she felt the soft brush of Noah's hand against her breast. 'Unless you're busy.'

Noah chuckled as he undid her top button. 'Definitely not busy.'

'Right.' Another button undone. 'Good.' Another.

Noah paused at the fourth, his gaze settling on the cleavage that was now visible. Thank the sweet lord that she put on a good bra this morning and not the worn-out one that was barely hanging on.

He leaned in and swept the hair from her neck with his hand. His breath skated across her skin before he kissed along her jaw bone.

'This is going to be fun,' he whispered, sending chills through Hazel's body. She had no doubt about that.

His fingers continued their trek down the front of her shirt undoing each button, slowly, torturously, while Noah kissed and sucked her neck. He tugged the bottom of her shirt from her pants to get to the last of the buttons and when he did, he pulled away from her neck and stood back.

Hazel was dazed, already so turned on she didn't know what to do with herself. The delicate skin on her neck tingled from Noah's lips and the scrape of his stubble. Her shirt hung open, the rapid rise and fall of her chest moving the two sides further apart.

'Much better.' Noah's smile was triumphant this time, his eyes dark and hungry and for the first time in her life Hazel understood what it felt like to be wanted. To be desired.

And it felt really damn good.

She wrapped her hands in Noah's tight black T-shirt and tugged him forward. She wanted more of this. More of him. More of feeling this damn good.

'Do you know how many times I've pictured you like this?' he murmured into her skin as he kissed down her neck. He traced the top of her breasts with his lips and then with his tongue and Hazel groaned.

He stood and put his hands on her hips and she was up on the countertop before she registered what he was doing.

'Every damn time I would come into that shop and see you there behind the register, all buttoned up. All prim and proper.'

'I'm not prim.' Hazel gasped as Noah's tongue dipped into the top of her bra and found her nipple. She wrapped her legs around his waist and tugged him closer.

He chuckled, his warm breath raising goosebumps in

the places he'd just licked. 'Well, I know that now. But then, I just wanted to rip open that damn shirt and...'

He demonstrated exactly what he wanted to do, burying his face between Hazel's breasts, his hands coming up to cup and squeeze them. Hazel arched toward him, wanting more, needing more. She slid the shirt the rest of the way off, letting it pool on the counter behind her.

Noah's hands came around her and undid the clasp of her bra. He pulled back, then, like he was unwrapping her and didn't want to miss a minute of seeing his gift. A moment of insecurity hit Hazel. It was a heady feeling to know someone had been fantasizing about you, but what if you didn't live up to the fantasy?

She met Noah's hungry gaze. Okay, maybe she was living up to it pretty well.

'So perfect,' he groaned, cupping a naked breast in his hand. He ran his thumb over the nipple and Hazel couldn't help the sharp intake of breath at the movement. He grinned. 'You are so damn sexy, Hazel Kelly.'

She might be starting to believe it. With the way he was looking at her, touching her like he couldn't get enough. She'd be an idiot not to believe it.

He ducked his head and took her nipple in his mouth. He sucked and Hazel's head dropped back. It thunked against the top cabinets but she didn't feel it. She didn't feel anything except Noah's mouth on her body and the growing ache between her legs.

'You okay?' he asked, lapping at her nipple between words.

Hazel groaned. 'Yes. Very okay.'

She could feel his smile against the curve of her breast.

'Do you want me to keep going?'

'God, yes.'

He chuckled and then ran his tongue over her other nipple. Hazel's body arched toward him. She wasn't in control of it anymore. This was a new body. A body that wanted and was wanted. This body was sexy and desirable, and even if those feelings hadn't totally sunk into her brain yet they had been thoroughly absorbed by her skin.

Noah alternated between sucking and flicking his tongue over her sensitized nipples until Hazel wondered if she could come just from this. Was that a thing? How had she come this far and still know so little about her own body?

And why had her past boyfriends paid so little attention to her breasts? They were right there!

Hazel's fingers gripped tight to the edge of the counter like she might float away if she didn't hold on. Her heels dug into Noah's lower back and her gaze had wandered down to where Noah was worshiping her body.

She moaned at the sight of his mouth on her breast. His eyes met hers and liquid heat flooded her veins. He licked her one last time and then raised his head to kiss her, his lips warm and soft now.

'Do you want me to keep going?' he asked between kisses.

'Yes.' Her voice was embarrassingly breathy but she couldn't help it. 'You don't have to keep asking, I'm okay.'

He pulled back, a crease between his brows. 'Of course I have to keep asking, Haze.'

'Oh. I just meant ... I don't want you to worry about me or anything.'

He kissed along her neck again. 'I want this to be good for you. Every time. I'll always ask.'

She pried her fingers from the counter and ran them across the wide expanse of his back. A little thrill ran through her at the touch, at the fact that she was allowed to touch him.

'Okay. I want this to be good for you, too.'

He kissed across her cheeks, nudging her glasses with his nose. 'Thank you. So far I'm enjoying myself very much.'

She huffed a small laugh as he kissed down the ridge of her nose.

'May I?' he asked, pausing before he lifted the glasses from her face. She nodded and he set them down beside her on the counter. He kissed her long and slow and deep.

'I want to go down on you.' The words were a low rumble in her ear and just hearing him say it out loud made her shiver. 'Can I?'

'Yes,' she squeaked. She cleared her throat. 'Definitely.'

He smiled, leaving another lingering kiss on her lips while he undid her pants. She lifted her hips so he could slide them off, leaving her in nothing but her underwear sitting on her kitchen counter.

Nothing so scandalous had ever happened to her in her entire life, which she realized said a lot about her life. But that was what she was trying to remedy, right? And Noah kneeling in between her legs felt like just the thing to do it.

His hands were on her hips and he pulled her forward so her butt was right on the edge.

'God, you're killing me Hazel,' he groaned, running a finger down the front of her underwear. The touch was light, barely a touch at all and still Hazel felt everything tighten, everything in her body coming to focus on that one single touch, that one finger.

'Killing you how?' Her voice wasn't hers. It was breathy and far away.

'These little cotton panties. I've been thinking about them since the beach.'

Shit. Should she be wearing some kind of lacy thong or something? Hazel owned exactly one lacy thong that she had worn exactly once for an anniversary. Joel, her boyfriend at the time, had given it a cursory glance before tossing it aside. Fancy underwear just hadn't seemed worth it after that. And they weren't very comfortable.

Hazel glanced down. But now with Noah face to face with her practical, polka-dotted, cotton underwear she could feel the sexy confidence seeping from her body. She was losing it.

Until Noah leaned forward and ran his tongue over the front of them.

He groaned and it vibrated through her entire body.

Maybe the moment was salvageable after all. 'I can...' Hazel went to take them off, but Noah grabbed her wrists, stilling her in place.

'No,' his voice was nearly a growl. 'Keep them on.'

'You ... like them?'

He looked up at her, a look of shocked exasperation on his face. 'These panties are all I've thought about for the past twenty-four hours. Well, these panties and seeing you in them. Ever since I got a feel of them yesterday, I've wanted to see you in nothing but these.' He grinned. 'And look at that. Dreams really do come true.'

Hazel's laugh dissolved as soon as Noah ran another finger down her core. She was sure her panties were already soaked through, but she forced herself not to be embarrassed by that, not to close her legs.

Instead she let her head drop back, gently this time, to the cabinets behind her, and let Noah tease her with his fingers and his mouth. By the time he finally tugged the underwear to the side and licked her bare flesh Hazel was so close to coming she was surprised she didn't fall apart after the first flick of his tongue.

'So perfect,' he murmured and Hazel's toes curled. He mimicked the same attention he'd paid to her breasts, alternating between licking and sucking until Hazel thought this man's mouth must be some kind of national treasure. Like maybe there should be a holiday designated to it.

Heat was building everywhere. Heat and a throbbing ache pulsed through her. Sounds were spilling out of Hazel that she didn't want to think too closely about or she'd be horrified. Deep guttural sounds that were being torn from her by the pleasure racking her body. Noah's fingers dug tight into her hips, holding her in place as he brought her to the brink.

And then he freed her hips to press a thumb to her clit, steady pressure right to the center of her. White-hot pleasure shot straight to her toes.

Hazel's life flashed before her eyes.

No, not her whole life, just all the mediocre sex she'd had until this very moment. No sound escaped her, no breath.

He switched back to his mouth, sucking relentlessly.

Hazel broke.

Her body shuddered, a low, keening moan tearing from her lips. It went on and on until she finally twisted her body away, unable to take another second. It was too much. Her whole body shook, her throat raw from whatever animalistic sounds she'd been making. Thank God the windows were shut or the neighbors probably would have called the police by now.

Holy shit. This man deserved two holidays, a parade and a statue in the town square.

Noah laid gentle kisses along her inner thighs before standing. She leaned forward and pressed her head into his chest. He wrapped his arms around her, letting his fingers skate over the naked skin of her back.

He was still fully dressed, but having his arms around her made her feel safe and not exposed.

His heart was thudding hard beneath her forehead. She should reciprocate. She needed to return the favor. She just needed a minute to catch her breath.

'Did you ... I mean, was it okay?' he asked.

Hazel pulled back, staring in disbelief. 'Was it okay? Noah, that was...

'Transcendent?' he asked, the slow smile returning to his face.

'Beyond.'

'Good.' He pressed a kiss to her forehead. 'I should get going.'

'Wait, what? You can't go.' How could you even think about leaving now? After ... that? Hazel's post-orgasm glow was threatening to fade.

'It's getting late.'

'But you ... but I didn't get to...'

He gave her a rueful smile. 'Haze, it's okay. This one was for you.'

She frowned. 'No. Now we're all lopsided.'

'Trust me, we're not. That was amazing.'

She ran a hand over the front of his jeans and the hard ridge of his erection. He sucked in a quick intake of breath. 'But I want you to feel as good as I do right now.'

He groaned, leaning his forehead against hers. 'I appreciate that, I really, really do. But I don't have a condom.'

She hadn't considered that at all. She hadn't even planned to have him come in.

'Me, neither.'

'So I should go.'

'No!'

'Hazel...'

'We could ... I mean ... I will...'

'Hazel it's fine, really. I'm a big boy. I can—'

'I want to go down on you, too,' she blurted, cutting him off.

Noah's eyes widened, the pupils swallowing the color. She didn't miss the stutter in his breath. She liked it.

Her smile grew. 'I want to go down on you, Noah. May I?' She licked her bottom lip and Noah's groan reverberated through the kitchen.

'I'm going to need an enthusiastic yes before I can continue,' she teased. Noah nipped her bottom lip and she yelped.

'Yes,' he held her gaze. 'Yes, I want you to go down on me.'

Chapter Fifteen

It was possible that Noah was having some sort of fever dream. But if he was, he sure as hell didn't want to wake up.

Not now. Not with Hazel in nothing but her underwear on her knees in front of him. He should have left. He intended to leave, to be a gentleman, to get Hazel off and then go on his way. He didn't want to pressure her into anything and he sure as hell didn't want her to think he expected anything from her.

But then she'd asked him, Hazel Kelly asked for permission to go down on him, and it had been the hottest thing that had ever happened to him.

Well, the hottest thing before Hazel undid his pants and slid off the countertop. And now here she was, her soft eyes on his, kneeling at his damn feet and Noah did not know what to do. He was not equipped for this. This was *Hazel*. Not some random chick from the bar. Sweet, smart Hazel

Kelly from the bookstore. Hazel who he hadn't stopped thinking about for the past year. Hazel, who he liked to think was slowly becoming his friend.

And now she was naked, and he knew what she tasted like and the noises she made when she came, and...

What if he hurt her?

What if she regretted this?

What if one time wasn't enough?

What if one summer wasn't enough?

She ran her tongue along his length and the questions stopped. The world stopped. His heart stopped.

'You have to tell me if I'm doing it right, okay?' she said, pulling away. The furrow was back between her brows. 'Like, let me know if it's good.'

'Jesus, Haze. It's already so good, I'm barely hanging on.'

A small, satisfied smile crossed her face and he nearly lost it.

'Okay, good.' She gripped the base of his erection and slid her mouth down around him. He moaned, long and low, unable to control it. He held tight to the counter behind him, wanting to wrap his fingers in Hazel's curls but unsure if she'd like that. He could ask, but he had no words available to him at the moment other than 'Oh, God,' and 'holy shit' so he kept his hands to himself.

Hazel worked her mouth up and down his length and Noah trembled. She must have noticed because her eyes flicked up to his, needing reassurance.

'It's so good. Just like that.'

She went back to the movement, using her hand to cover where her mouth didn't reach and her tongue to swirl around the tip when she pulled back. Noah was seeing stars. *Transcendent.*

He couldn't hold back anymore. He wrapped his fingers in her hair and her little moan vibrated through him, like a purr. Her curls were so damn soft.

'That okay?' he choked out and she moaned again. One more time and he would come for sure. 'I'm almost there.'

She moved faster, taking him deeper each time, and pleasure worked its way up his spine. He looked down and seeing her there, doing things he'd never allowed himself to even fantasize about, combined with the feel of her mouth, so warm and sweet, did him in. He pulled out just in time and came messily in his own hand, not wanting to do anything Hazel might not want to do, feeling so thoroughly thrown off his game, like this whole thing was the first damn time a woman had made him come.

'Hazel.' Her name seemed to be the only word he was capable of at the moment. She stood up and handed him a towel for his hands. He wiped them off and then tugged her closer.

'It was good?' she asked.

His breath was still ragged when he answered. 'God, yes.'

He could hear her smile rather than see it. 'Good.'

'Very good.'

'So, I think that went well... I mean that was a good first ... um ... experience.'

'Hazel, please tell me you've done that before.'

'I have. Just not that often... Could you tell?'

He huffed a laugh. 'No, I couldn't tell.'

'I just meant, first experience for us together ... I mean as part of our ... fun.'

'Right.' Why did it sting to be reminded that this whole thing happened purely because Hazel was throwing caution to the wind for the next two months? He was just a part of her reckless era.

He shook it off. This was good for him, too. He'd finally get Hazel out of his system and he could move on with his life.

'Is it always that good?' she asked quietly, and again he had to wonder about her past sexual experiences. Who were these losers that didn't properly take care of this woman? But if he was being honest, things were rarely *that* good.

'No ... that was above and beyond.'

'Do you want to stay over?' The question caught him off guard. He was still trying to untangle why everything that just happened was so much better than his usual hook-ups. And trying desperately to ignore the answer the little voice in his head was screaming at him.

'Um...'

'You don't have to.' Hazel was already pulling away and he found himself pulling her back, tucking her warm, soft body against his. He found himself telling her yes, he wanted to stay.

He found that it was true.

He stuffed the little voice in his head that warned this

was a bad idea into a box and followed Hazel's polka-dotted panty-clad ass into her bedroom because if Hazel was going to be reckless, he was, too.

It was morning and Hazel was propped up on her elbow staring down at him. They were in her bed. He was in Hazel's bed. A place he never thought he'd end up but was pretty psyched he was.

It was soft and cozy and had just as many pillows as he'd expect her to have, which was a lot. The sun was filtering in through the gauzy curtains and while this room didn't have quite as many plants as the living room, there were still a few on the windowsill, cactus and small succulents, which he only knew because Hazel told him last night while they talked in the moonlit darkness.

And then they'd just slept.

And it had been really freaking nice.

She'd even evicted the stuffed frog from her bed and made him sleep with the giant penguin he had won her, which had been perched on an overstuffed chair in the corner.

'Did you sleep okay?' She was wearing the Yale T-shirt with an ugly bulldog on the front that she'd slept in and a fresh pair of those cotton panties he was now inexplicably obsessed with.

'I slept great.' He crossed his arms behind his head and smiled up at her. He was wearing nothing but his boxers and he loved the way Hazel's gaze warmed when her eyes flicked to his bare chest.

Her hair hung down into her face and he couldn't resist pushing it back.

'Can I kiss you?'

She covered her mouth with her hand. 'I haven't brushed.'

'I don't care.'

She scrunched up her nose. 'Really?'

'Hazel, who did you date before ... this?'

'A few different guys, why?'

He scooted up to a seat, leaning against the headboard. 'Were they all right? I mean, did they treat you okay?'

Hazel shrugged. 'They were fine.'

'Fine?'

She twirled a curl around her finger, avoiding his gaze before bringing her eyes back to his. She was still without her glasses and he could see the silver ring around her pupils in the morning light. 'I've never really felt ... I don't know ... like I turned them on. No one has ever called me hot before ... before you.' Her cheeks turned red as she spoke.

She was sitting now too, and he tugged her closer, wrapping an arm around her waist. 'I don't know these guys, Haze, but I can only assume they were idiots.'

'They were all really intelligent, actually.'

He huffed. 'Then how did they miss what was right in front of them?'

She shrugged against him. 'Maybe it was me? I didn't feel very sexy ... I mean I never really have.'

He rolled her over then and she squeaked in surprise. He caged her in with his arms. 'And how do you feel now?'

She smiled that mischievous smile he was addicted to. 'Sexy.'

He dipped his head and kissed her neck. 'Good.' He sucked on the delicate skin and Hazel arched into him, her legs came up to wrap around his hips and he cursed himself for not running out to buy condoms last night.

But the moment didn't last long, anyway.

His phone buzzed on the nightstand where he'd tossed it the night before.

'Should you get that?' Hazel asked, as he continued his ministrations on her neck. He really *should* get that. He was a one-man business. It could be someone wanting to book a tour, and with the summer winding down he really needed to take all the work he could get.

But Hazel was so warm and she wasn't wearing a bra. He could feel her peaked nipples against his chest.

His phone stopped and immediately started up again. He groaned and pushed himself away from Hazel's welcoming body.

'Sorry.'

'It's okay.'

Noah glanced at the screen. It was an incoming video call from his sister's number. Damn it. He tugged on his shirt before answering. There was only one person this could be, well two, actually, and he never ignored their calls. He glanced at Hazel apologetically once more before accepting the call.

Two little faces filled the screen.

'Uncle Noah! You didn't answer!' Ivy's voice was full of six-year-old indignation.

'Hi, Uncle Noah!' Cece was the more forgiving of the two cousins. His sisters had given birth to a girl each only a week apart and now the two were inseparable, unless they were fighting and then they were sworn enemies. Until they weren't anymore. Similar to how his sisters had been his whole life. And he had been the baby brother they doted on. Until he ditched them.

He cleared his throat. 'Well, excuse me, ladies. I was ... busy.'

Ivy frowned. 'You said you were never too busy for us.' This kid knew how to go for the jugular.

Cece nudged her cousin. 'Maybe he was pooping,' she suggested and both girls collapsed in a fit of giggles. He glanced up to find Hazel with her hand clapped over her mouth stifling her own laughter.

He rolled his eyes. 'What are you two little menaces calling me for, anyway? This is not our usual chat day.'

His nieces both immediately looked guilty. He'd tried to teach them about poker faces but it had gone terribly. 'Well, Mommy doesn't know we have her phone.'

'Ivy...'

'It was an emergency!' she protested and he only now realized the girls were huddled under what looked like a Bluey blanket. The pattern cast a blue tint to the girls' faces.

'Is everything alright?'

Cece's face scrunched up like she was trying not to cry and Ivy put a comforting arm around her. Noah's heart rate ratched up.

'Girls, what's going on?'

'Mommy's having another baby!' Cece wailed. 'And I don't want one!'

Ivy nodded. 'Babies cry all the time and they poop in their pants,' she said with the deep wisdom that comes with being six.

At the mention of poop, Cece started giggling again and Noah felt like he was losing his mind.

'Hey, wait a minute!' Ivy pointed at the screen. 'That's not your house! Where are you, Uncle Noah?'

The girls' inability to stay on topic was giving him whiplash like usual, but he hadn't been prepared this morning. He hadn't even had any damn coffee.

He glanced up and found Hazel slipping from the bed like she needed to hide in her own home. Which he hated. But he never introduced the women he ... slept with to his family. And certainly not his little nieces. What would he even say?

'I'm at a friend's house,' he said.

'Did you have a sleepover?' Cece asked. 'Mom says I can't have one until I'm older. Only with Ivy.' She rolled her eyes.

'That's probably a good idea.' He actually had no idea what age was appropriate for sleepovers but he knew his oldest sister was crazy protective of Cece. And now his sister was having another baby. Was he even supposed to know? It stung that no one had told him, not that he would admit it.

Ivy's eyes widened, her little face craning away from him. 'Uh-oh. We gotta go...'

The blanket was snatched from their heads and both girls started screaming bloody murder.

'Give it.' His sister's voice brokered no room for argument.

'Bye, Uncle Noah!' the girls called as Kristen's face came into view.

'Hey, sorry about that.'

'Hey, Kris.'

Her eyebrows raised as she took in his surroundings but she didn't ask where he was.

'Hope the girls didn't interrupt anything.'

'No, not really.'

'You don't always have to answer for them.'

Noah frowned. 'I like to.' His nieces were the one part of his family that didn't feel complicated. His love for them and theirs for him was simple and unconditional. He'd always answer the phone when they called.

Kristen nodded, studying him like big sisters do. What she was looking for he didn't ever know, but he always felt like he came up short. Noah, the little brother, the flaky, high-school drop out, the perptetual screw up.

'Are you coming home for the holidays this year?'

Noah looked up from his phone. Hazel was gone. And this was the last conversation he wanted to have in the middle of her bedroom. He hadn't been home for the holidays in years and didn't have any intention of going this year, either.

Hazel had called him a good uncle. She didn't know that he'd only seen his nieces in person a grand total of three times.

He swallowed hard, the memory of their little bodies crashing into him in delighted hugs the last time he'd been home bringing unwanted emotions to the forefront.

'Not sure.'

'Noah...'

'I can't right now, Kris.'

'Yeah, okay. But I just ... everyone wants to see you. That's all.'

Noah swallowed hard. He knew she meant it, but he also knew it wasn't that simple. Going home meant facing everyone's questions, everyone's expectations. What are you going to do with your life now, Noah? The last time he'd visited he hadn't even stopped by his parents' house. He couldn't have the same conversation with his dad again.

He'd left.

And he couldn't go back until he had something to show for it. He couldn't sit across the table from his father until he had more of a plan for his life than fishing tours and bartending, something to prove that leaving school and leaving the business had been the right thing to do.

None of this was shit he could talk to his sister about while he was mostly naked in Hazel's bed. 'I gotta go.'

Kristen sighed 'Okay, love you.'

Noah looked into his sister's worried face. She always looked at him like that. Like she wondered how he managed to survive in the world without all of them. Like how did he even manage to feed himself without his big sisters or his parents' business to fall back on?

He was sure she didn't do it on purpose. But he could feel it, her lack of faith in him. Was it so wrong that when he went home he wanted to be able to say, he did it. That he left and made a life for himself?

Maybe it was.

Maybe he was just a stubborn asshole.

'Love you too, Kris.'

Chapter Sixteen

Hazel was sitting on her couch with a cup of tea and a blanket pulled over her bare legs, since she hadn't thought to grab pants, attempting to act like she knew what to do after a night of purely casual sex.

Which of course, she absolutely did not know how to do. She rearranged the blanket and took a sip of her too-hot tea and glanced toward the bedroom again.

She'd probably already messed it up by asking Noah to stay but she'd felt all wobbly and vulnerable and orgasm drunk and the words were out of her mouth before she could consider their implications. And he'd stayed. And it had been really nice. Like really nice. Like sleeping wrapped up in Noah's arms had been just as perfect as she'd imagined it would be.

And something about waking up with a hot man in your bed, really did wonders for a girl's self-esteem.

But was this right? Should she feel all soft inside for this man? How could she not after he took a call from his adorable little nieces in front of her and talked to them like they mattered? And that was after the mind boggling, super hot, kitchen oral he'd performed the night before. Any person with a brain would be in her same position right now. Hazel was not at fault here.

'Hey, sorry about that.' Noah emerged from her room still dressed in nothing but a pair of boxer briefs, running a hand through his copper hair and looking so adorably sheepish that Hazel had to look away or she might accidentally propose another crazy layer to this arrangement. Like marriage. Or carrying his babies.

Hazel cleared her throat. 'No problem. Are your nieces okay?'

'Yep, they're fine. Uh ... coffee?'

'In the kitchen.'

Hazel took some deep breaths while Noah prepared his coffee and tried to control her libido that had decided to finally wake up after nearly thirty years of being asleep. It didn't work. Especially not when Noah shuffled back out into the living room and lowered himself onto the couch next to her, gingerly, so he didn't slosh his coffee.

She forced herself to look at him.

He gave her a lazy smile over his coffee mug.

'So what do we do now?' she blurted out and watched Noah's eyebrows rise in return.

'Well, we still don't have any condoms but I could...'

'No!' Hazel's cheeks heated. 'That's not what I meant.'

Noah chuckled. 'I know.'

'Jerk.' Hazel smacked his shoulder.

'What we do now, Haze, is exactly what we've been doing.' He shrugged and took another sip of coffee while Hazel pretended not to stare at his bare chest. 'We keep following your clues and giving you the best lead up to your birthday ever, and if that includes more of this…' he gestured between them and somehow even that was hot, 'then that's great.'

'Okay.' How did he make it sound so simple? Like they didn't just alter everything between them. Maybe they hadn't? Maybe she was overreacting.

'And if you don't want to do more of this part, that's fine with me, too.'

She knew he meant it, knew he wouldn't do anything she wasn't one hundred percent on board with. He'd already proven that plenty of times.

'I want more of this part.'

His smile grew. 'Great, me too.' He leaned back on the couch and stretched his legs out and rested his feet on the little tufted ottoman she'd ordered in a moment of online shopping frenzy. Something she used to do when she was bored. Now she apparently just had sex with the town sex god.

'So your sister's pregnant?'

'You change subjects almost as fast as my nieces.'

Hazel winced. 'Sorry. Bad habit.'

Noah's head was resting on the back of the couch and his eyes were closed but he was still smiling. 'It's okay. Keeps me on my toes.'

Said toes wiggled happily on the ottoman and Hazel couldn't help the way her gaze slid from his feet up the long lean lines of his legs, over his taut stomach and across his chest. She followed the breadth of his shoulders with her eyes and the strong curves of his arm muscles. His forearm flexed as he adjusted his hold on his coffee mug, the friendship bracelets sliding down his arm as he brought the cup to his lips.

His eyes were open again. Caught. Oops.

She thought he might tease her for staring but instead he just winked and went on. 'According to my niece Cece, her mother, my oldest sister Rachel, is pregnant, yeah. But I don't think I'm supposed to know yet.'

He shrugged like it didn't really matter to him either way, but the lines of his body had gone tense.

'You love them, your nieces.'

'Of course.'

'And your sisters, you love them, too.'

He paused for a sip and maybe to figure out his answer. 'Of course, yeah. It's just more complicated with them. You know how family can be.'

'I guess. I don't have any siblings.'

'Really? I thought I heard your dad, uh one of your dads, talking about someone ... a Frida?'

'Frida is one of my mom's dogs. Diego and Frida.'

'Right. I forgot you have a mom, too.'

'Yep. No shortage of parents, just no siblings. At least no human siblings. My mom is overly dedicated to her dogs, some might say.'

Noah huffed a small laugh but his gaze was far away.

'Why'd you leave home?' Hazel was definitely not doing the 'morning after a casual fling' right, but she also felt like she and Noah had become friends and she was curious about him.

'Aw, Haze, you don't want to hear about that.' He leaned toward her and waggled his eyebrows. 'There's so many more interesting ways we can spend the morning.'

She frowned and Noah sat back.

'Okay fine, you really want to know?'

'Yes.'

'It's not some big dramatic story. I told you, I dropped out of school, wildly disappointing my parents, and then I tried for a year to help out with their seafood business, I really did. But I hated it. It's a big company now. The work was all at a desk, dealing with distribution and markets and all kinds of other shit I didn't care about and I just ... I couldn't do it.'

'And then you ran away.'

'Jesus, Hazel.'

'Sorry.'

'Don't apologize.' He blew out a long breath. 'I'm sorry. You're right. I ran off after that. Took my boat up and down the coast for a while until I landed here. My nieces miss me and I never go home. That's it. That's the whole story.'

'The book club thinks you were an underwater welder in Florida.'

Noah raised an eyebrow.

'And half the PTA thinks you smuggle goods on the black market.'

'The black market, huh?' The corner of Noah's mouth hitched up into a smile.

'Yep. And there was definitely a town meeting once in which it was heavily debated whether or not you were a male stripper.'

Noah choked out a laugh. 'A stripper?'

'Yes.'

'Well, that part's true.'

Hazel's eyes widened but then Noah burst out laughing. 'Just kidding.'

'Jerk.'

He put his cup down on the ottoman and crawled over to her, caging her in with his arms. He dipped his head and kissed her and Hazel forgot to care that she hadn't brushed her teeth. He nipped at her bottom lip and she moaned so wantonly she might have been embarrassed if she wasn't so busy being turned on.

'I'll strip for you, though, Haze. Anytime.'

She laughed and his teasing smile grew. 'You're already practically naked,' she pointed out.

He glanced down at himself in mock surprise. 'You're right!' He shook his head. 'But you are wearing far too many clothes.'

He pulled the T-shirt over her head and tossed it aside and proceeded to show her all the much more fun ways they could spend their morning.

Chapter Seventeen

'Earth to Hazel!'

Hazel blinked. Annie was standing in front of her, waving a hand in front of her face. She was thankfully not at the front counter today but getting some work done in the office. She hadn't even heard Annie come in.

'Oh, hey.'

'Oh, hey? That's all you have to say to me?'

Hazel frowned. 'What else would I have to say?' She'd been daydreaming again. She couldn't help it. It had been a week of the new, very special kind of fun she'd cooked up with Noah, and even when she wasn't with him she couldn't stop thinking about him. And more specifically, everything they'd done. And where.

She could barely look down at this desk now without blushing.

Noah was so damn good with his mouth and his hands and they hadn't gone further than that, but Hazel was more satisfied than she'd ever been. It was distracting to say the least.

'You've been MIA all week!'

Annie came back into focus. Right. Her angry best friend.

'I've been busy.'

'Busy with what? Or should I say with who?'

'Isn't it whom?'

'Hazel Delphinium Kelly!'

'You know I don't have a middle name.'

'And you know that's why I have to make one up for you.' Annie put a hand on her jutted-out hip. 'Now stop distracting me. What is going on with you and the fisherman?'

Hazel shrugged but she could feel the furious blush working its way up her face. 'We've just been hanging out.' Ironically, Hazel had kept all her new stories to herself. She'd started this whole summer of fun because she'd wanted to shock her friends, to have something new to talk about, to just be generally more interesting and now here she was holding out.

She just ... everything happening with Noah now seemed ... private.

'Hanging out? You missed trivia night and now half the town thinks you've been kidnapped.'

Hazel huffed. 'I'm clearly right here.'

'Hazel...'

'What? Can't a girl have a little fun?'

'Of course you can, but this just feels like—'

'Like what Annie? Like not my type of fun? Like it's totally out of character for me? That's exactly the point! I can't ... I just needed ... something different.'

Annie plopped down on the old couch. 'I didn't know you were unhappy, Haze.'

'I'm not unhappy. I'm just ... I don't know...'

'Afraid of turning thirty?'

Hazel's eyebrows rose.

'You're not the only perceptive one. I notice things, too.'

'I just don't want to turn thirty with regrets, that's all.'

'And you regret not sleeping with the town hottie?'

Hazel laughed. 'Well, I might.'

Annie smiled. 'We wouldn't want that.'

'Sorry I didn't tell you.'

Annie shrugged, leaning back into the couch. 'That's okay. You don't have to tell me everything, although we did make that pact back in tenth grade.'

'True. Well, in the spirit of honesty, have you been trying to leave me clues or something?'

'Clues? No, Haze, I usually just go with a text.'

'Hmm.'

'What do you mean by clues?'

Hazel pulled out one of the defaced books from her bottom drawer. She'd been keeping them as evidence or souvenirs. She didn't really know which.

'Someone has been highlighting lines and then putting them back on the shelf.' She slid the book across the desk and Annie looked down at the page. It was the line about eating berries, the one she'd followed by accident.

'Wait, is this why we found you drunk in a blueberry field?'

Hazel shrugged. 'Yes.'

Annie's eyes lit up. 'I know who's doing it!'

'You do?'

'It's so obvious!' She slammed the book shut. 'It must be Noah!'

'Noah? No, that can't be right. He's been helping me follow them. He seemed just as surprised as I was about them.'

'He's been helping you follow them?'

'Well, he was here when I found the first one ... and I don't know, he seemed interested ... and then I don't know, we started having fun...' Hazel sighed. This was why she hadn't brought any of this up. Because it all sounded completely insane.

'Hazel, come on,' Annie said, like the whole thing couldn't be more obvious. 'Then it's definitely him. He's been hanging out around here for months now. He's clearly into you and look, he figured out a sneaky way to spend time with you!'

Wait. Could that be true? Did Noah set up this whole thing to hang out with her? And sneakily made it sound so nefarious.

Hazel's heartbeat had ramped up over the course of this conversation and now she felt dizzy. Could Annie be right? And did she want her to be? Devising a sneaky, scavenger hunt did not sound casual at all. But the more time she spent with Noah the more she liked him and...

She shook her head. She was getting way off track here.

'Annie, have you gone down a romcom rabbit hole already?' Her friend had a tendency to binge-watch seasonal romantic comedies from September through to the new year.

Annie huffed. 'My viewing habits have nothing to do with what is very obviously going on here.'

'And that is... '

'And that is that the sexy fisherman, who has had the hots for you for months, has been leaving you little love notes so you guys can go on dates together.'

Hazel frowned. That couldn't possibly be right.

'But Noah doesn't do relationships, remember? This feels very relationship-y.'

'There's a first time for everything.'

Noah had said those exact words to her at the carnival. *A first time for everything*. Was Hazel about to be the woman who got the infamously promiscuous Noah to settle down? Did she want to be? Wasn't she trying to *un-settle* herself?

She groaned and leaned her forehead on the desk.

'Or...' Annie paused, thinking. 'It could just be some sociopath who likes to highlight books and then leave them on the shelf.'

Hazel groaned louder.

'Haze.'

'What?'

'Are you coming to the town meeting tonight?'

'I guess so,' she mumbled.

'Great.' Annie got up and patted her head. 'I'll see you then. Love you.'

'Love you, too.' Hazel gave her a little wave and went back to staring at the next month's book orders she'd been attempting to work on for the past hour.

There was no way Annie was right about Noah and the clues, which was fine. It was good, actually, because Hazel didn't want anything serious with Noah. So really it worked out perfectly. And she could just continue with her reckless summer of fun even though it was nearly September and thinking about the end of her little experiment gave her a stomach ache. But it was all perfectly fine.

Really.

Fine.

Chapter Eighteen

It wasn't hard to spot Hazel at the town meeting since she always sat in the same seat next to Logan and Jeanie and because Noah's gaze seemed to find her no matter where she was in any room. He headed over to them, glad he wasn't late. He'd rushed right here after his tour ended. It had been a mellow afternoon with a father and his adult sons out for an afternoon of fishing for their dad's birthday and Noah had enjoyed spending the time with the family. Even when it brought back memories of fishing with his own father. Memories he usually tried to avoid. Memories from before he'd let his dad down.

He actually used to like spending time with his dad when he was a kid. Being out on one of their boats was always his favorite thing to do. His dad wasn't a man who talked a lot but he showed Noah everything he needed to know about boating and fishing and weather and the tides.

Watching him work, Noah had learned more than he ever had in a classroom.

Too bad his father couldn't teach him world history while he was at it.

He wasn't sure if it was the last few weeks with Hazel and wanting to show her he could be more than a fun time, or if he was thinking too much about his family lately, but he felt ready to finally share his plans with the town board.

Or at least his initial ideas.

He knew there would be plenty of paperwork to file and townsfolk to convince and licenses to apply for but he wanted to get the ball rolling. It was a good idea. A solid idea. And maybe it could be the start of something bigger for him here in Dream Harbor.

And if that just happened to make Hazel see him in a different light, then that would be a happy side effect. Because if the last week of fooling around with Hazel had taught him anything, it was that this woman wasn't getting out of his system anytime soon.

She turned as he approached and a secret smile crossed her face, reminding him of exactly how much she was embedded in his system.

He really freaking liked this girl.

'Hey, Noah.'

'Hey.' His gaze was stuck on hers until Logan's voice cut in.

'You gonna sit or just stand there and stare at Hazel all day?'

Noah grinned at his friend. 'Hello to you, too, Logan.

Hey, Jeanie.' The café owner gave him a wave as he slid into the seat next to Hazel. Annie was in the row ahead of them, whispering furiously with Isabel.

'What's going on?' he asked, tipping his head toward Hazel.

'Newbie.'

Noah glanced around the old meeting hall, only finding the familiar faces. He lifted a hand in greeting to Tim and Tammy before turning back to Hazel.

'She's not here yet, but supposedly she's on her way,' Hazel went on.

Noah chuckled. 'Okay, so what's new with you, then?'

'Since you saw me this morning?' she asked and heat zipped through Noah's veins at the memory of what they'd done in her office before the bookstore opened that morning. Hazel on her desk, her legs spread wide...

'I found another clue.'

'Really?' He'd almost forgotten about them, about how this had all started. About how lucky he'd gotten with those damn clues.

'Yep.' Hazel was looking at him now, studying him, like she was trying to figure out a puzzle.

'So what did it say?'

Hazel pushed her glasses further up her nose. 'Something about drinking hard cider.'

'I know just the thing!'

'You do?' Hazel's eyes narrowed like she was suspicious.

'Yeah, there's this great new brewery I've been wanting

to try. They do beers and ciders. We could go this weekend?'

Hazel muttered something that sounded an awful lot like 'how convenient' but Noah didn't have time to question it before Mayor Kelly was doing his damnedest to start the meeting.

'Attention, Dreamers!' he called over the din. 'We have a lot to get through tonight so if everyone could settle down …'

Mindy's whistle pierced through the noise and the mayor flinched. The crowd quieted and he cleared his throat. 'Right. Thank you, Mindy.'

Pete adjusted his glasses 'So, first order of business. We have a new resident in town. Ms Kira North recently purchased the Christmas-tree farm up on Old Spruce Road.'

The crowd started to glance around, whispers about this mystery resident were quickly circulating through the room. Noah couldn't help his smile. This town was too much sometimes.

'And where is she, Pete?' Tim asked the mayor from the front row.

'Well, I invited her tonight to discuss her plans for the land.'

'Is she going to reopen the tree farm?' Nancy asked.

'The place is in shambles,' Tim quickly pointed out.

The crowd took this as their cue to shout out whatever they saw fit.

'I used to love going there as a kid.'

'Used to have the best trees around.'

'And Santa! Remember in the old sleigh?'

'We have to convince her to reopen! Right Pete?'

Noah almost felt bad for the flustered mayor.

'Now hold on!' he shouted over the voices of his constituents. 'I'm sure we'll figure it out!'

The loud creaking of the back doors interrupted the room's excitement. Heads turned just in time to see a woman enter the room. A woman who clearly had not expected to be facing half the town's population.

She froze in the doorway. She had straight black hair with blunt bangs and holes in her baggy jeans. That's about all Noah managed to notice before the crowd reared up again.

'Dear God,' Logan groaned beside him, pinching the bridge of his nose.

Mindy whistled again.

The woman held up a hand in greeting. 'Uh, hello.'

'Kira, welcome!' Mayor Kelly beckoned her toward the podium and the poor woman had no choice but to make her way through the crowded room. 'Thank you so much for coming.'

Kira glanced around, a shell-shocked look still on her face. 'I ... uh ... didn't realize it was this type of meeting.'

Pete's eyes widened in dismay. 'Oh, I probably should have specified.'

Hazel sighed. 'Oh, Dad,' she whispered, shaking her head. Noah gave her hand a squeeze and she gave him a grim smile. 'He has good intentions.'

Noah chuckled. 'I know.'

'The town has a rich history of discussing town business in a public forum.' He smiled but Kira just scowled back.

'And my property is town business?'

'Well ... uh...' Pete cleared his throat. 'We were so delighted when the land was purchased. That tree farm holds a lot of special memories for the town and...'

'I'm going to stop you right there.' Kira held up a hand and Noah was impressed with her bravery. But he also worried about how the town would react. His nerves swirled in his gut thinking about his own little presentation and how it would hold up under town scrutiny. The old shacks were technically owned by the town so if he couldn't get the council on board, the whole idea was a non-starter.

'I'm not reopening the tree farm,' Kira said, voice firm. 'That's not why I bought the land.'

A hushed disappointment rolled through the room but no one spoke.

'I'd love to discuss it further, uh, privately if you prefer,' Pete pushed on.

'There's nothing to discuss.'

'It's just that you might change your mind. You see, I had a dream that...'

Kira shook her head, ignoring Pete's bizarre dream-claims, a feat Noah found impressive. 'I won't be changing my mind. And I need to go. If that's all?'

The mayor looked crestfallen, Noah really felt bad for the guy. 'Of course. Sorry for the confusion.'

Kira gave a curt nod and made her way back down the

center aisle, not bothering to glance at anyone else on her way out.

'Yikes,' Hazel whispered. She leaned over Noah's lap toward Logan. 'Maybe you should talk to her, grumpy farmer to grumpy farmer.'

Noah stifled his laughter in his arm, pretending he was catching a cough the way his nieces taught him.

'Ha. Ha,' Logan said.

'Good one,' Noah leaned down and whispered in her ear. He caught a whiff of whatever it was she put in her curls; it smelled the same as her pillow. He resisted the urge to breathe in. Not here. Not now, when he was already half hard just thinking about being back in her bed.

He shouldn't be thinking about that right now. He should be thinking about what he was going to say about his short-term rental idea. Things had gone terribly with this Kira but the town was eager for that business. Maybe they'd be open to his, too.

But the mayor had moved on to the next item, something about a change in trash pick-up days, and the PTA was up next on the agenda to discuss bus schedules for the fall; and Hazel was leaning against him in a very distracting way.

When had she started tracing the designs on his arm with a single distracting finger? And why when he glanced down at her was she looking at him with that look in her eyes?

No. He had to focus. This meeting was the perfect opportunity to present his plan. He'd even looked up pricing comps and spoken with a realtor in the area that specialized in vacation properties. He'd done his homework!

'Hey,' Hazel murmured, sending goosebumps skittering along his skin. 'Want to get out of here?'

Hell, yes, he wanted to get out of here. But for once in his damn life he was trying to be responsible. Hazel would want a responsible guy, wouldn't she? One with more to his name than an old boat?

'What would the townsfolk say?' he whispered, trying to joke his way out of the situation.

'Who cares?'

She cared. He knew that. But for some reason, she didn't seem to mind the rumors that were circulating about them. That had to mean something good in his favor, right?

'Don't you want to stay for the rest? We might miss something important.'

Her head rose sharply at that, a furrow between her brows. 'You don't want to ... I mean, I thought we could…'

God, she looked so sweet when she blushed like that.

His foot tapped nervously against the old floorboards. He could just tell her, explain that he needed to stay for the open forum part at the end so he could bring up his new idea, but he found his throat closing up at the thought. Who was he kidding? If he couldn't even explain his idea to one person, how was he going to present it to a room full of people? Maybe he didn't even want to. Isn't this what he left behind in the first place? He had a good life right now, a fun one, filled with beautiful women and few responsibilities.

Why mess with that?

'I just thought we could do something more interesting than listen to town business,' she went on, quietly, 'I know somewhere no one will find us.'

Her voice was so tempting, her breath warm on his face. *This* was what Hazel wanted him for. This was all she'd asked for. Not a relationship. She'd been upfront about the whole thing: two months of reckless fun. He was the one blowing things out of proportion. He was the one who convinced himself she could want him for more.

But Noah knew where his strengths lay. And they sure as hell weren't with business and certainly not with serious relationships. He could stay here and get laughed out of town by the terrifying residents of Dream Harbor, or he could go make out with this sexy woman. It was an easy decision, really.

'Yeah, you're right. Let's get out of here.'

Hazel's smile grew.

An easy decision.

You can't always take the easy way out, Noah. It was the last thing his father had said to him before he left home for good. And here he was, still doing it the easy way.

Noah shook the old memory from his head and grabbed Hazel's hand. They made their way out of the meeting hall, turning plenty of heads on their way. But the only opinion he cared about in this room was Hazel's.

Even if she did only think of him as a good time.

Chapter Nineteen

'I think you're better at this fun thing than you let on, Haze.' Noah's voice was a low rasp in her ear, his hands on her butt, tugging her closer.

'I'm improving.' She found his lips in the dark and he gave a quiet groan. She leaned into him and his back hit the shelves behind him, rattling the contents of the bins Hazel knew were stored there.

'What is this room, anyway?' he asked, pulling away from the kiss long enough to glance around.

Hazel pulled the overhead light switch and lit up the tiny storage room. The shelves behind Noah were filled with oversized plastic Tupperware stuffed full of seasonal decor. She knew because she'd been the one to organize them. It was nearly time to pull out the multiple bins labeled 'fall' and decorate the town hall with garlands of fake colorful leaves and plastic pumpkins.

'Supply room.' She flipped the lock on the door. 'Don't

worry, no one ever comes in here. Especially after hours.' Her father's office was down the hall along with a meeting room for the town council and some other town employee offices.

Other than the over-full metal shelves, the room contained some old office furniture, several artificial Christmas trees with the lights still on, and a stack of traffic cones. Actually, with the fluorescent light on, the room was kind of depressing.

Hazel frowned. 'Maybe this was a bad idea.' She'd been sitting in that meeting realizing that it was nearly September and her birthday was only a month away and her time with Noah was running out and she just...

She already missed him.

And she didn't want to waste any time. Certainly not to listen to the pros and cons of a new trash company.

But now that they were in this room where Dream Harbor hid its charm in between seasons, Hazel was thinking she'd miscalculated.

'Nah, it's not a bad idea.' Noah stepped forward and ran a finger down her nose, gently forcing her to stop wrinkling it in dismay. 'Just needs a little adjusting.' He walked over to the biggest tree and stooped down to find the end of the lights. He plugged it into the outlet and the tree lit up with tiny white lights. He did the same with the other two trees and then pulled the overhead light chain, bathing the room in the soft glow of the Christmas lights.

Hazel smiled.

'Much better,' he said, pulling her close again.

'You're really good at that.'

'At what? Setting the mood?' He winked but Hazel didn't miss the shadow that crossed his features at the joke, like he thought that was all he was good at.

'No. At making me feel good.'

His eyes widened a little at that, his expression so genuinely surprised that Hazel wondered how he really saw himself. Did he not know how sweet and loving he was? How he made everyone around him happier just by being himself?

She should tell him but he was already dipping his head, already kissing her, nipping and sucking his way down her neck, breathing new words into her skin.

'I'm going to make you feel even better.'

Hazel groaned. She didn't doubt it.

He flicked open the buttons on her shirt one by one, exposing her to the soft glow of the room. A grin spread across his face.

'I'll never get tired of that.'

There was a lot packed into that statement, wasn't there? Did he want to keep doing this after their time was up? Did she want to?

The questions were washed away by Noah's tongue on her skin, tracing the tops of her breasts and dipping lower. Her nipples peaked beneath her bra and she couldn't help the arch in her back, the moan from her lips.

She felt it, too. That she would never get tired of this.

But that was crazy. That's not what this was supposed to be. It wasn't what Noah signed on for.

Noah's large hands spread around to her back, smoothing over the bare skin, holding her close as he kissed her. His face was covered in a rough stubble today and it scraped Hazel's cheeks and lips and neck, the slight burn distracting her from her thoughts. He smelled like a sunny day, fresh air and freedom.

He was summer and she was fall. He was adventure and she was comfort. But right now, on the cusp between the two seasons, in this liminal space they'd carved out for themselves, they fit just right.

'God, Hazel, you're so damn perfect.' His hands traced the curve of her waist, the fullness of her breasts. She kissed him, tasting his words. She wanted to keep them.

Shouting erupted from the room below them and they froze. The reality of where they were and the possibility of being caught crept back into the room.

Noah chuckled, low and deep. 'Town drama.'

Hazel huffed. 'Always something.'

He held her gaze, his eyes dark and hungry like he didn't give a shit what scene was unfolding downstairs. And then he was kissing her again, hard and deep and like they were running out of time.

He managed to undo her pants with one hand, the other was tangled in her hair. He kissed her, his tongue twined with hers while he shoved a hand in her pants, suddenly desperate to get to her.

She was already wet and aching when his fingers swiped her sensitive flesh and her moan vibrated between them. He held her tight, a slight pull on her hair that sent sparks skittering through her body and his fingers rubbing her right where she needed it. His lips launched a brutal assault on her mouth and all Hazel could do was stand there, her legs trembling in the forgotten Town Hall supply closet and take it.

She clung to Noah's shoulders, the orgasm barrelling toward her so fast she thought it might knock her clear off her feet.

'Noah,' she gasped, pulling her mouth free. 'I'm...' She pressed her forehead to his and he flashed her devilish grin.

'Come for me, Hazel. Right here. Right where anyone could catch us.' His voice was low and deep and wicked and his gaze nearly burned right through her.

She came fast and hard, biting down on her bottom lip to keep in her screams. Her legs trembled but Noah banded an arm around her waist and held her up as the aftershocks rolled through her. He pulled his hand slowly from between her legs and licked his fingers. Hazel's eyes widened at the obscene gesture.

His low chuckle rumbled through her. 'You are just full of little kinks after all ... the thrill of getting caught. I didn't know you were into that.'

'I didn't know I was into a lot of things.'

He pressed a kiss to her temple. 'Good thing we're getting it all figured out.'

Hazel's hand wandered between them to where his erection was still straining against the front of his jeans. She freed him from his pants and Noah's groan filled the tiny room.

'Shh...' she whispered, gripping him in her fist.

'Jesus Haze, I can't shh when you're doing that.'

She flashed him a grin. 'Well, you have to.' She caught his mouth with hers and kissed all the moans from his lips as she stroked him. She knew how he liked it now, after this week of experimenting, fast and a little rough. His hands wandered while she touched him, squeezing her breasts, her ass, tugging her hair. He pumped his hips into her fist the closer he got, his movements becoming more erratic.

'Hazel, I'm close...'

She dropped to her knees and took him in her mouth, surprising them both.

'Are you sure?' Noah asked, holding still, his voice choked and raw.

Hazel nodded, swirling her tongue around him and Noah broke. The jagged sound from his mouth was nothing more than a wounded gasp. His hands came to her face, a thumb caressed her cheek. In a week of firsts, Hazel added one more and swallowed.

Noah tugged her up off her knees. 'Hazel, you didn't have to ... that was... I mean...' He tipped his forehead against hers and she couldn't help her smile.

For once in her life she felt sexy and powerful and she was claiming it right here, right now, in this bizarre little supply closet. Maybe she hadn't needed to change her life, maybe she'd just needed to change how she *saw* her life. How she saw herself.

And right now, in the twinkling lights of the old trees,

with Noah panting against her, she saw herself as pretty damn hot.

'You liked it?'

'Hazel.' He wrapped his arms around her. 'I really, really liked it.'

She kissed the tip of his nose. 'Good. Me too.'

Noah shook his head a little. 'This has been the most surprising summer of my life.'

Hazel laughed. 'Mine, too.'

'You're a very fun girl, Hazel Kelly.'

'Yeah, maybe I am.'

Chapter Twenty

The brewery was more charming than she thought it would be. It was small and rustic with a cozy interior for ordering and plenty of outdoor seating at several rows of wooden picnic tables. Lights were strung up in the trees above them and music that sounded like a mash up of country, folk, and rock came through the speakers. The air smelled like hops and over-ripe apples and the sun had just dipped below the horizon, bathing the space in a violet glow.

'So, how did you find this place?' The spot was new, Marlow & Maeve's, but it was already drawing a crowd.

'Mac got some of their new beer to serve at the bar and I'm always happy to taste test.' Noah smiled at her over his beer. 'When I found out they were opening up a spot like this, I thought it would be the perfect date spot. Good thing your clues led us here.' He winked.

Good thing.

But had it been her clues? Or Noah's? Hazel had lost the thread of what was going on here. Could he actually be the one leaving the clues like Annie said? And what did it mean if he was? It was September third which meant she had exactly twenty-five days until her birthday, and what exactly had she accomplished?

Some fun outings.

A new appreciation of summer.

Plenty of orgasms.

Discovered her own sexuality.

Caught feelings for the sexy fisherman.

Damn it. It was that last one that was the problem.

'What's the matter, Haze? Cider's no good?'

Noah's hair had grown out a bit over the past few weeks and it stood up a little on one side today; Hazel wanted to pat it down, but despite all the things they'd done together that gesture seemed way too intimate and she was lost again. What the hell was she doing?

'What?' Hazel glanced at her glass. 'No, it's perfectly good. Quite good, actually.'

'Then why are you making that face?'

'What face?'

'Like the cider has personally insulted you.'

She huffed a laugh and grabbed one of the bags of chips they'd laid out between them. The brewery had beer, cider, and snacks. She opted for salt and vinegar, letting the salty sourness coat her tongue.

'Nothing's the matter.'

'Liar.' He smirked.

'I just…' *Like you far too much for my own good and I am already dreading the end of this little arrangement.* 'I just think I liked the first one better.'

They still had a few weeks to go and she was not going to ruin it by making Noah feel uncomfortable with her new, inconvenient feelings. Feelings would fade. Right? It was just all the amazing orgasms clouding her judgment.

Right.

'Do you want me to get you another one?'

Hazel shook her head, not wanting another cider and also to rid herself of the ridiculous thoughts that wouldn't leave her to have her reckless summer in peace.

'No, I'm good.'

Noah quirked a brow and stole back the salt and vinegar chips, but didn't argue.

The tables had filled up around them as the evening darkened. Groups of people talked and laughed over their drinks. Kids ran between the trees and groups of adults. Couples sat in Adirondack chairs around little private fires. Under the table, Noah's legs tangled with hers.

Even though the day had been warm, the air cooled off quickly with the sinking sun. Hazel ran her hands over her bare arms and rubbed them to warm up, wishing they'd snagged a seat with a fire pit.

It would be even cuter here in the fall, she thought. She could imagine all the be-flanneled Dream Harbor residents making the short drive to enjoy the changing leaves and a hard cider.

'Cold?' Noah asked, already unzipping his hoodie.

'Oh, no, I'm fine.'

'Full of lies tonight, Haze,' he said with a teasing smile. He came around to her side of the table and draped the sweatshirt over her shoulders. It was big and warmed from his body and Hazel couldn't help but snuggle into it.

It was completely absurd, but no boy, or man as the case may be, had ever given her their sweatshirt or jacket or even a damn scarf to keep her warm. And it was equally absurd how freaking happy she felt now that she had Noah's.

He rubbed a hand over her back, creating more heat with the friction and his nearness.

'Better?'

Hazel smiled at him like the besotted idiot that she was. 'Much.' Her inner nerdy teenager was shrieking obnoxiously in her head. The cutest guy in town had given her his sweatshirt and she could barely stand it.

Good thing she was a mature, grown woman, though, and was totally keeping it together on the outside. Probably. She couldn't really tell what her face was doing.

Noah wrapped an arm around her as he finished his beer and Hazel let herself lean into his side. She was sure there was a Dreamer or two around here somewhere and the rumors would beat them back to town, but she really didn't seem to care.

For all the energy she put into wondering what people thought about her, whispers about her and Noah didn't bother her at all.

Maybe because you really like him and he seems to like you and why wouldn't you want the whole damn town to know?!

God, that inner voice was really getting sassy.

'You're never getting this sweatshirt back, by the way.'

Noah laughed. 'Okay, consider it a HANSOF souvenir.'

Hazel's dreamy you've-got-a-crush-on-a-boy thoughts stuttered to a stop. A souvenir. A souvenir to remember something that had a hard end date like a vacation.

'Yep. Exactly.' She finished off her cider and focused on the intricate artwork on the can instead of on Noah's words and his arms and his absurdly cozy sweatshirt.

This thing was temporary. That was the whole point, wasn't it? Hazel honestly didn't know anymore.

'Hey, can I show you something?'

Hazel glanced up and found Noah looking uncharacteristically uncertain.

'Sure.'

'Great, let's get out of here.'

They gathered up their trash and headed back across the gravel lot to Noah's car. Hazel held tight to the too-big sleeves of his hoodie and the very important fact that this thing between them was just some reckless fun.

'Um ... ta da?' Noah flipped on the battery-powered lantern he kept by the door, illuminating the small space.

'Noah, where are we... Wait, do you live here?' Hazel glanced up at him and she looked so small and sweet wrapped in his sweatshirt he had to look away or he might just kiss her and forget his whole plan to tell her about, well, about his whole plan.

'Sort of,' he huffed a laugh. 'Don't tell your dad. I'm not actually sure this isn't all very illegal.'

Hazel's eyebrows rose. 'Oh, it's definitely illegal.' They were standing in his partially renovated beach cottage, the one he hadn't actually paid for or got any sort of permission to work on or live in... Maybe bringing her here was a mistake.

Another impulsive idea. Just like dropping out of school, just like leaving home, just like getting involved with this woman. The one that was currently staring at him like he was insane and possibly a criminal.

Shit. He shouldn't have brought her here. He'd just simultaneously blown up this thing between them and his crazy plan in one dumb move. Was it too late to reverse course? Just lie about the whole thing?

'But it's beautiful,' she said, cutting off his thoughts.

'It is?'

'Of course. Noah, it's gorgeous in here. Did you do all this?' She ran a hand over the butcher block countertops he'd put in the kitchenette. Her gaze traced over the tiny house and he followed along as she took in all the work he'd done. The floors he'd refinished, the ceiling he'd patched after he fixed the roof, the walls he'd painted, the windows he'd replaced. She took the lantern with her, shining the light on his work. Noah had never been good at sitting still and this little house had become his hobby in his downtime. It did look pretty good, actually, if he was being honest with himself.

Even better as he watched the look on Hazel's face.

'Uh ... yeah. I mean, I had an idea to do the others, too. And then maybe do like a short-term rental thing...'

Her eyes lit up. 'Noah, that's a great idea. People would love these! And it's like staying in a little piece of history. Oh, my gosh, we could look up who built them and when, and what they were used for in the past. We could put little plaques on each one!' She was walking the perimeter as she spoke, past the chair he'd found at the flea market and the mattress he'd piled with extra pillows he'd found on his last trip to the home-goods store. Pillows he'd bought for her as he pictured her in his bed.

She finished her lap and was standing in front of him again in the little kitchen where he'd stalled out next to the front door, listening to her be excited for him, listening to her use the word *we* when she talked about future ideas for the houses.

She was smiling. Beaming, really. She *liked* his idea.

'So, you think it's a good idea?'

'It's a great idea.' The worried wrinkle appeared between her brows. 'You have some obstacles in your way, though. The main one being that these old shacks are owned by the town.'

'Right.'

'You should bring it up at a town meeting.'

Noah ran a hand through his hair, remembering what happened at the last town meeting. Heat rushed through his body at the memory of Hazel on her knees in front of him. Hazel must have remembered at the exact same time because her cheeks flushed red and her eyes widened.

'You wanted to stay.'

He shook his head. 'No, I very much wanted to go with you.'

'Noah.'

'Hazel.'

She frowned, hand on her hip. 'You should have told me. We could have stayed.'

He flashed her a cocky grin, hoping to cover up how insecure and panicked he'd felt at the thought of presenting his idea to the whole damn town. 'I think we had a lot more fun in that closet than we would have if we stayed.'

Hazel didn't take the bait. The little frown stayed put on her perfect lips. 'You need to at least bring it up with the mayor.'

'Your dad.'

'I like to refer to him as the mayor when I'm speaking about him in a professional capacity.'

Noah bit down on a smile. 'Of course.'

'I'm serious. You should talk to him. I think this is a really great idea, Noah. You did beautiful work here and if you kept going with it, I think it could be really amazing for the town and for you... and...'

She faded off when he cupped her face in his hands. He needed to kiss her, he needed to stop all these beautiful and wonderful words spilling from her mouth because he couldn't take them all in. He needed to slow them down. He wanted to explore them one by one, slowly. He wanted to put them on his windowsill like secret treasures.

Hazel Kelly thought he'd made something beautiful.

For the first time in a long time, he didn't feel like a screw-up. And for a minute, he felt like he could be worthy of a girl like Hazel.

He wanted to stay in that minute forever. So he kissed her, long and slow and sweet. Sweet until it wasn't anymore, until it was aching and desperate, and Hazel was making little moans and whimpers against his lips and her fingers were clutching tightly to his shoulders.

He wanted to back her up toward the bed, he wanted to lay her down in all those pillows and kiss her everywhere. He wanted to taste her. He wanted to feel her legs wrapped around his hips as he dove into her.

She pulled away suddenly. 'Wait.'

Noah stopped, hands still tangled in her curls, his mind still five steps ahead of what they were doing. 'What's the matter?'

'You can't keep doing that.'

'Doing what?'

'Distracting me like that. Whenever we're actually talking about something real.'

'This is real, too.' He lowered his head to kiss her again but she extracted herself from his touch.

'This is you running away.'

Her words stung. 'You think you really have me pegged, huh, Hazel?'

'I just want to have a conversation without you using your...'

'My what?'

'Your body to distract me.'

He knew his smile was cruel, he knew he was only lashing out because he'd been so happy a minute ago and now here he was feeling like he had nothing to offer all over again, but he couldn't seem to stop himself.

'Isn't that why you're here? I'm showing you a good time before you turn thirty. That's what you wanted from me.'

Her face fell and he didn't know how this night had gone so horribly wrong.

'Then maybe we should stop.' Hazel's words were loud and final in the small space. Panic surged through him. Panic at losing her. Panic at this thing ending before he'd had the chance to convince her to stay.

He needed to back up, to rewind, to fix it before she walked out.

'I don't want to stop.' Not exactly a riveting argument, but at least Hazel paused in her path to the door.

She turned back to face him. 'I'm sorry.'

Noah blinked. Why was she apologizing when he was the one clearly being an asshole?

'I'm sorry if I made you feel that way, that I was only using you for ... for physical stuff. That's not my intention. It's just . . . I thought that's what you preferred . . . and I didn't want to make you uncomfortable, but obviously I screwed that up.'

She gave him a weak smile. 'So let's just end this as friends, okay? Before we make things worse.'

Friends? Suddenly, the worst word in the English language.

'Hazel, no listen. I'm sorry. I'm acting like a dick. This summer has been amazing. Spending time with you is amazing.'

She let out a little disbelieving laugh. 'You don't have to lie to me, Noah.'

He stepped toward her then, but didn't grab her. He wouldn't use his body to distract her. Not about this. *This* he needed her to know in no uncertain terms.

'I have loved spending time with you, Hazel Kelly. I've loved all of it.'

'You have?'

He reached out and brushed a curl behind her ear. 'Yeah, definitely.'

Her smile grew.

'And I'm just ... sorry. I'm insecure about this plan of mine and I took it out on you which is a totally shit thing to do.'

'True,' she said.

He stepped closer, her face in his hands again. 'I'll talk to your ... the mayor.'

'Good. But don't do it on my account. Do this for you, Noah.'

Her ability to cut right to the heart of him, still caught him off guard. 'You're very wise, Hazel Kelly.'

She shrugged. 'It's because I'm so much older than you.'

He laughed. 'Luckily, I find older women to be very attractive.'

She reached up to press a kiss to his mouth, but didn't linger. 'I have to go.'

'You sure?'

He watched her weigh the pros and cons in her head, her thoughts playing across her face. He'd screwed up tonight for sure and maybe she'd forgiven him, but apparently not enough to stay and roll around in his pillows.

'Yeah, I'm sure.'

'Okay, I'll drive you.'

'Thanks.'

'And ... um...' He cleared his throat. 'The clues?'

Hazel gave him a small smile. 'I'll let you know if there are any more.'

It was embarrassing how much relief flooded through him at her words. He wasn't ready for things to be over with Hazel yet. He was going to hang onto this crazy summer with both hands for as long as he could.

For as long as she would let him.

Chapter Twenty-One

The bookstore smelled like cinnamon, butter, and vanilla icing. It was Sunday. Cinnamon-bun day and the place was bustling. The weather had turned gray and rainy, forcing an abrupt end to the short-lived summer heat, and now suddenly the town was more than happy to be inside sipping their coffee from Jeanie's and pulling apart cinnamon buns while they searched for their next read.

Hazel tried not to worry about sticky fingers on her books. She'd warned Melinda that having a gooey, frosting-covered treat in here every week might have unintended consequences like ruined merchandise, but her boss was having none of it.

Melinda wanted cinnamon buns. So Melinda got cinnamon buns. Hazel had worked out a deal with Annie for a weekly limited order of fresh cinnamon buns and the town flocked to the bookstore to get their hands on one.

She had to admit, it had been good for business. Most

people left with a sugar high and a book. Plus, the store smelled amazing. And Annie had already slipped her a warm bun under the counter to snack on between customers.

'Hey, Hazel.' Logan had a to-go bag of cinnamon-y goodness in one hand and the latest book in the romance series Jeanie was working her way through in the other.

'Hey. Is Jeanie swamped this morning?'

'Oh, yeah, but she needs her cinnamon-bun fix.' He held up the bag with a small smile. He looked happy, her friend. It was like he was the same old Logan but with a new shine. It was nice. She was glad he found Jeanie. Or she found him, as the case may be.

'So, Annie mentioned something about book clues...'

Hazel rolled her eyes. No secrets in this town. But she didn't really care if Logan knew. Of all people she knew he wouldn't say anything to anyone. He glanced behind him, but there was no line at the register. Everyone was gathered around the table they'd set up in the back for the cinnamon buns. Alex and Lyndsay were manning it this morning. Hazel glanced over to her fellow employees and found the last tray of buns was nearly empty.

'Yeah, it was strange, but I haven't seen one in over a week, so ... I guess it's over. Whatever it was.' She tried to keep the disappointment from her voice but the way Logan's brows rose, she knew she wasn't pulling it off.

'And ... Noah?'

'What about him?'

Logan cleared his throat, shifting on his feet. 'I just wanted to make sure ... I mean ... did he...?'

'Ruin me for the marriage mart? I think you're reading too many Regency-romance novels, Logan.'

Logan scowled and she couldn't help but laugh. She didn't know what was going on with Noah. She hadn't seen him since their sort of fight at his house. After maybe she'd called him out on his bullshit one too many times.

If Noah had been the one leaving the clues, he'd stopped. And if he hadn't been the one leaving them, no one else was, either, and she couldn't seem to fabricate another way to see him. So she hadn't. For a week. And she was perfectly happy to pretend that was fine with her.

'That's not what I meant. I just wanted to make sure you're ... okay.'

She smiled at him, her sweet old friend who just wanted to look out for her. 'I'm fine, thank you.'

He nodded, relief evident in his posture. 'Okay, good.'

'Nine ninety-five.'

'What?'

'For the book.'

'Right, sorry.'

He tapped his card and Hazel emailed his receipt. 'Happy reading,' she said with a grin only to be met by Logan's scowl.

'It's not for me.'

'Oh, don't pretend you don't read them when Jeanie's not looking.'

The blush that rose above Logan's beard told her she was spot on. 'They're very informative.'

Hazel laughed. 'I bet.'

'See you later, Haze.'

'Bye. Tell Jeanie to stop in after closing. Oh, and is Bennett coming to visit?'

Logan paused on his way out the door. 'Yep. He's going to stay above the café.' Logan's smile grew. 'And Jeanie's going to stay with me.'

'And that ring Nana gave you?'

Her best friend was nearly grinning now. 'On her finger by the end of the year.'

'How very cocky of you.'

He shrugged. 'When you know, you know.'

Hazel nodded as he pushed open the door and left with a wave. When you know, you know.

What did Hazel know? Well, at the moment, she knew she was happy for rainy days and ooey-gooey breakfast treats. She knew that she did love working here, even when sometimes she thought she didn't.

She knew that she was sexy. That was new. And she liked it.

Her thoughts wandered back to that interlude in the supply closet, and that day on the beach, and that kiss in the blueberry patch. But this time, instead of thinking about Noah, she thought about how brave *she'd* been, how passionate she'd been, how she'd taken the lead.

The realization she'd had the night of the town meeting rang even more true in the days after it. She didn't need a new life or to be a new person. She just needed to look at herself, at her life, in a new light.

In the romantic glow of some dusty old Christmas trees, or the late afternoon light of an empty beach, or the blinking lights of the Ferris wheel, Hazel was fun. And interesting. And maybe Noah had been by her side when she'd realized it and maybe he'd brought it out in her, convinced her that she was desirable, but Hazel could hold onto all of that even if she and Noah ended right now.

With her birthday only two weeks away, Hazel felt like she was finally ready to embrace thirty. It was just a number after all.

But even as she felt and believed it, she couldn't keep her gaze away from the romance section and the books lined up neatly on the shelves. Just in case. Because even though she knew she could be interesting and sexy without Noah, she also knew how much fun things were with him by her side. And she couldn't help but want a little bit more time with him.

Or a lot more time.

She tore off another piece of cinnamon bun and stuffed it in her mouth before Kaori made her way to the counter, letting the sugar spike through her bloodstream.

'Good morning, Hazel,' she chirped.

'Good morning. Did you find everything you needed?'

'I sure did!' Kaori lowered the stack of books in her arms onto the counter. 'Couldn't help myself. Too many good ones this week!'

'Well, I've been taking your suggestions into account.'

'I can tell. And the Dream Harbor Book Club thanks you.' Kaori tucked one side of her sleek bob behind her ear with a smile. 'Oh, but I don't want this one.' She pulled the top book off the stack. 'It's damaged.'

Hazel's heart stuttered in her chest as she glanced down at the book. A page at the center of the book had been turned down in the corner. When she looked up, Kaori winked at her.

'Did you ... do that?'

The woman put a hand to her heart like she was highly offended. 'I would never!'

Hazel huffed. 'Well, then who did?' She stuffed the book under the counter beside her breakfast. She would deal with it later.

Kaori shrugged, glancing around the crowded store. Alex and Lyndsay were packing up the trays and paper bags, a sign proclaiming the buns as 'sold out' now hung on the front of the table. 'Could have been anyone. I think most of the town was in here today.'

Hazel frowned. Most of the town except a certain red-headed fisherman.

'Who do you think is doing it?' Kaori asked, leaning forward conspiratorially.

Hazel focused on scanning the stack of books and piling them into Kaori's bag. 'I don't know. But it needs to stop. They are ruining my stock.'

'Mmm-hmm.' Kaori agreed, lips pursed. 'It's kind of a fun little mystery, though.'

'It's criminal.'

A small laugh escaped Kaori's lips before she regained her serious expression. 'So true.'

Hazel narrowed her eyes at the book club president. This woman knew more than she was letting on, which meant everyone knew more than they were letting on, which meant Hazel was once again on the outside of an inside joke. She hated that feeling.

'Don't worry, Hazel,' Kaori cut into her thoughts. 'I'm sure it's all in good fun.'

'I'm sure.'

'See you on Wednesday!' Kaori slung her bag of books over her shoulder.

'Bye. Thanks for shopping!' Hazel barely remembered to be professional in her goodbye, too caught up in the new clue beneath her counter and who left it and why, and if this meant she could text Noah again...

She'd promised to let him know if she found another clue.

Hazel didn't break promises.

The crowd thinned out significantly once the baked goods were gone and Hazel took the opportunity to peek at the book. Maybe this time the highlighted sentence would make it obvious. Maybe the perpetrator was ready to come clean.

The ship cut through the waves, tossing Arabella's curls around her face. Salt spray misted her face, and the wind whipped around her skirts. She felt like she was flying.

Well, damn.

She looked up from the page, half expecting to find

Noah grinning at her, but the store was suspiciously devoid of smiling fishermen. She supposed he could have recruited someone else to leave the clues. Someone like a certain busybody book-club president. Or maybe even his best friend, Logan?

As she stood with the book in her hand, her stomach already swooping with the thrill of seeing Noah again, Hazel found that she didn't care how this clue got here, but only that it was here.

She pulled out her phone and sent a quick text to her HANSOF partner and just hoped he was still up for a few more adventures.

Chapter Twenty-Two

Noah was reading the latest fantasy novel Hazel had recommended when his phone buzzed on his bed.

Hazel.

Hazel, the woman he'd been sort of avoiding but thinking about constantly for the past week. He'd wanted to see her, of course. He'd nearly wandered into the bookstore a half dozen times last week, but the way things ended the other night, he thought maybe Hazel wanted a little space between them. Maybe a little distance, a little breather was a good thing.

But now with her name flashing on his screen, Noah realized what a complete idiot he had been and how happy he was to see her message. And how he didn't want any distance between them at all, like not even an inch.

Another clue! You in?

Hell, yes!

Maybe he should have played it cooler? Waited more than half a second to respond? He didn't care. He wasn't cool around Hazel.

All he got back was a smiley face so he assumed she was busy at work. Not that that made it any easier to wait to hear more from her.

He flipped his book back open and lost himself in the pages. These epic fantasy novels seemed to be the antidote to his normally fidgety behavior. When he was in the story, everything else faded away. If you had told him a year ago that he would regularly be tearing through five-hundred-page books, he never would have believed it. But he loved these things. What had started out as a flimsy excuse to see Hazel had turned into something real.

If nothing else, his little infatuation with her had given him a new hobby, a way to quiet his mind and calm his body. It was nice, laying here on a rainy day in his sweats, totally absorbed in another world. If school had been like this he definitely would have finished.

But you probably can't learn calculus from a werewolf.

He'd made it through a few chapters before his phone rang. He was expecting the call, but still his heart lurched at the idea that it might be Hazel.

It wasn't, but it was his two, second favorite people to talk to.

'Uncle Noah!'

'Hello, ladies.' He propped himself up on his new pile of

pillows. His nieces' faces were crowded around the screen. 'You're looking fancy this morning.' Cece was wearing a tiara in her dark hair, bright pink lipstick slashed across her mouth. Ivy on the other hand, was in full zombie mode, face powdered an eerie white, complete with fake blood dripping from the corner of her mouth.

'We're testing out some Halloween costumes,' Cece informed him, straightening her crown. 'I think Ivy's is too scary.'

'Halloween is supposed to be scary! Right, Uncle Noah?'

'I think you could go either way with it.' He didn't bother to point out that Halloween was still a month and a half away. He knew that Halloween was serious business for these two and the costume process started early. He also knew these costumes were likely to make an appearance at every holiday following Halloween.

Ivy frowned and he had to bite down on his smile at the grumpy little zombie.

'Are you coming to visit soon?' The girls were jostling the phone between them, and for a moment he was looking at nothing but his sister's ceiling, but Cece's question came through loud and clear.

'Yeah! Are you coming for Halloween?' Ivy's face filled the screen again, her blue eyes big and imploring.

Christ. How was he supposed to say no to those little faces?

'Girls, you know Uncle Noah is very busy.' His sister's voice came from somewhere in the background. They were at Rachel's this weekend. He knew his sisters took turns babysitting on Sundays so they could each get a break.

The way Ivy nodded, like of course he wouldn't come visit and she had already come to terms with it, nearly killed him.

'Maybe Thanksgiving, though.' The words were out before he could stop them.

'Really?!' Cece squealed. 'Did you hear that, Mama? Uncle Noah's going to come for Thanksgiving and you can tell him all about the baby in your belly!'

Noah winced. There was no taking it back now.

'All right, let me talk to your uncle, please.' Again the screen was filled with snatches of Rachel's home, of his sister's life that he rarely saw because of his own stubbornness.

'Hey, Rach.' She was frowning. Off to a good start.

'Please don't get their hopes up, Noah.'

'Jesus. Give me a chance to actually let you down before you get mad at me.'

She blew out a long sigh, her eyes to the ceiling like she was looking for strength up there. 'Look, Noah. There are two little girls here who love you, and, frankly, I'm too sick from this pregnancy to sugar-coat things for you right now.'

'Congrats by the way.'

'Thanks.' She pinched the bridge of her nose like she did when she had a headache coming on. 'We were going to tell you soon, there's just been a few complications so we didn't want to jump the gun . . .'

'Complications?' Noah's heart dropped into his stomach.

'Yeah, we weren't sure at first if it would ... if we would...' She waved her hand in front of the screen, brushing away her worry, but suddenly the dark circles under her eyes were obvious, the furrow between her brow deeper. 'Everything's better now. Just hoping I don't have to go on bedrest.'

'Bedrest?' he croaked. 'Jesus, Rach.'

She gave him a weak smile and Noah's heart broke. His strong, seemingly invincible sister was hurting and here he was only thinking about his own bullshit.

'Just come home for the holidays, okay? I don't know what story you've been telling yourself about everyone being mad at you or disappointed or whatever. All any of us care about is you.'

First his nieces' little faces and now this?

'It's not a story, Rach. You know how Dad felt about me dropping out. And then leaving the business...' All his excuses seemed so feeble now in the face of his sister's stress.

'Yeah. He wanted what was best for you! But you need to let it go. He has. And the business is just fine, thank you very much.'

'I didn't mean it like that.' He knew his sisters did an amazing job with the business, but he also knew his parents were upset with his decision, that for years they'd imagined all their children working together on what they'd built. And he'd ruined that.

Noah had talked to his parents since he left, but there was always an undercurrent of disappointment, of them waiting for him to get his shit together. But maybe he was wrong? Maybe they just wanted him to be ... okay.

'Just think about it, Noah. I don't want your new niece or nephew to only know you as a face on a screen, okay?'

He nodded, the sudden emotion at the thought of having a new little person in his life clogging his throat.

'And if you want to bring a guest for Thanksgiving ... we can make room.'

'What guest would I bring?'

Rachel tried to look innocent but she'd always been a terrible liar. 'The girls mentioned you'd had a sleepover the last time they called you. Sorry about that, by the way.'

Noah shrugged. 'It's okay.'

'Anyway, if that sleepover person is serious, feel free to bring them.'

'It's not serious.'

Rachel arched a dark eyebrow. His sisters both ended up with dark hair. He was the only one who got the ginger hair from their father's family. 'And why not?'

He huffed. 'I don't do serious, Rach.'

Somehow she still had the uncanny older sister ability to sniff out his bullshit. 'You could, though. You could make it serious with this person.'

'Woman.'

'With this woman. What does she think?'

What did she think? He thought he knew, but in his

current state he wasn't feeling super confident about anything.

He shrugged. 'She's just looking for some casual fun, like me.'

Rachel frowned again, a deep crease forming between her brows. 'Casual can turn into serious. You know me and Patrick started out as a one-night stand.'

'I didn't need to know that.'

'Well, I wasn't going to get into the details!'

Noah laughed and it felt good. It felt good to be chatting with his sister again. Maybe he really would go to Thanksgiving with his family. Maybe he wouldn't spend the whole time thinking about all the ways he'd screwed up over the years.

Maybe he would bring Hazel.

'I'll think about it. About bringing a guest, I mean.'

Rachel smiled. 'Great. That makes this emotional, pregnant lady really happy.'

The next words left his mouth before he could think about them. 'Maybe I should come home sooner...'

Rachel's eyes widened. 'Sooner?'

'Yeah, I mean, I have a few more weeks of tours booked, but then maybe I should come home and help out for a bit ... you know, until you're feeling better.'

The relieved smile that lit up his sister's face sealed the deal. He needed to go home.

'Noah, that would be ... wonderful.'

'I can't do most of what you do.'

'Oh, I know that,' she said with a laugh. 'But we have

plenty of ways we could put you to work. With Patrick still on deployment, having you here would be a huge help.' She wiped a tear with the back of her hand, shaking her head. 'Sorry. Pregnancy emotions.'

'Don't worry about it.' Noah was on an emotional roller coaster of his own. What had he just agreed to?

Shrieks from the background caught Rachel's attention.

'Yikes, sounds like you should go.'

Her eyes rolled heavenward again. 'Mom will be here soon to take over, but wish me luck in the meantime.'

'Good luck. Talk to you soon.'

Rachel gave him one more watery smile before a crash had her scrambling off the phone to go investigate.

Noah leaned back into his pillows again. Rachel's words swam around in his head. What story was he telling himself? That his family didn't want him around because he hadn't met their expectations?

No, the story he was telling was that he didn't want to go home until he proved to himself and everyone else that his choice was the right one, that leaving school and home and the family business was the right thing to do.

He wanted to be *successful* when he walked in that door.

But maybe that was all bullshit, too. Maybe he just needed to go home to the family that loved him. Maybe they loved him even if all he ever had was an old boat and some crazy ideas. Maybe Hazel could too...

And now his family needed him. He couldn't shake the look of stress and fear on his sister's face when she talked about the pregnancy. He'd never once seen her look like that, not even when he'd managed to get himself stuck too high in the apple tree in their yard while she was babysitting, or when that freak, coastal blizzard knocked out all the power to their freezers jeopardizing hundreds of pounds of frozen seafood, or when Kristen announced that Ivy's father wouldn't be sticking around.

Rachel didn't get scared. Except now she was. And if Noah could do anything to fix that, he sure as hell had to try. He just didn't know what any of it would mean for him and Hazel.

It was a lot to take in. A lot to process all at once.

So he made the healthy choice and grabbed his book, comforted in the fact that at least he didn't have dormant magic powers or the tendency to turn into a wolf.

He'd read just one more chapter and then deal with his own shit...

Chapter Twenty-Three

It was early when Hazel pulled her little Prius into the marina parking lot. The sun was up but the sky was still streaked with cotton-candy pink. It was a Tuesday in September and the docks were relatively empty. Anyone that had been here for the summer was gone for the season and the locals with boats were either at work or still in bed. So she was alone as she grabbed her bag from the passenger seat and made her way down to the water.

The day was shaping up to be a sunny one but the air was chilly, the breeze off the water making Hazel glad she'd worn a sweatshirt. Well, technically it was Noah's sweatshirt. She didn't know if that was weird but it just so happened to be her new favorite one. Just the right amount of big-ness paired with the perfect coziness. And the exact right amount of Noah's summery scent. Not that she would be mentioning that last part.

A boat trip was the pinnacle of outdoor adventure. At

least to Hazel who sure as hell wasn't about to climb a mountain anytime soon. But she was feeling proud of herself for agreeing to do this.

It was all about stepping out of her comfort zone. And nothing to do with the sexy fisherman waving to her from the dock.

Ha! *Yeah, right.* One and a half weeks from her thirtieth birthday and she probably shouldn't be lying to herself anymore. She wanted to be with Noah. Like for real. Like she wanted Noah past her birthday, past the end of HANSOF. She just wanted him.

But how he felt about the whole thing was still ... fuzzy.

Which was why after this little adventure she had every intention of talking to him like the adult she was and just laying it all out there. Probably. Maybe. She still hadn't worked out all the kinks in that plan. Like what if he didn't want that, at all. What if he wanted to stick to their original agreement and Hazel was left embarrassed and exposed? What if Noah was perfectly content to walk away from all of this in a week and Hazel's summer of adventure ended with a broken heart?

It wasn't exactly what she'd had in mind when she'd started this whole thing.

'Hey! You made it.' Noah greeted her with his signature grin.

Hazel pushed down her growing worries and forced a smile. 'What, you thought I wouldn't show up?'

His smile grew. 'Nope. I'm just happy to see you.'

Hazel's heart actually fluttered, something she would

have sworn was physically impossible just a few weeks ago. 'I'm happy to see you, too.'

She fidgeted under his gaze. Was a sweatshirt and jeans not appropriate boat wear? She didn't own any of those boat shoes they wear in the LL Bean catalogs her mother still had stacked in her mail tray, so she'd just gone with her white canvas sneakers.

'You're wearing my sweatshirt.'

Oh, right. That.

'It's comfortable.'

'Mmm. I remember.'

'Do you want it back?' She'd already started undoing the zipper when Noah's hands came to stop hers.

'No, I like seeing you in it.'

'You do?'

'Of course. It satisfies some deep masculine urge to mark you as mine.' His smile was full of teasing mischief. He was kidding but a little part of her, a part she'd never confess to anyone, wanted it to be true. She wanted to be his. And in the spirit of equality, she wanted him to be hers.

She shoved all that aside and instead feigned outrage. 'Ugh, in that case...' Her fingers went back to the zipper.

Noah laughed, the sound startling the nearby seagulls. 'I'm just kidding. You look cute in it.'

'Oh. Well.' Hazel shrugged even as her stomach swooped at Noah's words.

'Anyway, this is *Ginger*.' He gestured with a flourish to the boat docked next to them, its name scrawled on the side. It looked like most of the other boats parked in the marina, at least to Hazel it did. White, with navy-blue trim, a few cushioned seats, steering wheel, two engines in the back. Typical boat, in her mind, but Noah was looking at her like he was introducing her to his baby.

'A little on the nose, isn't it?' she teased, glancing at his copper hair, glinting in the sunlight.

He ran his hand through the coarse strands, leaving one side sticking up. Hazel reached up and smoothed it down. Noah caught her by the wrist and tugged her closer.

'I missed you.'

'You could have stopped by.' She hadn't meant to say it, had nearly convinced herself that she didn't care that he'd disappeared for a week, but apparently the not-lying-to-herself started now.

'I should have. I just thought maybe you wanted some space.'

'Nope.'

Noah smiled at her quick response and ran his nose along hers. 'Good, me neither.'

'Good.' He stole the word from her lips and she smiled against him.

'Now,' he said, pulling away from their kiss. 'Are you ready for your first voyage?'

Hazel eyed the boat where it bobbed menacingly in the water. It wasn't very big. Hazel had been on exactly two boats in her entire life. One had been a cruise she went on with her dads and her mom for her mom's sixtieth birthday. And the other had been the ferry out to Martha's Vineyard with Annie for a girls' weekend.

Those boats had been large. Large enough to feel ... sturdy. Safe. This boat looked like it could easily be tossed around.

'Uh ... yes?'

'You don't sound very confident about that.'

'Because I am not at all confident about it.'

He kissed her again, sure and swift. 'Trust me, Haze. It's going to be fun.'

'Hmm.'

'Come on.' He grabbed her hand and tugged her toward the boat. He was vibrating with excitement and it was almost contagious. If she wasn't also a bit terrified she might have caught it.

'Here, give me your bag.' He took the large, straw bag from her hand and his eyes widened. 'What's in here? Rocks?'

'No.'

He continued to study her with an amused expression, waiting for her to go on.

'Mostly snacks and a water bottle and a couple of books.'

His eyebrows rose at that. 'You brought books?'

'Yes.'

'Several?'

'Of course.'

'Of course. For what?'

Hazel sighed. 'To read. You know, in case there is a lull in the ... excitement.'

Noah smirked. 'There won't be any lulls, I can assure

you.' His gaze skimmed the top of the bag and delight lit up his face. 'Oh, wait, you brought book three of the Wolf Brothers series!'

'It just came in.'

'Thank God!' He hefted the book from the bag and hugged it to his chest with one arm. 'The last one ended on a cliffhanger and I was dying to know what happened to the seer.'

Hazel grinned. 'So maybe there will be a lull or two today?'

Noah nodded as he turned the book over and read the back. 'Oh, yeah, there might have to be.' He squeezed her hand and looked up at her. 'Thanks, Haze. This is great.'

'My pleasure.' And it was. Seeing how excited Noah got over these books made her feel like maybe they had more in common than she first thought. That maybe they *could* make sense together. They'd been making plenty of sense so far.

'Okay, let me give you the tour.' He easily stepped onto the boat and then gave Hazel his hand and helped her over. The water was relatively calm today, but the ocean always had a rockiness to it, one that Hazel immediately felt when she stepped on board.

'What if I get seasick?' she asked as Noah stowed her bag in the cockpit. Cockpit? Was it the same on a boat as on a plane? She'd have to find out.

'You won't,' he said. 'I brought motion-sickness tablets and ginger candies. They always work.'

'Hmm.'

Noah spread his arms wide. 'The open sea awaits us, Hazel! Doesn't that thrill you?'

'It's the openness that concerns me, actually. And the sharks.'

'There are no sharks on the boat, Haze.'

'What if I go overboard?'

'You won't.'

'Hmm.'

He came toward her and wrapped his arms around her. It was chilly so she let him. And she liked his arms around her. That, too.

'Trust me, okay? I'll keep you safe. Promise.'

She tipped her face up to his. 'I do trust you. There's just a lot of ways this could go wrong.'

'Yeah, but think of all the ways it could go right.'

Were they still talking about this boat trip or everything else between them? Hazel wanted to believe it could go right, she really did. But there was a reason she'd done the same thing for fifteen years, kept the same job and the same friends. Hazel liked to play it safe, and somehow that hadn't occurred to her until she stood on this rocky boat, held by this man who might not be a safe bet. Who might end up hurting her in the end.

But adventures weren't safe, right?

Getting out of your comfort zone was by definition, uncomfortable.

And if these last few weeks had taught her anything, it was that good things came from being a little bit unsafe, by taking a few risks now and then.

By trusting this man.

'Yeah, okay. Let's do it.'

Noah's smile brightened his whole face. He planted a kiss on the tip of her nose and then continued the tour of the little boat.

'All right, so first off, general boating terms. The front of the boat is the bow and the back is the stern.'

Hazel nodded.

'Right is starboard and left is port.'

'Okay.'

'And this is the helm.'

'The steering wheel?'

'On a boat, it's the helm.'

'Fancy.'

Noah laughed. 'Very.'

'Will there be a quiz?' she asked, running a hand over the steering wheel.

'Maybe.'

'I plan to ace it.'

'I would expect nothing less.'

'Wait, didn't you say you lived on this boat when you first got here. How is that possible?' Hazel looked skeptically at the bench seats. There was no way a man of Noah's size could have slept comfortably on them, not to mention he would have been totally exposed to the elements.

'I saved the best part for last.' He gave her a cheeky grin and then lifted a latch near the helm. It opened up and revealed a small door that led down into a living space.

'A secret door!' She peered down into the compartment. It had a bed, a small one-burner stove and two more benches. 'Wow, it's like the inside of a camper.'

'Yeah, it's not much but it worked for a while. I got a gym membership and showered there. But the tight space got old after a while.'

'I bet.' Hazel pulled her head from the doorway and found Noah fiddling with some important-looking boat levers and knobs. She watched him, enjoying seeing him in his element. He was serious as he readied the boat, a side of him she'd rarely seen. She could see why people trusted him with their safety and their fun on his fishing excursions.

'Ready to go?' he asked, finding her staring at him.

'Ready as I'll ever be.'

Noah winked at her, the playful excitement returning to his face. He closed the door to the below-deck apartment. The boat was untied from the dock and they were off into the great unknown.

Or the coast of Dream Harbor.

But either way, it felt a little scary and a lot exciting.

And the perfect adventure to round out their summer of fun.

The trip went smoothly for a while. Hazel did a lot of staring at him while he steered the boat which Noah had to admit he liked a whole lot. It got cooler, Hazel pulled up her hood, reminding him of that day on the beach and the things they'd done, the things they'd talked about.

He was joking when he said that his sweatshirt on her made him feel like he'd claimed her. Mostly joking. He did love seeing her in it. Like a little proclamation to the world that something really was going on between them. Like they were in high school and she was letting everyone know she was taken.

It was ridiculous but it was true.

She looked so damn cute, sitting there, her cheeks pink from the air, her eyes bright. He wanted her there all the time. With him.

He shook his head. 'Got any more snacks in that bag?' he asked, distracting himself from the direction of his thoughts. Last week he wasn't even sure if Hazel wanted to hang out with him at all and now here he was thinking about forever again. He needed to cut that shit out. Especially if he really was going to go through with his plan to help his sister. He might not even be here a week from now.

'I brought scones from Annie's or...'

Noah smiled as she rummaged through her giant bag. 'Scones? Are we having a tea party?'

Hazel looked up with a scowl, but he could see the amusement in her eyes. 'You can take the girl out of the bookstore, Noah, but you can't take away her scones.'

He laughed and Hazel flashed him a smile.

'I also have chips, granola bars, trail mix, pretzels...'

'Chips!' He cut her off before she could continue her list.

Hazel tossed him a bag.

He let them drift for a bit while they ate, enjoying the late morning sun. Hazel was stretched out on the bench across from him, popping little bites of scone in her mouth, sipping her tea from her travel mug.

'So, pretend I'm a customer,' she said after a while, her gaze out at the water. 'How would that go?'

'Well,' Noah put his arms behind his head, leaning back in his chair, 'we would have agreed on a set amount of time when we booked the tour.'

'Sure, of course.' She was watching him now, her big eyes taking him in like she always did. She looked at him like maybe he didn't come up short in her eyes. Hazel was the one person in his life who looked at him and he didn't feel like she was searching for something that wasn't there.

And God, wasn't that addictive? That feeling that maybe you were enough.

'Right.' He cleared his throat. 'And then I'd take you out to my best fishing spots, depending on the time of year and what you're interested in catching, of course.'

'Do people get mad if they don't catch anything?' she asked.

'Sometimes, but I try to make sure it's a fun day, even if we don't catch anything.'

Hazel nodded, looking back out over the water. Clouds were rolling in, casting shadows over the waves.

'Want to drive?' he asked and Hazel's surprised gaze found his again.

'Is that part of the package?' she asked, eyebrows raised.

He chuckled. 'Only for you.'

She grinned at that and stood from her spot, brushing crumbs off her lap. 'What if I hit something?'

'Haze,' he laughed. 'What could you possibly hit?'

'You'd be surprised.'

He tugged her closer. 'I think you'll be okay.' He sat her on his lap, his arms around her waist. She was warm and soft and smelled like whatever Annie had iced those scones with. Sweet and a little spicy, like Hazel. 'Hands on the wheel,' he instructed.

'This feels like a flimsy excuse to get me in your lap,' she grumbled but he could hear the smile in her voice.

'And it worked,' he whispered in her ear and she shivered.

'Aye, aye, Captain.' She put her hands on the wheel and then wriggled further into his lap. Noah groaned and she laughed, knowing exactly what she was doing to him. Hazel's round ass nestled between his thighs was the best distraction.

'Haze,' he groaned and she did it again, a little squirm against him. Why had he stayed away from this woman for a week? If this was the only time he got with her, he needed to stop wasting it.

He pressed a kiss behind her ear, keeping his arms around her waist while she steered the boat in the open water, savoring the feel of her against him.

And if it wasn't such a perfect day, if Hazel hadn't been so delicious in his arms, then maybe he would have been paying more attention to the weather.

He'd meant to be back on shore before late afternoon. The nor'easter wasn't meant to hit them this time around. It was forecast to be just south of Dream Harbor. He'd checked. He'd watched the satellite all morning. But now here they were, farther from home than he'd intended, and the sky was quickly filling with dark clouds. The earlier soft breeze had rapidly turned harsher, colder.

The satellite no longer showed the nor'easter skirting past them. In fact, now it showed the edge of it falling right over their current path home.

'Shit,' he muttered.

'What is it?'

Hazel had retired from piloting the boat and was curled up under the blanket he'd tossed her when the wind picked up. Her big brown eyes watched him, a worried crease appearing between her brows.

Damn it.

He'd told her to trust him and he was royally screwing it up. So much for not coming up short.

'A bit of weather coming our way.'

'I assume that doesn't mean good weather.'

'Uh ... no, not really.' He ran a hand through his hair, his mind racing with ideas on what to do. The water was already choppy, the white tops of the waves crashing into the sides of the boat.

Where had this damn storm come from? He'd been so confident it wouldn't hit them. And then he'd let himself get distracted. He'd dropped the ball. Again.

There's just so many ways this could go wrong.

'Noah...' There was fear in her voice and he hated it.

'Hazel.' Her face was turned out toward the water, her hands clenched tight to the metal bar beside the bench she was sitting on. 'Hazel, look at me.' His voice was stern, serious, so different from his usual tone that her head whipped back to face him.

'I got this, okay? I have a plan.'

She nodded, her gaze frozen on his.

'Promise.'

'Okay.' Her response was nearly lost in the wind. But he heard it. Small but sure. Trusting. She was trusting him with a whole hell of a lot more than her fun summer now.

'Put this on.' He tossed her a life jacket and her eyes widened. 'Just as a precaution.'

It was raining now and her glasses were speckled with water but it didn't hide the fear in her eyes as she pulled on the life jacket and buckled it over her chest.

'And remember, if you see any sharks just punch them in the gills.'

A little whimper of fear escaped her.

'I was kidding! God, Hazel, I'm sorry. I was just kidding. We're going to be fine, okay? I know a place where we can wait out the storm, all right?'

She nodded. Just barely. No witty response.

'And then maybe you can finally get some reading done, okay?'

He got a small smile from her at that and that was all he had time for at the moment. He had to turn this damn boat around and get them to safety. Now.

Chapter Twenty-Four

Wind, whipping her wet curls against her face.

Rain, soaking her jeans and these stupid, canvas sneakers.

Endless gray waves with white peaks.

Dark clouds racing across the sky, like the storm was in a hurry to arrive, eager to rage.

Noah's handsome face set in grim determination as he steered the boat.

That's what Hazel focused on. Noah's face. Not her cold feet or her wet hair or the violent rocking of the boat or the thoughts of how horribly cold the sea must be right now, how terrifying it would be to plunge into that dark water.

Hazel was wearing the giant raincoat Noah had tossed her when the rain started and she pulled the hood further over her hair. They were under the small roof that covered the cockpit but the wind was driving the rain sideways and into the open sides of the boat. The life jacket she had fastened around her middle, squeezed around her ribs with each deep breath she tried to suck into her panicked lungs.

Noah's face. Calm, determined, competent. She watched him, stared as though if she kept her eyes pinned to him, everything would work out. They would be safe. He glanced at her and winked. *Winked.* With water dripping down his face and his hands clutched tight to the steering wheel, he winked at her.

'Nearly there,' he shouted over the wind and the motors.

That was when Hazel saw it. The island coming up fast ahead of them, just a gray smudge against the gray sky. But the closer they got the more it resembled actual land, safety. Hazel nearly cried at the sight of it.

Relief was written on Noah's face too, as they pulled up closer to the rocky coast of the small island. Waves crashed brutally against the big boulders.

'There's a dock around the other side of the island,' he told her, keeping the boat close to the shore but not close enough to come up against the rocks. There were more hidden beneath the waves, she was sure. The area around Dream Harbor wasn't known for its soft sand beaches. The sand they did have was coarse and rough and the rest of the shoreline was covered in rocks.

They made their way around the coastline and miraculously the wind lessened as they approached the other side of the island.

'Less windy on the lee side,' he said, flashing her a confident grin.

An old dock stuck out into the water and Hazel was

immediately skeptical. It didn't look sturdy enough to hold onto a canoe much less this boat. Would it even keep them here or would they just be tossed back out to sea?

'It's stronger than it looks,' he said, reading her mind. 'Been here for years.'

'That doesn't comfort me.'

A new layer of relief struck Noah's features at Hazel's words and she realized she hadn't spoken in a while. He flashed her a smile.

'Hang on tight.'

Noah turned the wheel, angling the boat to come up even with the dock, but with the storm, Hazel didn't know if they'd make it. He dropped the boat into reverse to slow it down, like he'd explained to her earlier in the day, but with the wind and the waves, they were still approaching the dock fast.

'Might be a bit of a rough landing,' he said, eyes focused on the dock.

Hazel held tight to the railing, bracing for impact.

They were coming in at an angle and Noah started straightening out the boat to come parallel with the dock, even as the wind kept knocking them out of alignment again. Hazel's insides churned as much as the water beneath them.

What if this didn't work?

What if they broke this ancient dock?

What if she died a cold and watery death?

The boat thumped against the dock, jarring Hazel out of her doom spiral and nearly knocked her off her seat.

'Sorry!' Noah yelled over the wind. He was keeping the boat steady next to the dock with the hull banging ominously against the old wood.

'Hold this.'

'Hold the wheel?!'

'Just hold it steady.'

Hazel got up on shaky legs and took the wheel because literally what else could she do? Noah hurried out of the cockpit and grabbed the rope to tie the boat to the dock. The boat, tipped and bobbed, pulling away from the dock and for one terrifying second, Hazel thought he would fall in.

But Noah managed to reach one of the dock pillars and grab on. He tugged and the boat came up flush with the dock and he wrapped the rope around an old metal cleat on the dock and did the same with the back of the boat.

If watching a man parallel park was sexy, watching him dock a boat in a storm was next level. He hurried back to where Hazel stood paralyzed with her hands on the wheel.

'Good job, skipper.' He kissed the tip of her nose and Hazel blinked.

She threw her arms around his neck and he let out a surprised laugh.

'You saved us,' she gasped.

'It's not actually that bad of a storm. I mean, I've sailed in worse.'

'Noah!' She pulled away, filled with righteous indignation. 'You. Saved. Us.'

He shrugged, his smile growing. 'I mean, if you want to tell people that I saved you, I won't be mad.'

'I'll be telling everyone this story.'

He huffed a quiet laugh. 'Okay, Haze.'

'Okay.' She glanced around. 'Now what?' The wind was less on this side of the island but it was still lashing rain against the sides of the boat and soaking its occupants. The boat still rocked beneath her feet.

'Now we ride it out.'

Hazel's brows rose. 'Here? On the boat?'

Noah grinned. 'Yep.'

'But ... isn't anyone here? To help us?'

'Nope. This island's been abandoned for at least a decade. Island living is rough out here. Most people can't hack it.'

'Oh. Shit.'

'The worst of the storm is past us. Look.' He held up his phone, showing her the weather satellite he'd been checking all day. 'That's the storm. And we're here-ish. This thing is moving fast. We'll be all right.'

'Hmm.'

He chuckled and grabbed her hand and she realized it was freezing cold and had been for some time but she'd been too preoccupied with not dying to pay attention. Now that they were relatively, sorta safe, she was cold and stiff.

'Come on, let's warm you up.'

Noah opened the sneaky trap door he'd shown her earlier and gestured down the few steps into the living space below deck.

'After you.'

Hazel didn't love the idea of going further into the boat

while the waves tossed them about but she also didn't love the idea of staying above deck and freezing her butt off, so she went down the steps.

There was about two square feet of standing room in the cabin. The rest of the space was taken up by a bed that was the shape of the front of the boat, sort of like a triangle with rounded sides, two small benches at the foot of the bed, and a small cabinet with the one burner stove on top.

'Just strip that wet stuff off and toss it under the bench. Open the other bench up and there's some dry clothing in there you can put on,' Noah instructed, his head poked in the doorway and then he closed it to keep the rain and wind out.

Hazel quickly changed into a pair of sweatpants that she had to roll five times just to be able to stick her feet out of the bottom, an equally large T-shirt and a sweatshirt. She kicked her wet clothes under the other bench and then crawled onto the bed to make space for Noah to come down.

He peeked his head in a moment later. 'All good?'

'Yeah, get in here. You'll catch your death.'

He stepped down, laughing as he closed the hatch. 'Okay, that sounded like an old lady.'

Hazel managed a small laugh even as the boat swayed in the water. 'That's what I was shooting for.' There was a skylight above her on the bed, but she couldn't see anything besides the rain pelting the outside of it. A few small lights glowed around the tiny cabin.

Noah shucked his wet shirt, he'd already left the wet

coat he'd been wearing above deck, and Hazel barely had time to catch her breath before his jeans were gone, too. He stood at the end of the bed in nothing but his boxer briefs and the braided bracelets around his wrist. His hair was wet and looked dark brown in the low light. He grabbed a towel from the storage bench and ran it over his hair, leaving it standing up in places.

She watched the muscles in his arms and back bunch and flex as he moved, remembering how he'd moved to get them here, to keep her safe.

She swallowed hard. 'I'm wearing all your clothes.'

He sent her a lopsided grin. 'Guess you'll have to keep me warm.' He crawled up onto the bed next to her and she quickly lifted the blanket to let him underneath. His skin was cool to the touch when he wrapped his arms around her and she hugged him back, nestling her face in the crook of his neck.

'I think this might have been a little bit too much adventure for me.'

'Nah,' he spoke to the top of her head, his breath rustling her curls. 'You did great.' His arms tightened around her. 'Haven't you learned to stop underestimating yourself yet, Haze?'

She pulled back far enough to see his face. Even in the low light, he was bright; the way he looked at her warmed her completely.

'You're Hazel freaking Kelly. Smart.' He brushed a kiss across her cheek. 'Funny.' A kiss to her other cheek. 'Sweet.' The tip of her nose. 'And sexy as hell.' Her lips, soft and warm. She sighed, letting her body relax against his. Even the storm seemed to quiet.

'You didn't need me to help you discover any of that,' he said.

'Maybe. But I'm glad you were here for all of it.'

'Yeah?'

'I really like you, Noah.'

'Yeah?'

She smiled, pulling him closer, feeling him respond to her touch even through the baggy clothes she was wearing.

'Mmm. A lot.' So much that she wondered if 'like' was even the right word anymore, that maybe at some point between the drunken blueberry-patch night and this crazy storm Hazel's feelings for Noah had catapulted straight from like to something much stronger.

Something that Noah certainly hadn't signed on for.

Something she sure as hell would be keeping to herself for the moment, until she was on dry land and had properly sorted out this alarming escalation. It probably had something to do with her recent near-death experience.

'I really like you too, Hazel Kelly.'

'Yeah?' She didn't hate hearing that, though. If she had leapfrogged from like to ... something else ... then maybe Noah could, too?

Noah grinned. 'Yeah.' He rolled on top of her. 'A lot.' He pressed the word into her skin with his lips. 'But if I'm going to properly show you, these things have got to go.'

He was tugging on the giant pants she was wearing and she laughed. 'You told me to put them on!'

'I was feeling chivalrous at the time.'

'And now?'

'And now I'm feeling like I want you out of these damn pants.'

Hazel giggled, his words tickling her neck. She helped him, wriggling out of them and yanking the sweatshirt over her head. Her glasses came with it and Noah rescued them from her hair, placing them on the little shelf built into the side of the boat.

'This is a clever space,' she said when he'd pulled her close again.

'Yeah it's not bad.'

'So you stayed down here during all your adventures?'

'For a lot of them, yeah.'

'What's the craziest thing you ever saw?'

She had a leg draped over his hip, his hands on her ass tugged her closer. 'Um...'

He thought about it but his eyes were dark, his cheeks flushed like he wanted to think about other things. Do things other than chat.

'I was up in Maine once, camping out and I swear I saw a werewolf.'

Hazel laughed. 'No you didn't.'

'You calling me a liar, Hazel Kelly?' He nuzzled against her neck, teeth scraping skin.

She sucked in a breath. 'Werewolves aren't real.'

'Maybe not. But I saw one.'

'How do you know it wasn't a regular wolf?'

'He was huge.' Noah's hands roamed freely over her body, his mouth, too. 'With glowing eyes.'

Hazel huffed but she couldn't concentrate well enough to argue, not with Noah's fingers tracing paths across her stomach, grazing the underside of her breasts. He groaned against her lips.

'Well, I'm glad you lived to tell the tale.'

'Mmm ... me too,' he rumbled, low and deep as he cupped her breast with one hand and squeezed her ass with the other. His erection was pressed hard against her center where she already ached for him. If the storm still raged outside, she was no longer aware of it.

'This body, Haze.' He groaned. 'It does things to me.'

Her laugh was breathy, stuttering out of her as his thumb brushed across her nipple. Back and forth until all sensation was distilled down to that one point. She still could barely believe it, that her body did things to this man, but she did believe it. She believed him.

'Does this boat come equipped with condoms?' she asked and Noah stilled.

'Haze,' his voice was gruff, thick with want. 'We don't have to ... I mean, I know you don't usually...'

'I don't usually what?'

He pulled back far enough so that they were face to face, his hand slipping from her breast to safer territory on her stomach.

'From what you've told me, I know you don't usually do casual sex and I know you're trying to do new things here, but this is more than a little fun and I know we're not actually ... I mean, we're not...'

Hazel's heart sank as Noah fumbled with his words. It was too painful, too embarrassing. She wouldn't make him say it, wouldn't make him admit out loud that they weren't anything serious, that this thing between them wasn't anything real.

She silenced him with a kiss. 'It's okay,' she said, even though it wasn't. 'I know what this is. Casual, fun. But I want this with you, for now.'

Noah was watching her, studying her face. And if they weren't so close, if she hadn't gotten to know him so well over the past month she might not have noticed the trace of disappointment on his face. But she did. It was there and then gone before she could catch it, quickly replaced with a sexy smirk.

'Great, yeah, me too. For now.'

'Right. Good.'

He held her gaze a moment longer before he kissed her. He kissed her until she forgot why she was disappointed, until she didn't care why he was kissing her only that he was.

It was the last week of her twenties, damn it, and she was going to enjoy it.

She could deal with her broken heart the day after her birthday.

Today, she'd survived a storm at sea and was currently tucked into bed with the sexiest man she'd ever had the privilege of touching.

Recklessness won the day.

Hazel's warm body was wrapped around his, plush and beautiful, but all Noah could think about was the look on her face when he'd said they didn't have to have sex ... that they weren't anything.

It was a lie.

Hazel was everything.

Hazel was getting lost-in-your-favorite-book good, sun-on-your-face good, the-perfect-cup-of–coffee good. If Noah thought helping her these past two months, spending time with her, tasting her, touching her, was going to get her out of his system, he was a bigger idiot than even he realized.

His crush on the sexy bookseller had only blossomed into his favorite friendship and his sexual obsession all rolled into one.

He didn't just have the hots for Hazel Kelly anymore, he was completely and inconveniently in love with her.

And for a minute he thought she felt it, too. That maybe that little look of disappointment on her face meant she wanted more, too.

But then she'd said *casual fun* and she might as well have tossed him overboard.

'You okay?' she murmured, her lips coasting down his neck.

'Yeah. More than okay.' *Get your head in the game, Noah. This is what you're good at.* He would not let his over-the-top feelings for this woman ruin this moment with her. He'd had more than one fantasy that starred Hazel right here in this bed and he wasn't about to let that go.

If this was the way he got to be with her then he'd take it every time she offered it.

And maybe that made him an idiot, but it made him an idiot with a nearly naked Hazel in his arms. Which was perfectly fine with him.

She was still wearing his T-shirt and he ran his hands over the soft material, feeling the warm weight of her breasts through the fabric. Her nipples strained against the front of the shirt and he took in the sight of her, in nothing but her panties and his white T-shirt, nearly see through after years of wear.

'Perfect,' he sighed and she smiled up at him, her cheeks flushed.

He dipped his head and took a nipple in his mouth, soaking the fabric with his tongue. Hazel moaned and squirmed. He ran his hand over her other breast, teasing her through the shirt. The thin layer between their skin somehow made the whole experience hotter, driving his desire higher.

'Noah,' she groaned and he would remember the sound of his name in her pleading whimper for the rest of his life.

'What do you need, Haze?'

'More.'

He chuckled even as inside his heart lurched. He wanted to give her everything. He wanted to be everything. But he still didn't even know if that was what she wanted and he was going home right after her birthday. How could he be everything to her if he was leaving?

He shoved the thought from his mind as he lifted her shirt and ran his tongue over her peaked nipples. She gasped, fingers going to his hair, tugging him, keeping him close. He loved it.

He sucked and licked until Hazel was writhing, her little pleading moans getting louder and louder, but now there was no one to hear them, just the open sea and a deserted island.

Make her scream.

The thought shot through him, hot and urgent.

He swirled his tongue around her nipple and then pulled away. Hazel's head came up off the bed.

'Where are you going?' she asked, sweet and indignant.

Noah let his laugh brush along her stomach. 'I have a lot of plans.'

Hazel's head dropped when he got to her plain cotton panties. He could not explain why these things drove him crazy but they really did.

He tugged them over her hips and down her ample thighs. Hazel kicked them off her feet and tossed them aside.

He dug his fingers into her flesh and spread her legs open in front of him, like a feast, his own personal treasure. The first taste ripped a broken groan from his chest. He pushed every thought about time running out, and that he would some day have to live without this, from his mind and settled in between Hazel's thighs.

'Noah,' she gasped as his tongue found her.

'Okay?'

'Yes,' she squeaked. 'Yes, yes, yes...' The yeses tumbled out as he licked, broad, flat strokes.

He held tight to her thighs, pinning her in place.

He'd always loved this. Sex. Bringing his partners' pleasure. But never like this. It was never like this, not like it was with Hazel. He wanted to stay here forever, listening to her moans and whimpers.

'Noah, please. *More*.'

More. Everything.

He slid a finger inside her slick heat, thrusting while he sucked on her. Her heels dug into the mattress, her hips rocking against him.

He replaced his mouth with his thumb, circling the spot he knew would make her come. He knew how to do it now; he held this little secret knowledge about Hazel Kelly.

'Come for me, Haze. Don't be quiet. Let me hear you.'

She lifted her head and looked at him, eyes wide, cheeks pink. He got to see her like this. Undone.

'I'm close. Please, Noah.'

He added another finger, a slow, slick slide. Hazel groaned. She held his gaze for a thick, heated breath, until Noah dipped his head to her center again, licking and sucking until Hazel was moaning loud enough to drown out the remaining wind.

'Noah!' His name broke through, screamed to the ceiling of the cramped space. 'Noah, oh, God, Noah...'

Her body shook, legs trembling with aftershocks. He

licked her gently, teasing more pleasure from her until she finally pushed him away, begging him to stop, saying she couldn't take anymore. Only then did he stop. Only when he'd given her everything did he crawl back up her body, trailing kisses along her flushed skin.

'More,' she said when he reached her.

He couldn't help his grin. He dropped a kiss on the tip of her nose before tracking down the condoms he kept tucked away on one of the little shelves. A sailor always had to be prepared.

'You sure?' he asked as he rolled the condom on.

'Mmm hmm.'

'Words, Haze.'

She gave a little exasperated sigh. 'Yes. I'm sure.' She tugged him toward her, fingers in his biceps. 'Come here.'

She wrapped her legs around him and he was at her entrance before he could fully take in the moment, before he could prepare himself for what it would feel like to sink into Hazel. It didn't matter anyway. He wouldn't have been able to prepare.

He slid in slowly and he was positive it had never been like this before. What was it? Was it Hazel's little breathy sigh, sounding an awful lot like relief when he was as deep as he could go? Surely women had sighed before. But not like this. Never like this.

Was it Hazel's thighs clenching around him, or her full breasts or her wild curls? Was it how she trusted him, how she gave herself over fully to the moment? He didn't know.

He didn't know anything as he thrust into her, each slow slide obliterating all rational thought.

'Noah,' Hazel gasped.

'Okay?'

'Yeah,' she paused, her gaze on his. 'It's just ... I don't usually come this way. I mean during this ... part. I didn't want you to be ... offended.'

Noah paused his movements, his forehead dropping to Hazel's. 'Offended?'

'It ... it feels really good. I just don't usually ... reach...'

'Yep. I got it.'

'Sorry. Does that make it less fun for you?'

Less fun for him? Jesus, this woman was going to kill him. He literally could not think of a single place he'd rather be right now.

'Don't be sorry. Don't ever be sorry for something like that.' His voice came out harsher than he intended but he was buried deep in the woman of his dreams and so irrationally angry at everyone she'd ever had sex with at the same time. It was a confusing moment, to say the least.

'Let's try something else, okay?' he asked, softening his tone.

'Okay.'

He pulled out and turned so he was sitting on the bed. His head brushed the low ceiling but they would fit.

'Come here.'

Hazel repositioned herself so she was straddling his lap. 'I don't usually do it this way. I mean, in the past.'

Noah bit down on the sharp response he wanted to give

to Hazel's past boyfriends. 'It might be a better angle for you.'

Hazel lowered herself onto his erection and Noah nearly came from the sight of Hazel's hand wrapped around him, guiding him in.

'Oh.' Her eyes widened.

'See,' he said with a grin. He put his hands on her hips and rocked her forward.

Her eyes went wider. 'Oh!'

'Yeah, exactly.'

She rocked on her own this time, a low groan echoing from her chest to his. 'Holy crap, Noah.'

'Better, sweet girl?' he rumbled and she stilled, holding his gaze, a beautiful blush crossing her cheeks at the nickname.

'Much,' she breathed, moving again.

'That's right. Find how you like it,' he murmured in her ear and she picked up her pace. She rocked again and every thrust sent pleasure skittering down his spine. He was surrounded by her, her scent, her smooth skin, her plush body. Hazel, Hazel, Hazel.

He took a nipple into his mouth and Hazel's back bowed. She held his head to her and he sucked while she rode him.

'Oh God, oh God, oh God,' she crooned.

'That's it,' he said, breaking away only long enough to say it before taking her other nipple in his mouth.

Her fingers tightened in his hair, her thighs squeezing his hips.

Hazel screamed.

Hazel babbled a string of filthy words Noah had never heard come out of her mouth.

Hazel murmured his name.

And Noah came harder than he ever had in his entire life.

Rain still pattered gently against the skylight but the wind had stopped. Noah had said they could sail back whenever she was ready.

But then he'd pulled out his book and stretched out on the rumpled bed, giving Hazel a little smirk as he'd done it. So she pulled out her book, too, cozy again in one of Noah's sweatshirts, and laid down beside him.

They were still reading an hour later, Hazel's head now resting on Noah's stomach, his fingers trailing through her hair. The cabin was dim, lit by a few small lamps and the gray light from outside. Her skin was sticky from the salt air and ... other things, and her hair was a tangled mess, but Hazel was having a hard time remembering the last time she felt this content.

'No way,' Noah murmured above her and she bit down on a smile. He'd been doing that all afternoon, too. Little exclamations of surprise and excitement as he read. It was almost as sexy as all the stuff he'd done to her before they started reading.

'What?! No way.'

Hazel giggled.

'Sorry. Am I disrupting you?' he asked.

Hazel rolled over so she could look at him. His coarse hair stuck up on one side and he was in nothing but a white undershirt and boxers. His tattoos flexed and danced as he moved his arms to put his book aside.

'Not disrupting me. I like it. I mean, I like this.'

He grinned and the room was suddenly bright.

'Me too.'

'I think this was my favorite day.'

Noah rolled so he was on his side too, his face close to hers. 'Of all our HANSOF adventures, this was your favorite?' he asked with a smile. 'The one where we almost died?'

'Died?! You said you had it under control!'

Noah laughed. 'I'm kidding! I totally had it under control.'

Hazel frowned and he kissed her nose. And in that moment, she could picture it. She could picture so many days just like this one. Well, maybe with less near-death experiences. But ones where they went on little adventures together and ended the day reading in bed and it was so freaking perfect, it hurt.

'No, I meant, my favorite day. Of all the days.' She held his gaze and watched as his smile turned serious. Her stomach rolled dangerously, much worse than it had in the storm.

He brushed a curl from her face. 'Me too.' His voice was

low and rough like those two words meant so much more than he spoke out loud. Like maybe he meant, *me too, you're my favorite person, too. Me too, I have all my favorite days with you.*

'Me too,' she repeated and she meant, *me too, I want to keep doing this with you. I want more than casual fun with you. I want everything.*

Noah leaned forward and brushed a kiss to her lips.

And she hoped that meant he wanted everything, too.

'I have something to tell you,' he said and Hazel's heart tripped over itself with excitement. This was it. *This* was the moment.

'Okay,' she breathed. Finally they would say everything out loud; she would tell Noah how she really felt about him and he would tell her. No more guessing. No more wondering. They could do this for real. Casual fun had become exhausting. Hazel was ready for serious contentment.

'I'm going away for a while.'

'Away?' What? No, that couldn't be right. Going away? That was not what Noah had to tell her. It couldn't be. She misunderstood.

'Well, home, actually. To ... uh ... help out.'

'Oh.' Home. Noah was going home. He was leaving just as abruptly as he'd arrived. And just like that, Hazel's hopes of forever blew out to sea. Everything she'd planned to say rearranged itself, the declaration of love quickly retreating to the safe confines of her heart. She'd clearly misunderstood everything.

'After your birthday.' He was watching her as he spoke, waiting for her reaction.

Hazel swallowed hard. She absolutely would not make a fool out herself about this. Their tryst had always had an expiration date. She *knew* that.

'That's ... uh ... good, right?'

Noah frowned, a crease between his brows. 'I mean ... I guess so. My sister needs some help with things and my tours are wrapping up, it seemed like a good time to go.'

'Right. Sure. That makes sense.' Hazel was attempting a smile but her face wouldn't move. This was good for Noah. He *should* go home. His family needed him. This thing between them was temporary. It all made perfect sense but that didn't make it hurt any less.

'Look, Haze, I...'

'I'm happy for you Noah. This will be really good for you.' She inched away from him, suddenly their closeness was unbearable. 'We should head back soon, right?' she asked, her voice too loud, too cheerful for the moment. But she wouldn't make Noah feel guilty about this. He'd try to hide how much the issues with his family hurt him, but Hazel saw it. He missed them and if he was finally willing to go home and fix things, she wouldn't dare tell him he shouldn't. She couldn't keep him here.

Maybe this was how things were meant to end, anyway.

Noah blinked. 'Yeah, I guess we should.'

'Thanks for making this day so memorable,' she whispered.

'Happy to help,' he said, but his smile was anything but happy.

Chapter Twenty-Five

'Let's review the facts one more time,' Annie said, her legs stretched out on the couch in Hazel's office. Jeanie sat at the other end with Casper in her lap. The little cat had taken to visiting the bookstore and Hazel often found him hidden among the stacks of books.

'Do we have to?' Hazel was behind her desk, a fresh cup of tea in her hands, courtesy of Jeanie, and a half-eaten muffin from Annie's in front of her. She'd caved and told her friends everything that happened on Noah's boat and the weeks leading up to that moment, the one she hadn't stopped thinking about for the past two days.

The storm, the sex, Noah leaving, all of it had turned into a confusing and nauseating mix of emotions in her gut. It had been so wonderful and then it had been so ... not. He hadn't said he was leaving forever but he also hadn't said they should continue whatever this was between them.

So now she was stuck in limbo again.

And stuck listening to Annie's theories about the whole thing.

'Yes.'

Hazel groaned.

'Exhibit A.' Annie held up one finger. 'Noah has had the hots for you for at least a year.'

'That's not an exhibit. It's conjecture,' Hazel grumbled, but Annie just stuck her tongue out and continued on.

'The man has purchased more books in the past year than anyone else in town. There's your evidence.'

Jeanie gave Hazel a sympathetic look. There was no stopping Annie when she was like this.

'Exhibit B.' Another finger in the air. 'Someone starts ruining your books at the exact time Noah just happens to wander in here and offers to help you.'

'It didn't happen exactly like that.'

Annie plowed forward, a third finger up. 'Exhibit C. He saves your life and then rocks your world on his boat, a boat that was specifically named in the last clue!'

'Not specifically named.'

'It's totally him leaving the clues, Haze, and he totally has a thing for you. Clearly. Obviously! I told you this weeks ago. I mean sometimes you're so smart and other times . . .'

'Him having a thing for me is not the same as him being in —' Hazel caught herself before finishing that very dangerous sentence but it was too late. Annie's eyes had gone wide and even Jeanie's dark eyebrows were up to her hairline.

'Hazel Jasmine Kelly—'

'Not my middle name.'

'Are you in love with the sexy fisherman?'

'No.'

'Hazel Marjorie Kelly—'

'Still not my middle name.'

'You are! You fell in love with him!'

'I tried not to!'

'Oh, Hazel.' Annie shook her head but Jeanie was already jumping to her rescue.

'I think it's great, Haze.'

'You can't listen to her, she's blinded by all that big, grumpy farmer love she's been getting.'

'Ew.' Hazel scrunched up her face.

'I'm not blinded. I just know how amazing it can be,' Jeanie said between laughs.

Annie harrumphed and slouched back into the couch. Casper took the opportunity to crawl onto her chest. He purred happily as Annie scratched between his ears.

'You're the one who said I should go for it,' Hazel reminded her.

'I meant, go have wild sex, I explicitly told you *not* to fall in love.'

'I tried not to,' Hazel said again, stuffing more muffin in her mouth. It was good. Pumpkin spice. 'I just didn't expect him to be so ... thoughtful.'

'Thoughtful, how?' Jeanie asked.

'Thoughtful like he's just always thinking of me. Of

ways to make me happy or make me comfortable or make me...' Heat rose to her cheeks.

'Or make you come? Blinded. Blinded by orgasms, the both of you,' Annie said. Casper hopped down and sauntered out the door as she sat up.

'Thoughtful is good,' Jeanie said, and it was nice to have an ally.

'It is, right?'

'Of course it is. I think he really likes you, Hazel.' Jeanie smiled over her mug and maybe they were both blinded by orgasms but it didn't seem like the worst way to go through life.

'Everyone likes you.' Annie frowned.

'Uh, thanks.'

Annie shook her head, blonde wisps escaping her messy bun. 'That came out meaner than I meant it. I meant that of course he likes you. Who wouldn't like you? You're smart and beautiful and sweet.'

'Aw, thanks Annie.'

Annie was still scowling. 'I just... He goes through women fast, Haze. And he's so young! I mean, is his prefrontal cortex even done developing?'

'I'm pretty sure that happens by age twenty-five.'

Annie huffed. 'I just don't want you to get hurt.'

'But...' Jeanie leaned forward, ready to make a counter argument. 'If he is leaving all these clues, that's a lot of effort, right? I mean if he's so good at getting women, why would he go through all this trouble for Hazel?' Jeanie's smile grew. 'Because he's in love with her,' she sang, happily.

'You two are the worst,' Hazel grumbled but she couldn't stop her stomach from swooping at Jeanie's words. Was she right? It was a pretty elaborate plan just to get into her pants. These clues had to indicate a pretty high level of commitment, didn't they?

Then she remembered the part of their boat adventure she'd been trying to block from her mind. 'It doesn't matter anyway because he's leaving after my birthday.'

'He's what?!' Jeanie's smile dropped.

'He told me he's going back home to help out with the family business.'

Jeanie frowned. 'For how long?'

'He didn't say.'

'So maybe it's temporary?'

Hazel glanced at Annie, knowing her best friend would give it to her straight. 'I mean, I guess it's possible...' Annie conceded. 'He could just be helping out for a few months or something.'

Now she was more confused than ever. If Noah was the person behind the clues then why would he take off afterwards? Did she misunderstand? Was he coming back?

'I still think it's him. Who else could it be?' Jeanie asked.

'What do I do now, then?' Hazel slumped back in her seat an odd mix of excitement and disappointment warring for control in her gut. How had her summer fling turned into such a complicated mess? It was almost as if she saw this coming and did absolutely nothing to stop it. In fact, she had dived in head first.

And now here she was, heartsick and confused.

Annie shrugged.

'He must have planned some way for these clues to end,' Jeanie said. 'Some kind of grand finale. And then he'll proclaim his love for you!'

'Okay, okay.' Annie waved a hand like she could shoo away Jeanie's romantic ideas. Hazel bit down on a smile. 'Don't get carried away. This isn't one of your romance novels. This is Noah we're talking about.'

'Says the woman who has watched *When Harry Met Sally* at least fifty times.'

'It's a classic,' Annie said, but Hazel cut off their debate.

'You don't think Noah's capable of a grand finale?' She didn't care about clues or grand finales, but Annie knew what she was really asking. Did she think Noah was capable of being serious about her, about wanting her for real. Would he stick around for her?

'I don't know, Haze. But I really hope so.'

'Me too.' Noah had already surprised her so much. When she'd recruited him for this two-month adventure, she'd only expected him to be fun and maybe a little reckless. She hadn't expected him to be so sweet and kind and sexy, well, that's not true, she knew he was sexy. She hadn't expected him to light up her world like he did.

She hadn't expected to learn so much about herself just by being around him.

She hadn't intended to do the most reckless thing of all. And she certainly hadn't expected to fall in love.

'Have faith, ladies,' Jeanie said, getting up from the couch and stretching her arms over her head.

'Easy for you to say,' Annie said.

'Have you talked to Mac lately?' Jeanie teased as the two headed out of the office.

'How dare you?!'

Jeanie's laugh filtered back to the office. Hazel got up and followed them out to the front of the shop. Alex was behind the register. They had a romance novel in their hands.

'Hey, Hazel. This book is marked up. What should we do with it?'

Jeanie and Annie simultaneously froze.

'A clue!' Jeanie's eyes were bright with excitement.

The three of them ran to the counter, but Hazel was fast when she wanted to be.

'I'll take it!'

Alex assessed them with surprised amusement. 'Okaaay...'

'Open it. Open it!' Jeanie was giddy beside her.

'You guys are acting weirder than usual,' Alex said, even as they also leaned over the book. Hazel opened it to the dog-eared page. It was a diary entry and the only highlighted line was the date.

September 28th.

Hazel's birthday.

In the margins was a note.

Mac's. 7:00, bring friends.

'A grand finale,' Annie breathed.

Jeanie clapped. 'I told you!'

'Weird,' Alex muttered.

Hazel let out a deep breath and tried to control the erratic swooping of her stomach.

She turned thirty in four days.

And it seemed someone was throwing her a party.

Was it too early to make a birthday wish about the identity of the host?

Chapter Twenty-Six

Hazel's text came at the perfect moment. Noah was desperately in need of a distraction. He was at the Dream Harbor Public Library attempting to print out the proper forms for a building permit, a historical site designation form, a town petition to run a business from the beach and others that he wasn't even sure he needed to or not.

He needed help.

He should ask for some.

He was incredibly stubborn in that area so instead he checked his phone.

Got another clue today.

Oh?

Yep.

Noah waited. He tapped his fingers on the table until the older woman across from him started glaring.

'Sorry,' he mouthed.

So are you going to tell me what it said?

Typing bubbles appeared and disappeared several times while he waited.

I think it was an invite to a birthday party.

Cool. Can I be your date?

The response was quicker this time.

Sure.

Good. Can't wait.

More bubbles appeared and disappeared, making him wonder what Hazel was typing and deleting. Was she dreading her birthday as much as he was? Did she expect things to be over between them after the party?

He needed to talk to her.

For real.

He needed to lay it all out there.

But not over text.

Whatever Hazel had been typing and deleting she never sent. A few minutes later he got the details for the day of her birthday and that was it. He was alone again, drowning in paperwork and design plans for the other houses.

It was like school all over again but worse this time. Worse because he'd already screwed up so many times and he just needed this plan to work. Worse because he'd convinced himself he needed this to prove to Hazel that he was worth her time. If Hazel wanted him, he'd be back in Dream Harbor as soon as Rachel was feeling better. If Hazel wanted him, he'd build a million of these tiny houses, paperwork included.

He sighed, rubbing a hand through his hair. He'd rather be working on the houses, hammering and painting and actually *doing* something. This was the shit he'd run away from before and somehow he'd ended up back here frustrated by paperwork.

Maybe if he'd finished school...

Maybe if he'd gone to college...

Maybe if he'd tried to actually learn something from his parents...

Maybe if he wasn't such a screw-up...

A failure...

He stood up suddenly, enough that the woman across from him looked up with a surprised scowl.

'Sorry,' he whispered again, stacking his papers and grabbing his phone. He had to get out of here. He needed a break. He'd almost learned to block out that voice that criticized him so harshly, the one that had kept him away from home and his family for so long. But sometimes it crept back in.

He used to think it was his dad's voice, but lately it was sounding a lot like his own.

He made his way through what could only be described as a herd of toddlers heading toward story time and out into the fresh air of the afternoon. It was cool today, fall weather starting to push out summer's heat. A few early trees had even started to turn yellow around the edges. His tours had started to slow down and in another week he'd be back home, crashing on Rachel's couch. He always felt melancholy as the weather changed, but this year the feeling was magnified. The end of summer, the end of long, hot days, the end of his time with the sexy bookseller.

He didn't want to think that last one was true.

The walk home was over a mile but he was glad he'd left his car at the marina. He needed the walk, the fresh air, the chance to clear his mind. He tried to organize his thoughts as he went, sorting through what still needed to be done. The list was long and didn't do much to ease his anxiety. Not to mention he didn't know how he would feel being home after so long.

But when he got closer to the water, the salt air filling his lungs, he felt better. Even more so when he saw the little shacks on the beach, especially the one he'd fixed up. It looked damn good. If he could just get this bureaucratic stuff taken care of, maybe he could actually pull this off.

His phone rang as soon as he was in the house.

He answered, expecting to see his nieces' faces filling the screen. He did not expect to be ambushed by his parents and his sisters. Panic shot through him. *The baby*.

'Uh ... hi? Is everyone okay?'

'Rachel mentioned you might come home to help out for

a while,' his mom said, diving right in. Her voice was filled with more hope than he deserved.

'Uh ... yeah. I was thinking about it.'

'I told you. Pay up.' Rachel held her hand out and Kristen slapped a bill into it.

'You bet on it?!' Noah said.

'Of course. No one believed me.'

'How much?'

'Twenty.'

'Kristen, you bet I wouldn't actually do it?'

His sister shrugged. 'This was just over whether or not you even said it. Higher stakes for if you actually come home or not.'

'Girls, that's terrible,' their mother admonished.

His sisters rolled their eyes in sync with each other.

'Don't bet on your brother not coming home. He would never let his nieces who adore him down. Or his big sister who needs him. Or his mother for that matter. Right, Noah?'

'Wow, Mom. Really laying it on thick,' Kristen said.

'By whatever means necessary,' their mother said, and Rachel laughed.

'Jesus, Mom,' Noah muttered.

'Don't take the Lord's name, Noah James.'

He huffed. 'Sorry.'

'We just shouldn't take these years for granted. We don't know how long your father and I will be here...'

'Mom!' Kristen's face was filled with mock horror. 'Too far.'

'Really underhanded move,' Rachel agreed.

'Well, he hasn't been home in so long...'

The three women were talking to each other now, each offering ideas on exactly how much guilt should be leveraged to get Noah home, completely ignoring the fact that he was still on the line. His father sat quietly, his gaze on Noah.

'Hey, Dad.' He'd only spoken to his dad a few times since he left home. Not for much more than obligatory check-ins his mother orchestrated. And every conversation had felt crowded with all the things they'd never said to each other, all the disappointment Noah was sure his father harbored against him.

'Hey, Noah. How are things?'

Noah shrugged but then straightened. He wasn't seventeen anymore. He wasn't a kid telling his parents he was quitting school. He wasn't twenty calling them off the coast of Virginia telling them he wasn't coming back.

'Things are good. The tours did well this summer. A lot of good word-of-mouth sent groups my way.'

The older man nodded. 'That's good.'

'Yeah, it is.' The papers were heavy in his hand. He wanted to tell his father more. He wanted to tell him all about his new plans. Maybe even ask for the old man's help on all this damn paperwork. But he didn't get the chance.

'I'm proud of you,' his father blurted out and all three women were shocked into silence.

'Uh ... for what?' Noah dropped into his only chair, laying the paperwork in his lap.

His father cleared his throat. 'You know, for you ... just because ... I'm just proud of you. You know, the man you've become. And all that.' He cleared his throat again. His father was never cruel to them as children or overly harsh, but this many words strung together about his feelings was ... unusual to say the least.

Noah swallowed.

'Uh, thank you.'

'I just wanted you to know. In case you were ... uncertain on that.'

Noah nodded because that was all he could manage at the moment. How was it that even at this age, his father's approval could still mean so much? He didn't know but it really did.

'Oh. Yeah. I ... uh ... maybe I was uncertain on that.' Noah cleared his throat. 'So ... uh ... thanks for clearing that up.'

His father nodded again but his mother's eyes were filled with tears. 'See!' she said, her hands clasped in front of her. 'Was that so hard?'

'What about me, Dad?' Kristen wrapped her arms around their dad's shoulders from where she sat perched behind him. 'Are you proud of me, too?' she teased.

'Yeah, I don't think you've told me that lately either.' Rachel nudged him from the other side and their dad harrumphed good naturedly.

'I'm proud of all my pain-in-the-ass offspring. There. How's that?'

'So beautiful.' Kristen gave him a squeeze.

'Thanks, Dad,' Rachel laughed.

It was their mother's turn to roll her eyes. 'You're all ridiculous.'

And as Noah sat there, watching his family teasing each other he could almost smell his mom's apple pie. He could hear the sound of the football game blaring from the living room. He could see his nieces running wild while his brother-in-law attempted in vain to wrangle them.

For the first time in a long time, Noah let himself feel homesick. He'd ignored it for so long, pushed it down and denied it, always managed to have some stranger in his bed on all major family holidays, that the feeling now was overwhelming. It washed over him, strong and fierce like a sudden storm.

'Oh, my God, Noah! Are you crying?' Kristen's voice was loud enough to drown out the rest of his family's bickering.

'What?' He hastily wiped his eyes. 'No. Why would I be crying?'

'Because you love us and miss us!' his sister crowed triumphantly.

'Shut up,' he said but couldn't help the smile on his face. He loved these ridiculous people and he'd let his stubborn pride keep him away for too long.

Maybe coming home wouldn't be the worst thing in the world after all.

Chapter Twenty-Seven

Mac's was suspiciously empty for a Thursday night, especially for a birthday party. Other than a few regulars at the bar, the dining room was quiet. Quiet except for the corner booth, where Annie's cackles and Hazel's voice could be heard as soon as Noah walked in.

He'd agreed to meet Hazel here even though he'd offered to pick her up. They hadn't seen each other since the day on his boat and he had thought of nothing else in the two days since then. His brain had been a twenty-four hour, non-stop Hazel-a-thon ever since. The feel of her lips, the way she looked in his clothes, her laugh, the way she'd trusted him, her taste, dear God, her taste. He had just barely been a functioning member of society and that had only been with the help of lots of coffee and twice daily cold showers.

But they'd both been busy. He had several unexpected

end-of-season tours, plus all his homework trying to get his vacation-rental plans in order and Hazel had been busy putting all her new 'spooky season' books out as she'd called them. And it just didn't seem appropriate to waltz into someone's place of business and declare your love for them. Although it had worked for Logan...

So he'd offered a ride to the party and had hoped they could talk on the drive over, but Hazel threw a wrench in that plan, too. She'd insisted on just meeting him there. So all his important declarations would have to wait until after the party. He glanced around the room on his way to the table. At the moment, it wasn't much of a party, at all.

'Hey, everyone.'

'Hey, Noah!' Jeanie smiled. 'We were just talking about you.'

'Uh oh.' His gaze landed on Hazel's glowing face and she grinned at him.

'Hazel was just telling us all about how you saved her life,' Annie said with a raised eyebrow. 'It was quite the harrowing tale.'

Noah's smile grew, his gaze never leaving Hazel's face. 'Oh, that. Yeah, that was a good day.'

Hazel's cheeks turned bright pink and Noah was sure he heard Logan groan but he didn't spare a glance for his friend.

'According to Hazel, there were twenty-foot waves and gale-force winds,' Jeanie added.

'The boat was rocking and you were taking on water!' Annie chimed in.

'Hazel nearly fell overboard into shark infested waters. She would have if you hadn't steered the boat to safety just in the nick of time.'

Annie and Jeanie nearly fell over each other in a fit of giggles.

'I may have exaggerated a little,' Hazel said with a shrug.

'Just a little,' Noah laughed. 'You'd make a good fisherman.'

Hazel's smile was big and bright. She was surrounded by her friends on her birthday and Noah knew HANSOF was mission accomplished. If nothing else came of this night at least he knew he'd given Hazel the adventurous send off to her twenties that she'd wanted.

'I'm going to get another round of drinks,' Hazel said, already scooting out of the booth. 'Noah, want to help me?'

'I'm sure he'd like to help you with a lot of things!' Annie nearly shouted as they walked away.

'Oh, God,' Hazel muttered. 'I might have to make Annie's a seltzer.'

Noah chuckled. He bumped her arm, leaning to whisper in her ear. 'Happy Birthday, Haze.'

She peered up at him, cheeks flushed. 'Thanks.' She was wearing a red shirt-dress, cinched at the waist to show off her curves, complete with a tantalizing row of little white buttons down the front. She looked beautiful, amazing, perfect. He should tell her that. He used to be good at this sort of thing. He forgot when that used to be.

Amber was at the bar. 'Another round,' Hazel told her. 'And add one for Noah.'

'Sure thing.' Amber gave him a little smirk, as though she remembered when he used to be different and that now she saw exactly what had changed about him. And why.

They leaned against the bar as they waited for the drinks and there were so many things Noah wanted to say that the words all jammed up in his throat. Should he lead with, so I may have accidentally fallen in love with you because you are kind and sweet and beautiful and funny and so freaking perfect for me, and I really hope you could someday love me too, even though I'm basically an irresponsible idiot? Or was that the sort of thing he should build up to? Maybe just, how are you? Or I've missed you? Or what are you reading, tell me all about it?

While he was debating with himself on where to begin, Hazel spoke first.

'I wanted to tell you that I know,' she said, her cheeks pinkening.

'Um... What?' *She knew?* She knew! She knew he was madly in love with her? She didn't look horrified or disgusted, so that was probably a good start.

'I mean, I know that it was you and I think it's really sweet and I'm not sure what else you have planned for tonight, but just know that I really appreciate it and I...' A wrinkle of worry appeared between her brows right as the realization of what she was saying dawned on Noah. And the expression on his face must have given away just how confused he was.

Hazel's face fell. 'Shit. I thought ... shit.'

Oh, no. Oh, no, no, no...

'Haze, wait, listen—'

'No, it's my fault. I jumped to conclusions and I should have realized when you said you were leaving that it couldn't have been you.'

'I'm not leaving. I mean, I am leaving but only for a few months, tops and...'

'Noah, really, it's fine, you don't have to pretend.' She was pulling away from him, her smile dimming and he hated it. He had to make it right.

'Haze, just let me explain.'

He reached for her hand but at that exact moment her dads, a woman holding two dogs wearing matching sweaters, the entire Dream Harbor Book Club, Hazel's bookstore employees, George from the bakery, and a half-dozen other residents Noah didn't recognize crammed through the door.

The mayor was holding a giant bundle of balloons.

Frank had a cake.

The dogs were also wearing bow ties.

The book club was yelling, 'Happy birthday!'

It was her party. And Hazel had thought he was the one throwing it. She thought he'd planned this whole summer for her and in reality, he hadn't done a damn thing.

Shit.

Noah watched the emotions flicker across Hazel's face in rapid succession. Shock, confusion, surprise, and he didn't miss the flash of disappointment, *disappointment in him*, before she plastered a happy smile on her face.

'Dad, Mom, Frank! What is this?'

'Happy Birthday, Hazelnut!' Mayor Kelly was beaming as he walked toward Hazel. 'We got you good, huh? It's like a reverse surprise party!'

'I surprised you?' Hazel asked and the Mayor frowned.

'No, no, that's not what I meant.'

Hazel laughed. 'Just kidding, Dad. I get it. This is so wonderful. Thank you.'

Mayor Kelly thrust the bundle of balloons at Noah so he could hug his daughter. Noah stood there, frozen, with balloons in his face and Hazel's words running on a loop in his mind.

'Did you like our little clues?' he asked, pulling away.

Hazel's gaze flicked to Noah before returning to her dad. 'That was you?' she asked and Noah hated the undercurrent of hurt he heard in them. Disappointment. Embarrassment.

'Yep. Well, I had help to hide them. A few of the book club members helped me pick the books and that sweet new employee of yours, Lyndsay, I think, she was very helpful. She hid them for us.' Mayor Kelly beamed. 'We thought it would be a fun little scavenger hunt for you.'

'Your father thought it would be fun.' The woman with the dogs moved in for a hug. 'I thought you'd be mad about your inventory.'

'Thanks, Mom.'

'I'm going to pay for the books!'

'I know, Dad.'

'It was all in the dream I had, except I think there was treasure in it somewhere and definitely something about pirates.' Pete shook his head. 'Anyway, it gave me this great idea for a scavenger hunt.'

'We know, Pete.' The woman, Hazel's mom, patted his arm affectionately. 'And look, it worked out perfectly.'

Noah would like to argue that it hadn't worked out exactly perfectly, but that definitely wouldn't help anything. Even though, judging by Hazel's face, she felt the same way.

'Thanks, Frank.' Hazel gave the other man a hug, the two dogs now circling Noah's legs. Despite their dapper attire they didn't have any manners and were aggressively sniffing Noah's shoes, making little excited snorts and huffs when they sniffed something particularly interesting. Between the dog inspection and the balloons he was trapped.

The rest of the guests were gathering around now, hugging the birthday girl and leaving presents on the bar. Mac had emerged from the back and was helping Amber fill drink orders. And Hazel was getting further and further away from him.

Amber lifted the balloons from his fist. He glanced at her and found her with a knowing smirk as she tied the balloons to the bar.

'You got it bad for her, huh?'

He slouched onto the nearest stool. The dogs had found someone else to sniff. 'Yeah.'

'You screwed it up?'

He ran a hand through his hair. 'Maybe? I'm not really sure yet.'

'Hmm.'

'What?'

'Noah.' She sounded exasperated.

'What?'

Amber sighed. 'It's her birthday. Just tell her the truth.'

'Right.' He watched Hazel greet her guests, smiling and thanking them, but that hint of sadness hadn't left her face. He could see it in the tightness of her smile, the furrow of her brow. Maybe he hadn't screwed it up yet. Maybe he just hadn't really tried.

Maybe it was time that he did.

'The truth,' he repeated. But Amber was gone, serving the party guests. The truth was he was in love with Hazel Kelly and it was damn time he told her that.

'I thought I'd find you out here.'

Hazel looked up from the bench outside of Mac's to find Logan standing over her. She'd been studying her feet, wishing she'd brought her purse out with her. She had an emergency book in there.

Music and laughter spilled out of the bar after Logan, lingering in the quiet night even after the door had closed. It was delightfully cool outside; a pleasant reprieve after the heat of the party.

Hazel sat in a pool of yellow light from the streetlamp until Logan's shadow loomed over her. *Caught.*

'Hiding from your own party?' he asked, sitting down next to her.

'No.'

'Haze…' He bumped his arm into hers and she leaned into his familiar warmth.

She sighed. 'I just needed a little break.'

'You know they mean well.'

'I know.'

'And they love you.'

'I know.'

'The town really showed up in force. I don't even know half the people in there.'

Hazel huffed a laugh. 'Well, some are from my Krav Maga class.'

'Ah! That explains it.'

'Explains what?'

'I knew you were stronger lately, pushing me around when I was being an idiot about Jeanie. Like a little ninja.' He bumped against her again and she smiled. 'So why are you really out here?'

Hazel let out another sigh, trying to pull together all the reasons she was hiding from her own party. And there were many. One, she didn't love big parties. Too loud, too crowded, and she never felt like she actually got to spend time with anyone. Two, she was still processing the fact that it was her father who'd left the clues for her, who'd basically orchestrated her summer of fun. Which led to three, the worst part of all, not that she would admit it right now or maybe ever, that this was not in fact Noah's grand 'I'm actually in love with you' gesture. Just the thought of Noah's confused face right before her party burst through the door was enough to have Hazel's cheeks heating up all over again.

Logan was quiet, patient, sturdy, while she thought of a way to explain it. In the end all she came up with was, 'It's all just so ... embarrassing.'

'Is it the singing? I've always hated the part when everyone sings to you at a birthday party. Everyone staring at you.' He shuddered at the thought.

Hazel laughed. 'I know. I remember your sixteenth birthday when you just walked out of the room when Nana brought in the cake.'

Logan huffed. 'I told her I didn't want the singing part.'

'It's not the singing. I don't know...' She shrugged. 'It's the fact that the whole town was like, "you know who really needs to get out more? Hazel Kelly. We should leave her a trail of clues to get her out of that bookstore and into the world. Dusty, boring old Hazel."'

'Hazel Rainbow Kelly.' Logan's voice was serious, stern, like she was in trouble.

'If you tell Annie my real middle name, I'll kill you.'

'I don't doubt it, but that is not what anyone thinks of you.'

'I guess,' she said, although she was not at all convinced. Why wouldn't people think that? She thought it about herself. Or at least she had before Noah showed her that maybe she was more fun than she realized. It was why she'd followed the damn clues in the first place.

'Your dad wanted you to have some fun. A birthday scavenger hunt. And this crazy town helped him do it. That's it. No one thinks you're boring. Especially not Noah.'

Hazel grimaced. 'Oh, God. The whole town knows he was helping me, don't they?'

Logan made a noncommittal noise that Hazel took as a definite yes.

She groaned. 'That makes it even worse.'

Why did she have to admit to Noah that she thought he'd planned this whole thing right as her damn party walked through the door! If she'd kept her mouth shut for thirty more seconds, he'd never have to know the truth. He'd never have to know that she harbored secret hopes that he'd planned the whole thing. That her secret birthday wish was he had deeper feelings for her than just a summer fling.

'He likes you.'

'As a friend. Or a hook-up?'

'No. No way. Not a friend.' Logan frowned. 'Certainly not a hook-up. He's got it bad for you, Haze. I've never seen him like this about anyone before. He's been different this summer. He's in there right now talking to your dad about a short-term rental plan he has for those old beach shacks. Like he has a whole business proposal and everything.'

'Really?'

Logan nodded.

'Must be that prefrontal cortex firming up.'

'What?'

'Never mind.'

'All I know,' Logan went on. 'Is that he's serious about you.'

'But I thought he was leaving.'

'Apparently his sister has been told to go on bed rest for a few weeks. He's just going home to help out. If the elaborate plan he's explaining to your dad is any indication, he's definitely coming back.'

'Oh.'

Hazel didn't know what to do with that information, but she was glad she had it. She'd file it away for later when she had time to process it. She already knew Noah was so much more than she'd initially thought he was, was it so surprising that he could have real feelings for her?

'Oh, and Jeanie is really sorry for convincing you that Noah was behind the clues. Obviously, your dad didn't fill us in on this little plan.'

'I'm not mad at Jeanie.'

'Okay, good. And don't be mad at Noah, either.'

'Yeah, okay.'

'Or your dads.'

'Fine.'

'Or this whole crazy town.'

'Ugh, I really feel like you of all people should be with me on this one, but fine. I'm not mad at anyone and I'll try to get past my overdeveloped feelings of embarrassment.'

'Very good.'

She leaned against him, her oldest friend. 'Sit with me for another minute?'

'Of course.'

'Thanks, Logan.'

'Happy Birthday, Rainbow.'

'I will kill you.'

He leaned over and planted a kiss on the top of her head. 'Love you, too.'

Chapter Twenty-Eight

It was Hazel's first full day as a thirty-year-old and she was running late. Alex had opened the shop this morning and Hazel wasn't supposed to be in until noon, which was good considering she'd slept until ten this morning after her big surprise party last night, but she was still behind schedule. Mainly because she'd spent a lot of her morning, in between showering and drinking tea, picking up her phone and then putting it right back down.

No texts from Noah. No calls. And she hadn't even summoned enough courage to talk to him at her party. If Noah planned on ending things between them, she didn't want to have that conversation at her party. No one wanted to be dumped on their birthday.

Instead, she'd surrounded herself with her guests and made sure she was never alone with him.

Even when she caught Noah staring at her.

Even when he tried to offer her a ride home.

She didn't want to hear Noah apologize on her birthday. She didn't want to spend her party, which did, in the end, turn out to be lots of fun, hearing about how he'd never meant to hurt her and how things had been great while they lasted.

Because, apparently, even though Hazel was a full-grown, thirty-year-old who had finally accepted that she was sexy and fun, she was also a coward. And even though her friends all seemed to think Noah was in it for real, their opinions were not a substitute for hearing it from him. She'd been wrong once with this whole clue thing, she didn't relish the idea of being wrong again. Not about this, not about Noah's feelings for her.

No, she'd saved all that for today.

But she'd spent so much time thinking about it, and worrying about it, and deciding to just call him and then abruptly deciding never to speak to him again, she was now late for work.

'Sorry, Alex! I'm here.' She hurried through the door and found her second in command behind the counter.

'Don't worry about it. I've got it covered.'

'I said I would be in at twelve and it's nearly half past.'

'Hazel, it's fine. I told you, you didn't even have to come in today.'

She knew that. Her employees were great. But if she had stayed home she only would have had longer to stew in her current discomfort over the Noah situation and she really didn't need any more of that.

She paused at the counter, leaning against it with her

hip, letting the familiarity of the bookstore seep into her. It was quiet this afternoon, but several customers contentedly browsed the shelves. The front table was decked out in the latest fall reads and Lyndsay had hung the cute fall banners with colorful leaves and sparkly cinnamon buns that Hazel found on Etsy around the shop. The smell of cinnamon sugar lingered in the air. It never quite left, even when they weren't selling the baked goodies, like the scent had seeped into the walls themselves. The low, fall sun streaked in through the front window and Casper, here for a visit, was napping in a sunbeam.

Alex smiled at her from their place at the register.

And Hazel remembered that she loved it here.

This was her place and she *loved* it.

And it was fine that she had never sowed any wild oats or ever had any wild oats to begin with. She was thirty years old and she knew who she was. Hazel Kelly, bookstore manager, tea drinker, book reader, blanket snuggler, indoor cat. And she was also fun and flirty and sexy if she wanted to be. And sometimes she might get bored or antsy and that was fine, too, but Hazel liked her place here. She was allowed to be content. She was allowed to not want anything more than this.

Because what more did one need besides good friends, good books, and the occasional cinnamon bun?

A certain auburn-haired fisherman came to mind but Hazel gently pushed that thought aside. She'd deal with it later. Or never. She still hadn't decided.

'Did you have a fun night?' Alex asked.

'I did actually.'

'You sound surprised.'

'I was.' Hazel smiled.

'Well, I had fun, too.' Alex lifted their eyebrows mischievously. 'Me and Joe...'

'No way!'

Alex's smile grew. They'd been lusting after Joe from The Pumpkin Spice Café for months.

'Yes, way.'

'It was a good party.' And it was. Other than avoiding Noah at all costs, Hazel had danced and laughed and basked in the love of her family and friends. In the end she was glad her dad had ambushed her and she even had to admit that she was glad for his summer of clues. She had, after all, had an amazing last two months of her twenties.

If nothing else came of it, at least she had that.

'Well, I'm here now,' she said, patting the counter. 'Let me just put my things down and you can go on break.' She hustled to the back office to drop off her coat and purse, firing off a quick text to Annie who had rather suspiciously disappeared right around the same time that Mac had last night. So either they'd hooked up or one of them had been murdered. Hazel figured it could have gone either way.

You alive?

Yep

The answer was immediate. Annie was never far from her phone.

How's Mac?

How would I know?

Hazel laughed to herself, tossing purse, phone, and coat onto the couch. Whatever was going on between her best friend and the bartender was not something she had time to dig into right now.

She looked up and found a precarious stack of books on her desk. What on earth was this? Alex would never leave books in here like this. Certainly not piled up all willy-nilly and about to tip over. Hazel frowned.

'Hey, Alex,' she called, sticking her head out of the office door. 'What is this pile of books?'

'Oh, those were dropped off for you this morning,' Alex called back.

'By who?'

'Uh ... not really...' Alex's voice faded away. 'Got a customer!'

Hmm. She popped back in the office and eyed the stack. They were a mix of genres and sizes all piled up in the center of her desk. She took the first one off the pile.

There was a dog-eared page.

Her heartbeat immediately ratcheted up.

She opened the book and found a highlighted line.

I met a girl this summer.

Innocuous. Innocent. And yet...

She grabbed the next book.

The kiss was incendiary. He could have sworn his entire body had gone up in flames.

A bit over the top but Hazel knew the feeling.

She grabbed another, working her way down the pile. Each book had a marked page and a highlighted line. Each book set her heart beating faster. This couldn't be...

Attraction: noun: the action or power of evoking interest, pleasure, or liking for someone or something.

She put down the dictionary and took the next book. A picture book.

'Will you be my best friend?' the fox asked the rabbit.

'But we're so different,' said the rabbit.

'That's why I like you.'

A scientific journal:

According to a team of scientists led by Dr. Monica Hunter at Yale, romantic love can be broken down into three categories: lust, attraction, and attachment.

The science-fiction novel that had been flying off the shelves:

She brought him back to life, reconstructed him into a better version than the original. And he felt alive. He was alive. He was real.

The latest in the fantasy series Noah had been reading on the boat:

Fierce sea birds swooped from the sky, but he held them back. Anything to protect the princess.

She couldn't help the laugh that escaped her at that. The next book was small and worn; the perfect size to smuggle in a purse. She didn't know when her hands had started to shake.

He dipped his head between her thighs and he found heaven.

Heat flared in Hazel's cheeks as she hastily closed that one, not at all surprised to find a half-naked pirate on the front.

The YA novel that was a surprise bestseller last year was next.

'You're all I think about. All I want. Me and you until the end.'

Oh, God. This was...

The second to last book. Another romance. Of course.

He realized he loved her and that he probably had all along. But it had snuck up on him somehow even though she'd been perfect from the start.

Hazel gripped the book so hard, the pages crinkled beneath her fingers.

This one had a note at the bottom of the page. Not a note, really. Just a few words.

It's me this time,
~Noah.

The last book wasn't a book at all but a weekly planner. Today's date was circled and in the box someone had penciled in:

Meet me by the water. Tonight. 8:00.

Well, holy shit.

The grand finale.

Noah had paced back and forth in the sand so many times, he'd created a small trench. Maybe he could bury himself in it if Hazel didn't show up. That would be a good use of his current resources.

No, this was fine. He was fine. Even if Hazel didn't want him. He'd be ... okay. Well, he'd be pretty damn devastated because he definitely loved this girl and he'd never loved anyone before and he was pretty sure it would hurt like a bitch to have her reject him, but he'd survive. Probably.

He glanced up at the little shacks on the beach. With some help from Cliff, he'd managed to get the electricity up to code and he'd strung white twinkle lights from each one. Even the one on the end that was basically falling over at this point had a string of white bulbs. That one was definitely going to take more work than the others, but he'd spoken to Mayor Kelly last night when he'd momentarily lost track of Hazel and the man had assured him that there was a way forward.

He hadn't been super clear on what that was, but Pete told him he was sure they'd figure it all out. The important thing was Noah had told him his plan and the mayor had liked it.

And Noah was even considering asking his dad for some advice on the whole thing while he was home which was pretty big for him. Like really big.

Movement on the path to the beach caught his eye and Noah froze in his trench. Until he remembered how not a path the path was and then he hurried to help Hazel down.

'Hey, Noah,' she said when he got close and his heart stuttered in his chest. She was so damn beautiful, even in the dark, just the shape of her was beautiful. Her curls were loose around her face tonight and a hesitant smile graced her lips.

'Hey.' He really needed to get better at this again and fast. 'Let me help you. It's kind of treacherous.'

She took his hand and he led her down the jagged pavement to the sand. He wanted to hold onto her but he wasn't sure if he should so he didn't pull her back when she untangled her fingers from his. She was looking at the houses and he was looking at her.

'I talked to your dad,' he blurted out and she turned toward him, the lights from the houses reflected in her glasses. He wished he could see her better. Why had he chosen this spot? The wind had picked up and Hazel pulled her cardigan further around her and Noah felt his plan rapidly unraveling.

'About the houses and he thinks we can make it work.'

'That's great, Noah—'

'I talked to my dad, too. To my whole family actually and I think maybe they've forgiven me and I'm going to go home and help out while my sister is on bed rest but then I'm coming back. I was always going to come back for you, Haze. I should have said that ... I should have said a lot of things. Oh, and you're invited for Thanksgiving ... I mean if you want to ... I mean if we...'

He shook his head, trying to straighten out his racing thoughts. 'I think we should date. I mean, for real, like not for clues or anything. I just ... I know I'm a little bit younger than you, but I don't think that matters and I just think we're good together...'

'Noah, stop.'

He blinked, Hazel coming back into focus. The wind tugged at her hair and the ends of her sweater. She had her arms wrapped around herself. She was cold. He should get her inside, make her some tea, tuck her in his bed, never let her go.

'What are you doing?' Her question broke through his fevered thoughts.

'Uh...' What was he doing? Trying to profess his love for her and apparently screwing it up?

'Why are you still trying to convince me that you're worth it?'

'I...' Noah swallowed hard. Was that what he was doing? 'I just wanted you to know, I'm working on things ... on myself. I want to be ... good for you.'

She'd stepped closer somehow without him noticing, probably because his brain was spinning in circles and had completely abandoned him on this cold, windy beach.

'Noah.'

'Yeah?'

'You brought me a giant hat and bug spray.'

'Well, that was just good sense.'

'You won me a giant stuffed penguin.'

What was *she* doing? 'I mean, anyone would have done that.'

'You showed me I was beautiful and sexy, not to mention, you literally saved my life.'

'Hazel...'

'Noah.' Her voice was serious, stern, like she was not to be argued with right now. 'You have shown me more care and thought than anyone I've been with before. You *are* good for me.'

He shook his head. 'I was just giving you everything you deserved.'

'You left me secret book messages.' Her lips had tipped up in the corner and he wanted to trace the shape with his tongue. He wanted to grab her and hold her, wanted to bury his face in her hair and breathe her in, but this was too important, these words were too important.

'Well, the second time, I did yeah. I'm sorry...'

'Noah.'

'Yeah?'

'I'm in love with you.'

'Oh.' The sound came out of him like he'd been punched in the gut, a gasp, a puff of air, a choked surprised sound. Hazel looked up at him with wide eyes, that small crease between her brows. She had something clutched to her chest. A folder? He didn't care. He only cared about her words.

He took her face in his hand, his thumb sweeping across her cheek and his forehead pressed to hers. 'Thank God.'

She huffed a laugh, the sound small and sweet.

'I love you, too, Haze.'

'You do?'

'Hell, yeah. Of course I do. I have for so long, Hazel, I don't even know when it started. I was prepared to read every damn book in that bookstore just to spend more time with you.'

She smiled, slow and mischievous before she captured his mouth with hers. He grabbed her then, wrapping his arms around her and lifting her clear off the sand. She squeaked in surprise and he licked the sound from her lips.

'Wait!' she said. 'I brought you something. We're crinkling it.'

He reluctantly put her down and she thrust the folder she was holding toward him. 'Here.'

'Um... Thank you.'

Hazel sighed in exasperation. 'You didn't even open it.'

He opened the folder, squinting in the dark.

'It's everything you need to fill out and file with the town and the state. I think we can by-pass a realtor and do a direct sale between you and the town but you'll need to contact your bank and I don't think it would be a bad idea to hire a contractor and definitely an architect for the structural assessments. Obviously, before we put this up for rent they would need to be inspected...'

'Haze.'

'Yeah?' She stopped, blinking up at him.

'Thank you.'

She beamed. 'You're welcome. But I want you to know I don't really care about these houses.'

'For someone who doesn't care, you sure did a lot of research.'

'No, I just meant that I don't care if you do this or you do fishing tours or bartend at Mac's or do whatever other plans you might come up with. You don't have to prove anything to me, Noah.'

He swallowed the unexpected emotion from his throat.

'Oh.'

She moved closer and leaned up on her tip toes. She planted a kiss on the tip of his nose. 'Yeah, *oh*. And I would love to come to Thanksgiving.'

Noah grinned. 'My sisters are going to lose their minds.'

Hazel laughed. 'Can't wait.'

'Let's go inside.'

'Yes, please.'

She took his hand and he led her to the house. He'd lit it up like a gift for her. Like he needed proof that he was worth it, like evidence that he was serious enough for Hazel, but she hadn't needed it at all. She'd just needed him.

He probably should have guessed that.

He didn't care if Hazel ditched the bookstore tomorrow and wanted to leave town and become a circus performer. She could shave her head or decide she wanted to take up rock climbing, and he'd be on board. Hazel wasn't her job or her curls or her cute button-up blouses. She was the tart spark of blueberries on his tongue, she was salt air and rainy days, she was the perfect book. She was kisses and secret smiles. She was everything. He just needed *her*.

And the fact that she felt the same about him was enough to make him feel like he could do anything. Like his feet didn't even touch the sand anymore. He floated after her into his half-finished project and for the first time in a long time, he felt confident. He felt like enough.

She opened the door and they tumbled inside away from the cold wind and the crashing waves. She didn't let him catch his breath before pressing him against the closed door. Her arms were around his neck, her lips on his.

'I love you,' she murmured and he couldn't help smiling against her mouth, happiness bursting bright and sharp in his chest.

'I love you too, Hazel Kelly.'

She made a happy little sigh as he pulled her closer against him and every happily ever after he'd ever read finally made sense. This was it.

Happy.

Forever.

He'd make sure of it.

Chapter Twenty-Nine

Noah tossed her folder of documents onto a little table as he pulled her to the bed.

'We'll work on those in the morning.'

'So many pillows,' she teased as she flopped back into the cozy pile.

An actual blush worked its way up Noah's cheeks. None of the filthy things he'd said to her had ever caused such a reaction as his confession. 'They're for you.'

'What?'

He crawled onto the bed next to her, pulling her flush against him like he couldn't bear to have even an inch between them, which was good because she wanted to be pressed against him for at least the next twenty-four hours or until this all felt real. Noah was in love with her. She was in love with him.

It was...

Unfathomable. Unbelievable. Unexpected.

Even if maybe she should have seen it coming. Maybe she should have seen all along what Noah's glances really meant, what him wanting to spend time with her was really about, but does anyone ever really believe they'll find something like this? That someone will love them for who they really are?

It was perfect. And Hazel wasn't expecting it.

But now that she had it, she sure as hell was going to hold on with both hands. Literally.

'I bought them for you,' Noah was saying as she traced the line of his pink cheeks with her finger.

'You bought me pillows?'

He smiled, lopsided and sweet and Hazel's stomach swung from the rafters. 'I wanted you to be comfortable if we ever ended up here.'

'Wow.'

'I've got it bad for you, Haze.'

She grinned. 'Oh, yeah?'

'Hell, yeah.'

'I've got it bad for you, too.'

His smile grew. 'And look at that, dreams really do come true.'

Hazel laughed even as her body went hot at the memory of the last time Noah had said that to her. The night in her kitchen, her in nothing but her panties on the counter and him kneeling between her thighs. A shiver ran through her and he held her tighter.

'Cold?'

'No. Not cold. Actually, I think we're both wearing too much clothing.'

His smile turned into a piratic grin. 'Agreed.'

Hazel shimmied out of her sweater, tossing it aside as Noah tugged his shirt over his head. Her shirt joined the pile and then she pulled him back on top of her.

'That's a bit better,' she said as he kissed down her neck, the heat of his skin scorching hers.

'Much,' he murmured, his lips traveling across her chest and over the swell of her breasts. He had her bra unhooked before she could register his hands behind her back. She pushed it off as his head dipped to lick and suck.

'Pants,' Hazel gasped, tugging at the waist of his jeans.

He groaned when her fingers dipped below the waistband. 'I feel like you're rushing me, Haze.'

'Pants. Please, Noah,' she groaned. 'We can do it slowly later or however you want, I just need it like this ... I just need *you*. Now.'

His gaze met hers, dark and steady. 'That's how you want it? Fast?'

She nodded, biting her lower lip. 'Fast. And hard. Please, Noah.'

He swallowed. She watched his throat work, listened to his jagged breath. A muscle ticked in his jaw. She'd never seen him so still, so quiet, like he was pulling himself together before he spoke, before he moved.

Hazel waited, not embarrassed about her request,

knowing Noah would take it and keep her safe. She didn't want him to be gentle with her right now, she didn't want sweet. She wanted Noah to anchor her in this moment. She wanted this time to feel as raw as she felt right now, like all her emotions were on the outside of her body, exposed nerves that didn't need gentle touches.

These past four months had been the most incredible foreplay, but now she needed Noah to press her into this mattress and make her believe him. This was real. She was his. He was hers. She needed him to convince her once and for all.

And she only hoped he understood as she held his gaze, love and want and still that little bit of fear that this would all go away, lodged in her throat.

'You need to tell me to stop. Okay? If you need me to stop, tell me.' His voice was rough, waves over the rocks.

Hazel nodded.

'Words, Hazel.'

'Okay. I'll tell you. I promise.'

He was already unbuttoning his pants, sliding them over his hips.

'Pants,' he said, a slight smirk tugging at his lips. Hazel quickly followed his order, shucking her pants as she watched Noah's boxers follow the path of his jeans. She pulled down her underwear, a plain white pair, as Noah watched, a hungry stare on his face.

This man wanted her.

A thrill she hoped never went away raced through her at the thought.

'Roll over,' he rasped.

She did as she was told, savoring the sound of Noah's soft groan as she did. He ran a hand down her hip. He gave her a little squeeze.

'Okay?'

'Yes.'

She heard the tear of the condom wrapper, waited as he rolled it on, and then his hands were on her hips, angling her up for him.

She'd never felt so exposed, so vulnerable.

She'd never trusted another human so completely.

Noah's hand came between her legs, opening her even more. He teased her a little where she was already so wet and aching.

'Noah, please.' She couldn't take any more, her legs had already started to tremble.

His hand was gone, back on her hip, and he slid into her in one smooth thrust.

The angle was so ... deep.

Hazel's breath caught. Her heart caught. Her brain caught.

And then Noah was everywhere. His arms around her, his legs surrounding hers, and his body so deep within hers she couldn't breathe.

'You okay?' he whispered, his lips on her shoulder, his words in her ear.

'Yes,' she gasped. 'More.'

'Hazel.' His voice sounded as wrecked as she felt.

'More.'

He twined his fingers with hers, their hands pressed into the mattress. The other hand was back on her hip, holding her steady as he pulled out part way and thrust back in. Hazel's forehead was pressed into a pillow and Noah's breath was hot on her neck.

'Again,' she demanded and he complied. Again. And again, Noah crashed into her, the ache in her building and building. She squeezed his fingers in hers and he stilled, his body buried deep in hers. He kissed her across her shoulders, the sensation so at odds with the relentless thrust of his hips that Hazel felt tears spring to her eyes.

A startled sob broke from her lips.

'Hazel?'

'I ... just...'

'We'll stop.'

'No!' She kissed the back of his hand, desperately, reverently. It was the only part of him she could reach from her position pinned to the bed. 'Don't stop. I just ... it's real. You. You're real. And I love you.'

She felt the press of his forehead between her shoulder blades.

'It's real,' he said, his voice as broken as she felt. 'You and me. I promise.'

She nodded, her cheek against one of his many pillows.

'I'm gonna make you come now, okay?'

Hazel huffed a watery laugh.

'Yeah. Okay.'

Noah pressed one more kiss into her shoulder and then gently untangled his fingers from hers. He lifted her hips up again, changing the angle and Hazel immediately felt it.

'Good?'

'Hell, yeah.'

Noah's chuckle was briefly her favorite sound until it was followed by his groan as he thrust in and out. Hazel moaned, her fingers grasping at the bedsheets.

'Touch yourself, Haze.'

And she did it. She'd do anything he said right now. She knew anything he said would bring her pleasure.

She touched herself while he dove into her, hitting a place that made her eyes roll back and her toes curl and the ache was so deep now, she didn't know if she could survive it.

'Keep going,' he demanded, his fingers digging into her hips and she did. Faster and harder as he did the same, that ache building, but she was safe. Safe with Noah. Safe and wanted and loved.

She whimpered, the tears back in her eyes, the sob back in her throat.

And she let it out as she broke.

She trembled and cried and shook.

And Noah held her up.

'Noah,' she groaned into the pillows, the pillows he bought to keep her comfortable, and his arms were around her again, her body flush with the bed, their hands intertwined and Noah found his pleasure with his lips pressed to her shoulder.

'Hazel,' he murmured her name over and over even

after he rolled off of her. Even after he'd cleaned up and come back to bed, wrapping himself around her. He murmured her name as he kissed her and held her. Like he couldn't believe it, either.

But it was true.

And it was a story they'd be telling for a long time.

Well, parts of it anyway. Some parts were private.

Chapter Thirty

Two Months Later

'Happy Friendsgiving!' Jeanie opened the door to the old farmhouse, her arms wide. Noah was immediately hit with the smell of sage and onions, cinnamon and ginger. His stomach grumbled. Hazel hadn't let him eat more than a bowl of cereal this morning and the half a bag of marshmallows he'd scarfed on the way over. Although to be fair, they'd been busy with other things. Several other things that started with applying for a bank loan and ended with Hazel spread out on her kitchen table in nothing but her panties. So maybe he hadn't just eaten cereal and marshmallows...

'Hey, Jeanie.' Noah let himself be enveloped in a hug by Jeanie, quickly putting aside his memories of the morning.

'Welcome back, Noah!' She gave him a squeeze and then moved on to Hazel.

'Thanks for having us,' Hazel said from inside Jeanie's arms.

'I'm so glad we decided to do this.' Jeanie took the bags from Noah filled with wine and the rest of the bags of marshmallows Hazel brought to add to the yams, and ushered them inside. 'It's such a busy time of year, I'm just happy we could all get together.'

Noah decided not to point out that they all saw each other almost every day, especially now that he was back and full time at Mac's for the season. They were constantly in and out of each other's shops, but he knew Jeanie was excited to host her first official Friendsgiving, so he bit his tongue and followed her inside. It was warm and welcoming with a fire crackling in the hearth in the living room right off the hall. Jeanie and Logan had strung together several tables that stretched from the dining room into the living room. Candles and gourds ran down the center, creating a tablescape he was sure his mother would love.

His six weeks at home had been long and tough at times, but mostly for his sister. He'd had a blast playing with his nieces and going out with the crew on the new lobster boat. He even spent time going over his rental-property plans with his dad.

And talking with Hazel every night certainly helped. But with Rachel cleared by her doctor to be upright again, Noah was back in Dream Harbor. At least for now. He was taking Hazel home with him in three days and he was a ball of nervous energy about her meeting the family. But excited nervous and not dreading-it nervous so he was taking that as progress.

'Oh, look who decided to finally show up!' Annie emerged from the kitchen, wine glass in hand.

'We're not late.' Hazel glanced at her watch. 'Well, we're not *that* late.' A blush rose up her cheeks and Noah grinned, knowing she was thinking about exactly why they were late.

'Gross, guys. I mean, really,' Annie said, also expertly reading Hazel's expression.

Hazel rolled her eyes, ready with a retort when a random man followed Annie into the entryway.

'Um ... hi,' Noah said, taking Hazel's attention from Annie to the man standing uncomfortably behind her.

'Oh, this is Trent.'

'Trent?' Hazel's voice rose incredulously.

'Hey, nice to meet you...'

'You brought a date to Friendsgiving?' Hazel asked.

'She sure did,' Mac answered from where he sat glowering in the corner of the living room. Noah hadn't even seen him over there. Trent shifted on his feet. Poor bastard.

Annie ignored Mac and turned back to Hazel. 'Trent is a new friend. It just seemed nice to invite him.'

Jeanie hustled out of the kitchen with several trays of cheese and crackers in her hands. 'And the more the merrier,' she said, eyebrows raised like she was communicating a very important message to him and Hazel. A message about how no one was to ruin her Friendsgiving with drama.

'Hmm.' Hazel's little noise of disapproval was all she contributed to the conversation.

'Well, it's nice to meet you, Trent.' Noah stuck out his hand and the man breathed a small sigh of relief. 'How'd you meet Annie?'

'I tried her cookies and I just had to have more.'

Hazel choked on nothing, sputtering and coughing. Noah patted her back, biting down on his own laughter. He may or may not have heard Mac grumble something about staying the hell away from Annie's cookies, but it was hard to hear over Trent's backpedaling.

'Uh ... from her bakery. Chocolate chip. I went to buy some and we got to talking. That's ... uh ... what I meant.'

Noah chuckled. 'Yeah, she's the best.' He winked at Annie and she smacked him playfully on the arm.

'Gee, thanks. Okay, now that we're all introduced, let's move on to having a nice day.'

More grumbling from Mac's corner.

Logan was the next to emerge from the kitchen and Noah was starting to wonder how many more people were hidden in there. His friend was wearing an apron with a giant turkey on it.

'Looking good, man,' he said with a grin as Hazel followed Annie into the dining room for snacks.

Logan glanced down at his apron and then back to Noah with a frown. 'Thanks. How's your sister?'

'Much better, no thanks to me, but I kept the kiddos occupied at least.'

'Good man.'

Noah leaned toward him. 'Did you do it yet?' he whispered.

'Shh!' Logan grabbed him by the arm and dragged him back into the kitchen. 'What are you crazy?'

Noah rubbed his arm. 'Sorry. Geez.'

Logan frowned. 'Sorry. I just don't want to ruin the surprise.'

'So you didn't do it yet?'

'No.'

'I thought you said, by the end of the year...'

'There's still time.'

'Hey, did you check the biscuits?' Jeanie swept back into the kitchen and Logan nearly jumped away from Noah like they were caught doing something nefarious. Jeanie eyed them skeptically. Oh, his best friend was *definitely* going to ruin the surprise.

'Uh, yeah. They need a few more minutes.'

Jeanie tucked herself next to him and Logan draped an arm over her shoulder. He dropped a kiss on the top of her head.

'So how are things with Hazel?' she asked Noah.

'Don't pretend she doesn't tell you everything,' he said with a laugh.

'Not everything! And besides, I like to hear it from you.'

Noah couldn't help the smile on his face. It was inevitable when he thought about things with Hazel.

'Things are great with Hazel.' Great, amazing, the best two months of his entire existence, no big deal.

Jeanie grinned.

'Uh, do you need help with anything out here?'

'Nope. We've got it under control.' She glanced over her shoulder as something bubbled over on the stove, hissing as the liquid hit the hot burner. 'Mostly. Anyway, maybe you could just go make sure Annie and Mac stay in their own corners.'

'Oh, is that all? Maybe I could figure out world peace while I'm out there.'

Jeanie laughed as she moved back toward the stove. 'Thanks, Noah! You're the best.'

'Yeah, yeah,' he muttered as he went back out to the living room.

Annie and Hazel were busy stuffing themselves with cheese and crackers while Trent and Mac seemed to be in the middle of some sort of staring contest. At some point, George had arrived with Jacob and Crystal, whose rumored NFL boyfriend was off playing in Texas today. And the three of them were busy mixing drinks at the little bar cart Logan had set up.

Nana and Grandpa Henry were in Florida for the winter, so they weren't around, but soon Alex and Joe arrived to round out the group. They'd been on again, off again since Hazel's birthday but apparently today they were on. With the way everyone was already drinking, Noah could picture this Friendsgiving rapidly deteriorating, but he was going to do his damnedest to make sure that didn't happen. He planted himself in the seat next to Mac and handed the man a small plate filled with crackers.

'You should probably eat something.' Noah eyed the empty scotch glass in Mac's hand.

Mac grunted but started shoving crackers in his mouth. 'I don't know why she brought him.'

Noah glanced at where Trent was now by Annie's side, looking at her all sweetly.

'Maybe he's nice to her.'

Mac scoffed. 'I'm nice to her.'

'Right.'

More grumbling. More cracker eating. 'She's the one that's not nice.'

'You are aware that you sound like a kindergartener, right?'

'I'm aware.'

'Okay, good. As long as we're on the same page.'

Hazel sat down beside him with her small plate and glass of wine. 'Hey, Mac.'

'Hazel.'

'For the record, I'm team Mac.'

'There's no team Mac.'

'Hmm.'

Noah laughed and leaned closer to Hazel. 'He's grumpy today.'

'I don't blame him,' she whispered.

'I can hear you.' Mac got up to refill his glass and Noah pulled Hazel's chair closer to his.

'You starved me all day so we could, and I quote, "save

ourselves for the feast" and now look at you.' He gestured to her plate filled with crackers, cheese, various cured meats, pickles and dried fruit.

'I can't resist a charcuterie board. Besides, we're here now so this counts as part of the feast.'

'Oh, is that the rule? Good.' He snatched a fig from her plate and popped it in his mouth.

'Hey! Get your own!' She turned toward him and he grabbed her face. Her cheeks were flushed pink from the warmth of the room and the wine. Her eyes sparked happily behind her glasses.

He thought about the ring Logan had been carrying around in his pocket for months. He thought he wanted one, too. Someday. Soon. He wanted it soon.

She quirked an eyebrow like she was reading his mind so he kissed her, quick and sweet, at the table.

'What was that for?' she asked.

He shrugged. 'Just thinking that I'm thankful for you this year.'

'That's sweet, but you should probably save it for later. I'm sure Jeanie's going to make us do that thing where we go around and say what we're thankful for.'

Noah chuckled. 'Okay, noted.'

Hazel's leg bumped against his under the table.

'I'm thankful for you, too.'

'Glad to hear it.' He found her thigh under the table and let his hand run over the tights she was wearing under her skirt.

'What are you doing?' she murmured.

'Nothing,' he said, giving her his best innocent smile even as his fingers coasted higher.

'Noah,' she warned.

'Yes?' he whispered, leaning close to her again. He found the edge of her skirt and slid his fingers up and underneath.

Hazel's breath caught.

He inched higher, keeping his expression neutral, placid.

'What are you doing?' she asked again even as her thighs parted for him.

'Just having a little reckless fun.'

She held his gaze and he winked at her. She huffed a little laugh. 'Oh, really?'

'Mmm-hmm.' He reached the apex of her thighs and slid a finger down the front of her. Hazel shuddered.

'Time to eat.' Logan thumped a plate with a giant pile of turkey down in front of them. Hazel coughed and Noah slid his hand from her skirt.

'Later,' he whispered before holding out his other hand for the bowl of mashed potatoes. 'Can someone pass the gravy?' he asked, not missing a beat. Hazel let out a breathy laugh next to him, catching his eye as their friends gathered around and took their seats. He smiled at her, letting the chaos of the room swirl around them.

Hazel sat at the center of it all, the calm in the storm. He didn't really know what had brought him here; he'd docked at a lot of places over the past few years, but Dream Harbor had stuck. And he was thankful for everything that led to this moment. Every screw up. Every rough day at sea.

Every fight with his family, with himself. It had all led him here.

He was meant to be here.

With her.

Hazel freaking Kelly. The girl of his dreams.

And for that he was thankful.

Epilogue

Six months later

Hazel was lounging under the shade of the cabana. Even in the shade she was wearing her giant floppy hat and a long-sleeved shirt, because this sun was no joke. She was pretty sure she was burning anyway.

They were in Aruba and had been for nearly a week now. It was the longest vacation Hazel had ever taken in her entire life but Melinda had insisted she take two weeks when Hazel had asked for some time off.

'You've earned it, darling!' she'd said over the phone. 'Of course you should take some time off.'

And so she had. Well, she had with lots of convincing from Noah and plenty of assurances from Alex that they had everything completely under control and promises from Annie and Jeanie to check in on the bookstore every few days and report back. Then she had dusted off the passport she'd used only once for a trip to Niagara Falls, packed her bags, and followed Noah for an island adventure.

After this week in Aruba they were headed to visit Noah's new nephew, Michael, before they returned to Dream Harbor. Noah was so in love with the baby, this visit would already be his fifth since the little guy was born in March. And of course, Hazel loved to see Noah with a baby in his arms. It was nearly as sexy as him docking his boat in a storm.

But he deserved a break too after all the work he'd done on the vacation rentals. After an investment from his dad, the sale had gone through with the town. Noah had hired an architect, and a construction team and worked through the winter to get the houses ready for guests. He'd made a lot of progress but there was still plenty of work to be done.

Hazel loved the little row of tidy beach houses, but mostly she loved that Noah was proud of them.

She took a sip of her fruity drink, eyeing the iguana that had crept up next to her beach chair.

'I don't like it when they get so close.' She tucked her legs up closer to her body while Noah tried to shoo the lizard from their cabana.

The little green monster just blinked at him, wildly unimpressed with his hand flapping.

Noah leaned back in his chair. 'I don't think he's going to come any closer.'

Hazel huffed. 'So, you only fight seagulls?' she teased.

'If that thing takes flight, I'll be sure to spring into action.'

He was sprawled out in his beach chair, his tan chest on display. Hazel couldn't help but reach out and trace his new tattoo, the little book over his heart with the letters HK+NB written inside.

Noah grabbed her hand and brought her fingers to his lips.

Hazel smiled. 'This is my favorite vacation.'

Noah hummed a happy little sound. Hazel could feel it vibrate through his chest where her hand still lingered.

'You know what would make a good story to tell when we get home?' he asked, eyes still closed.

'What?' They had already complied quite a list: snorkeling over the top of the shipwreck that Hazel was sure housed a fleet of sharks and probably a few ghost pirates, eating their weight in shrimp, the fight Noah got in with that pelican, drinking more 'happy punch' than was advisable on their sailing trip. Not to mention all the stories they wouldn't be telling anyone like the day they hadn't left the room at all...

'If we got married while we're here.'

Wait. *What?*

'Married?' Hazel squeaked.

Even the iguana looked surprised.

Noah turned his head toward her, a mischievous grin on his face. 'Yeah, married.'

'Noah...'

'Say you'll be my wife, Haze.'

He squinted a little in the sun, creases forming next to his eyes. His hair glinted copper and gold, his smile competing for brightness. He was so beautiful her heart ached.

His *wife*.

'It'll be fun. I promise.'

'Noah, I...'

He sat up, swinging his legs over the side of the chair and took her hands in his. 'And sometimes it won't be fun. Sometimes it will be boring and sometimes you'll be mad at me and sometimes I'll be mad at you. But, Haze, it will be me and you. Forever. Do you want that?'

The mischievousness was gone now, the grin, the smirk, the casual playfulness Noah did so well. Now he was earnest and sweet and serious. He was good at those, too.

Did she want that?

Did she want him forever?

An adventure partner and a reading buddy.

'Yes. Of course I do. Yes.'

Noah whooped loud enough to scare the iguana and several nearby sunbathers before he grabbed her face in his hands and kissed her hard and strong and real.

She was laughing and crying by the time he pulled away.

'We'll get a ring. Whatever you want,' he was saying. 'And I did all the paperwork, Haze. I got things apostilled, and I learned what that word meant, and we can get married right here on the beach, if you want.'

He still had her face in his hands and he brushed the

tears from her cheeks. His eyes sparked with excitement and love and happiness.

And she knew her life with Noah would be filled with good stories. This one would be one of her favorites, for sure. The time she married her best friend on a tropical island and promised to love him forever.

It would be hard to beat, but they had a lifetime to try.

Acknowledgments

I dedicated this book to you, the readers, because without you Dream Harbor is just a place I go to in my head, and Hazel and Noah are just my imaginary friends. So thank you, thank you, thank you for reading! The response to *The Pumpkin Spice Café* so exceeded my expectations that two books in, and I am still pinching myself. Thank you to everyone who read it, talked about, and posted beautiful pictures of it sitting on your gorgeous autumnal shelves or next to your favorite pumpkin mug. I am so happy you decided to come back to Dream Harbor with me and I hope you love Hazel and Noah as much as I do.

Another huge thank you to Charlotte Ledger and the amazing team at One More Chapter for letting me continue on this crazy journey (again, still pinching myself). A big shoutout to Jennie Rothwell for making sure Hazel wasn't too frumpy and that Noah actually had a backstory (and all her other advice, support, edits, and brainstorming chats along the way!). Thank you to everyone at One More Chapter and HarperCollins for all the work you do on these books and for getting them out into the world!

Thank you to Kelley McMorris for the stunning cover

art! These covers are so cozy and wonderful and I couldn't dream of a better fit for the series.

Sometimes as an author you have the perfect scene in your head and then it comes time to write the scene and you realize you know essentially nothing about the thing you wanted to write about in said scene. And that is what happened to me when I pictured Noah and Hazel stranded on a boat, but I know nothing about boats, or boat words, or tides, or coastal geography, or apparently, weather patterns. So a big thank you to my brother-in-law, Aaron, for lending me his nautical knowledge for this book. He saved the scene I had in my head and saved me from having to watch too many YouTube videos about boating (although I did still watch some). Aaron is very knowledgeable and any mistakes in boating lingo are definitely mine.

And finally, thank you, as always, to my family. To Liz, Steve, Janzer, and Sean for your excitement and encouragement. To Molly for always reading. To Ashley for insisting that I'm a really big deal now (not sure I believe it, but it's nice to hear). To my in-laws for being totally cool about a daughter-in-law who writes smut. To my parents for continuing to be my biggest cheerleaders. To my kids for continuing to ask if I'm famous yet. And to my husband for continuing to bring that big romance hero energy into my life. You guys are the best.

Read on for an exclusive extract from *The Christmas Tree Farm*

Kira North hates Christmas. Which is unfortunate since she just bought a Christmas tree farm in a town that's too cute for its own good. Bennett Ellis is on vacation in Dream Harbor trying to take a break from his regular life.

Somehow fate finds Ben trapped by a blanket of snow at Kira's farm, and, despite her Grinchiest first impressions, maybe, just maybe, the glow of the fairy lights might give these two lost souls a Christmas they'll remember forever...

The Christmas Tree Farm: Extract

Chapter 1

Kira North hated Christmas. Which was unfortunate considering she was currently the proud owner of a Christmas tree farm in a town that was far too cute for its own good with residents that couldn't seem to take the hint and leave her the hell alone.

She breathed out a frustrated sigh as she closed the door on her latest visitor. Some guy named George, dropped off a complimentary sample of Christmas gingerbread cookies from the bakery in town and a business card, and more than a few hints about a plan to do business together. He was the third one this weekend.

Yesterday, Deputy Mayor Mindy Walsh dropped by on behalf of the town council to hand her a flier for the annual Tree Lighting next week, as though Kira hadn't seen half a million of those every time she went into town for food.

And just this morning an entire family showed up, kids in tow with matching Christmas sweaters asking if they could cut down a tree. She'd pretended not to see the children's tears as she turned them away.

It was all a bit much. She slid down to the floor, her back against the door, and tore open the red and green cellophane protecting the cookies. She picked a Santa-shaped one and bit off his head. Unfortunately, he was absolutely delicious, all nutmeg and cinnamon. Damn him.

The cold seeped through her back as she finished him off one decadent bite at a time. The door was freezing. The floor was freezing. The entire crappy old house she'd moved into three months ago was freezing. She leaned her head back against the door with a soft thud, attempting to pretend that she was fine. It was fine. She would just put on another sweater even though she was already wearing two. She'd put on a warmer pair of socks. People sometimes wore hats inside, right?

The ancient radiator beside the door let out a defeated whine.

Right. Time to get up. Time to get up and get back to work because the 'quaint farmhouse' she'd bought sight unseen was actually a decrepit, old farmhouse with a heating system on life support, and the 'acres of scenic farmland' was actually a beloved, but totally run down Christmas tree farm and even though she'd sworn not to re-open it, now she had to in order to make some money and fix up this place, seeing as how she'd spent all hers buying it in the first place.

If she wanted to survive the winter and not be found frozen to death by a nosy but well-intentioned neighbor, she needed to get this place up and running. And fast. It was already the Sunday after Thanksgiving and judging by the family she'd devastated this morning, people were dying to get their trees up.

She grabbed a blanket on her way past the couch and shuffled over to where she'd left her laptop on the ancient wooden dining room table the previous owners had left behind. They'd left a lot of junk behind actually. She kept finding old mail tucked away in odd places but hadn't bothered opening any of it. The table was nice though. It fit her farmhouse aesthetic.

She flipped open her computer. Still no wifi. It hadn't worked right since that power outage last week.

Damn it.

How was she supposed to hire people, set up a website, *and* create a social media presence for this place without wifi and an incredibly unreliable cell signal? In like two days? She slumped down in the closest chair and practiced not crying. Her tears would probably freeze on her face if she did. She sniffled them back in and tried not to think about how pitiful she must look right now wrapped in a worn comforter, packed into way too many layers of clothing, nose red from cold and crying.

This wasn't at all how things were supposed to go.

First of all, she wasn't supposed to be alone. Her sister should be here with her. Her other half. Her much more competent, reasonable, level-headed half. Her twin and best friend since birth. Chloe never would have bought this place on a whim. Chloe never would have agreed to the sale without a visit and an inspection at the very least. Chloe would have asked questions like: why do you want to live on a farm in New England despite having no idea how to grow things or cook things or really do anything on your own? Questions that Kira had no desire to answer.

Because this whole plan wasn't so much a whim as it was a last ditch effort to start over. To get as far away from her old life, her old self as possible. It wasn't a whim so much as a radical reimagining of who she wanted to be.

But Chloe had abandoned her. Ran off and got *married*. And moved to *Denmark*. Denmark! Of all places. And what was one supposed to do when their soulmate, their other half, finds a new other half?

Well, apparently they absorb too much homesteading social media content, decide they can totally do that, use their trust fund money to buy a farm, and essentially, ruin their lives. Okay, so maybe this specific plan was a little bit of a whim…

But here she was. Miserable and alone. And really freaking cold.

Kira wiped her cheeks with the back of her hand. This was ridiculous. She had to do something or that image of herself, frozen to death in her bed, was about to become reality. She shoved another cookie in her mouth for strength, grabbed her phone, wrapped her blanket around her more securely, and headed for the back door. She slid on her new boots and stepped outside. It might have been warmer outside than it had been in her house. The sun, however weak this late in November, definitely helped.

If she was going to survive this, she was going to have to get used to these northern winters. It hadn't even snowed yet and she already felt wildly unprepared. The temperature in Georgia rarely dropped below 50 degrees and certainly not in the middle of the afternoon. Today couldn't be warmer than 30.

She was so screwed.

No tears. Not right now. Not until later when she was huddled under her blankets in bed instead of out here in the backyard where any roaming resident of Dream Harbor could pop up like some kind of jack-in-the-box nightmare of glad tidings.

She held up her phone and started wandering through the rows of trees just past her tiny yard. Surely, if she walked far enough she'd get some kind of signal. She could probably go into town and work at the library or that café everyone seemed to love, but that would require being out in public which she did not feel up to in her current state of mental breakdown. So…wandering the fields in her flannel pajama bottoms, ratty old sweaters, and down comforter it had to be.

The trees stretched in tidy rows ahead of her ranging in height from her waist to at least a foot or two above her head. Luckily, the trees had just continued being trees even without an owner for the past few years. They could use some trimming and shaping, but overall, her crop was in good condition. It was the barn that was nearly falling down and the house that required significant work.

But first, money.

And before money, employees, and a real live business. Something Kira had never done nor aspired to do in her entire life. Her nose burned, and tears pricked behind her eyes.

But she didn't have time to cry. Not before a giant black blur raced across her path with two smaller blurs at its heels.

Kira shrieked.

The dogs barked.

The man following them skidded to a stop.

'Elizabeth, come.' His voice was stern and harsh and the biggest dog loped happily to his side. 'Good girl.' He patted her head.

'Odie, Pudgy, come.' He tried to get the other two dogs' attention with the same stern tone, but it was far too late for that. Kira was already squatting to pet the two little wiggly bodies at her feet.

'Look at you, sweet babies,' she crooned. 'Little angels.' The smallest dog, some sort of Westie mix with wiry white hair, pushed its cold snout into her palm, huffing in excitement. The other one, who must have been at least a hundred years old in dog years, waited patiently for scratches between its floppy ears, its tongue lolling out of its mouth.

'What good doggies you are, so sweet,' Kira went on, petting and scratching and so generally delighted to have such precious babies on her property that she'd nearly forgotten the man until he was towering over her.

'Uh, sorry about that,' he said. 'I didn't realize…I mean, I thought this place was abandoned. Otherwise, I would have had the dogs on their leashes.'

'It's okay,' Kira said, still crouched low, but now paying proper attention to Elizabeth who was starting to whine at not being part of the love fest happening with the other dogs. 'Look at you! What a beautiful girl you are,' Kira told her and it seemed the larger dog smiled at her. Kira smiled back, for the first time in days. It was nice.

Until she finally stood and looked at the man who had brought the puppies to her farm. The smile dropped from her face. He was staring at her with a mix of confusion and horror.

It was then that Kira remembered her unwashed hair and her red eyes and her blanket-as-outerwear fashion statement. Ugh. This day, this town, these people! They were everywhere!

'Yes, well, actually, I own this farm,' she said, standing to her full height. 'So, you are trespassing.'

Elizabeth whined and Kira scratched between her ears. 'Not you, sweetheart. You didn't know.'

'To be fair, I didn't know either,' the man said, a slight smirk on his face.

'How is that possible? Everyone in this nosy town knows about it.'

He shrugged. 'I don't live in this nosy town.'

Kira frowned. 'Then what are you doing here?'

'Visiting.'

She didn't like his tone. Or his face for that matter. It was too…too…handsome. But in like an obnoxiously conventional way. Too much symmetry. Too much perfect dark hair. It was annoying. And entirely uninteresting.

Too wholesome.

'Well, whoever you're visiting should have told you that I own this land now so you can't just traipse through here on your little hike or whatever you're doing.'

The man's obnoxiously straight smile grew. 'Little hike or whatever?'

'I don't know! What's with that vest? You look like you're going on a hike.'

He looked down at his puffy vest and dark jeans and hiking boots and then let his gaze wander over Kira's ensemble.

'You're wearing a blanket,' he observed.

'Yes.'

'And you're making fun of my vest?'

'Yes.' She crossed her arms over her chest, not that he could see that since they were tucked under her blanket, but still. Her stance was defiant. She was pretty sure that came across. She didn't like this guy and his teasing smile. And his light eyes with dark lashes. Really? Ugh, could he be more basic?

Kira only went for men that had 'bad idea' tattooed across their forehead (sometimes literally) and this guy looked like the model for 'the guy your mother wants you to bring home for the holidays to sip cocoa under the tree in your matching pajamas'. Highly undesirable. Downright unattractive in every way, really.

Except for maybe the way his thighs were filling out those jeans.

But that was neither here nor there.

'Sorry again for the misunderstanding. We'll get going.'

Oh, right. He was going to take the dogs with him. Shoot. She *liked* the dogs. She looked down at the three precious faces in front of her and she would swear she could hear their thoughts.

'You might as well finish your walk,' she blurted out, ignoring how his dark eyebrows rose in surprise. 'I mean, you're here now and the dogs need their exercise and I would never deprive them of that.'

'You're a big dog person, I take it.'

'They're better than people in every way.'

His laugh was low and deep and did absolutely nothing for her.

'I agree.'

She gave him a curt nod, expecting him to go on his way, but he was still looking at her like he was working on a puzzle.

'What?' she snapped.

'I just…are you okay?'

Was she okay?! How dare he?! How dare he presume just because she was wandering around outside wearing bedding and waving her phone in the air like she thought it worked via witchcraft that she wasn't okay?

She smoothed her blanket down with a hand as though it were an evening gown. 'I'm fine, thank you.'

A small crease of worry formed between his obnoxiously perfect eyebrows and Kira wanted to throw something at him and see if she could hit it.

'It's just…you're walking around with your phone over your head. I thought maybe you were having trouble with it. I work in tech, so I thought…'

A tech bro? Oh just what she needed! Always trust your first instincts and her first instincts were right. She didn't need some Silicon Valley, let's go for a hike wherever we damn well please because we think we own the whole world, Clark Kent look-alike, to rescue her. Not today, buddy!

'No thanks, Elon. I'm managing just fine.'

'Elon?' Now he looked highly offended. Hm…*that* did something for her. 'Wow, I was just trying to help.'

'No one asked you to.'

He held up his hands. 'Sorry. You're right. I'll…uh…get out of your hair.'

'Thank you.' She didn't look at him as she said it. The hurt look on his face had taken some of the fun out of the whole thing. Instead, she crouched one more time to say goodbye to her new friends.

'Bye, sweet babies. Enjoy your walk.' She gave them enough pets to last for a while and by the time she was standing again, the mystery man had already turned and was walking down the row of trees, whistling for his dogs to follow.

And unfortunately, they did.

Chapter 2

'You can stay and sit with me for a few minutes, can't you?' his sister asked, already pulling out a chair at the closest table and gesturing to the one across from it. 'While it's quiet in here? I need a break anyway.'

Bennett glanced around the temporarily empty Pumpkin Spice Café and then back at his sister, Jeanie. She flashed him her sweetest smile. 'Please.'

'I do actually have to work while I'm here, you know,' he grumbled but sat anyway. He was visiting Dream Harbor for a month, living in his sister's apartment above the shop while she got settled at her new fiancé's house, and he was staying to celebrate the holidays. But he did have to work. He'd set things up to work remotely for the next few weeks which plenty of his other coworkers already did regularly, but Jeanie seemed to think he was on an extended vacation.

'Just for a few minutes! Geez, do they not give you coffee breaks at this job of yours?'

'They do, but it's the week after Thanksgiving. I have a lot to catch up on.'

'Right. Computer-y work to do.'

He nearly opened his mouth to explain to his sister for the umpteenth time that he was a software engineer and that he wrote code for multiple online retailers, but he'd given up on that years ago. Probably around the time when she started telling people he was some kind of personal online shopper for lack of a better explanation. Computer-y work was close enough.

'So what did you do yesterday?' Jeanie asked, in between sips of her coffee. Her new engagement ring glinted at him from her hand wrapped around the mug. Logan had proposed to her just before Thanksgiving and Bennett had had to endure the two of them making heart eyes at each other for the entire seven-hour drive back here from Buffalo where they'd all spent Thanksgiving with their parents. He'd been very thankful to have his own space when they arrived in Dream Harbor and to have a break from the love birds.

Logan was a good guy and Bennett was happy for them, but the ring was another little reminder of how epically bad his dating life had been lately. He couldn't imagine going on a second date with most women he'd met, let alone commit to a lifetime together. Was long-term commitment a thing people even did anymore?

'Slept in, took the dogs for a walk.' He shrugged. 'Nothing much.'

'Where'd you take the dogs?'

'The old Christmas tree farm up on Spruce.'

Jeanie's eyes widened. 'Oh.'

'Yeah, would have been nice if you'd mentioned the new owner.'

'Sorry! I forgot all about it.'

Bennett leaned back in his chair remembering the woman he'd met in the fields yesterday. The woman who'd simultaneously greeted his dogs with such warmth and affection and froze him out completely. Who looked like maybe she was in the middle of some kind of crisis but held herself like she was better than him. Who when he offered her help had made fun of him instead.

Yeah, he wasn't a big fan of the new Christmas tree farm owner. Despite how cute she looked all wrapped up in that blanket and how bright her smile had been when she was petting his dogs.

Ben knew plenty of cute women and cute wasn't worth the trouble. In fact, all cute had gotten him in the past few months was roped into helping a woman he just met move out of her ex's apartment while he begged for forgiveness from the front porch, a second date with a woman he met on a dating app that consisted of a quick drink and then her asking for a ride to the airport which he gave her because what else was he supposed to do, and three separate women who all disliked dogs, one of whom seemed to have a strong dislike for animals in general. He saw her scowl at a bird.

The last thing he needed was another cute woman.

He was done with cute women.

'Did you run into Kira?' Jeanie asked, a guilty grimace on her face.

Bennett shook off the grim thoughts floating through his head and refocused on Jeanie. 'If Kira is the hostile new owner, then yes, I met Kira.'

'She's…' Jeanie paused, tapping her lip as she searched for a kinder word to describe Kira. She didn't find one.

'Yeah, she's sort of hostile, but I think she's probably got a soft spot somewhere. We just have to find it.'

'*I* don't have to find anything. *I* have to get back to work,' he said, rising from his seat. Besides, he already knew what Kira, the hostile Christmas tree farm owner's soft spot was. He'd heard her croon sweet words to his dogs, her dark eyes lighting up at the sight of them. If the residents of Dream Harbor wanted to get on her good side, he imagined all they'd have to do is head up there with a basket of puppies and Kira would be putty in their hands.

But he had about zero percent interest in getting involved in town drama, of which he already knew too much thanks to Jeanie. And even less interest in having Kira in his hands.

Jeanie frowned. 'You work too much.'

'Ha,' Bennett scoffed. 'Says the woman who runs her own successful business and is here all the time—which I'm very proud of you for, by the way.'

'Thanks, Ben.' Jeanie waved away his praise as she stood. 'Oh! I have a great idea.' Her eyes lit up in a way Bennett found to be incredibly ominous. 'You should come to the town meeting tonight!'

'I'm going to have to pass on local politics, but thanks anyway.'

'No, it's fun. It's a whole thing and you can meet my friends and then we all go out for drinks after. Please, Ben.'

'Don't look at me like that Jean Marie.'

'Like what?'

Bennett sighed. He had never been very good at saying

no, hence the moving services and airport rides he'd provided lately, but his sister made it particularly hard. 'With those big eyes. You know exactly what you're doing.'

'It'll be fun, I promise. And besides, aren't you here to spend time with me? The loving sister you abandoned to live all the way on the other side of the country.'

'Excuse me, you left Buffalo before I did.' His sister still didn't know the real reason he'd moved out to San Francisco after college and he had no plans to fill her in.

Jeanie blinked. 'Oh, right. I forgot. Whatever, just come, okay? It starts at seven.'

She brushed a quick kiss to his cheek before hurrying back behind the counter just as a group of retired folks in workout gear ambled in through the door.

'How was your walk today? Chilly out there!' He heard his sister chatting happily to her customers as he slipped away and up the back staircase to the apartment. He was greeted by three wagging tails and a pile of work to do.

And apparently, tonight he was attending the town meeting.

This wasn't even close to a vacation, despite what his sister believed.

Available to pre-order now!

As a renowned chef, single-dad **Archer** never planned on moving to a small town, let alone running a pancake restaurant. But Dream Harbor needs a new chef, and Archer needs a community to help raise his daughter, Olive.

Iris has never managed to hold down a job for more than a few months. So when Mayor Kelly suggests Archer is looking for a nanny, and Iris might be available, she shudders at the thought.

As Archer and Iris get used to their new roles, is it possible that they might have more in common than they first thought…

Available to pre-order now!

The author and One More Chapter would like to thank everyone who contributed to the publication of this story...

Analytics
James Brackin
Abigail Fryer
Maria Osa

Audio
Fionnuala Barrett
Ciara Briggs

Contracts
Sasha Duszynska Lewis

Design
Lucy Bennett
Fiona Greenway
Liane Payne
Dean Russell

Digital Sales
Lydia Grainge
Hannah Lismore
Emily Scorer

Editorial
Arsalan Isa
Charlotte Ledger
Bonnie Macleod
Jennie Rothwell
Caroline Scott-Bowden
Emily Thomas

Harper360
Emily Gerbner
Jean Marie Kelly
emma sullivan
Sophia Wilhelm

International Sales
Peter Borcsok
Bethan Moore

Marketing & Publicity
Chloe Cummings
Emma Petfield

Operations
Melissa Okusanya
Hannah Stamp

Production
Denis Manson
Simon Moore
Francesca Tuzzeo

Rights
Vasiliki Machaira
Rachel McCarron
Hany Sheikh
Mohamed
Zoe Shine

The HarperCollins Distribution Team

The HarperCollins Finance & Royalties Team

The HarperCollins Legal Team

The HarperCollins Technology Team

Trade Marketing
Ben Hurd

UK Sales
Laura Carpenter
Isabel Coburn
Jay Cochrane
Sabina Lewis
Holly Martin
Erin White
Harriet Williams
Leah Woods

And every other essential link in the chain from delivery drivers to booksellers to librarians and beyond!

YOUR NUMBER ONE STOP
ONE MORE CHAPTER
FOR PAGETURNING BOOKS